Pursuing Cicely

By Luana M. McDowell

CHAPTER 1

Cicely sat on the top stair looking out of the window on the landing below. It was a sunny day in early June.

She had just put the finishing touches on the bedrooms in preparation of her sisters' visit. Everything was spit polished and clean like their mother had taught them. She debated putting fresh cut flowers from the yard in each of the three bedrooms, but decided that was too much. After all, they were coming to talk her out of her home.

They didn't think she knew. But she was good at reading between the lines. Every sister had called her long distance more frequently. Each asking wasn't she lonely staying in that big house by herself.

Madeline, the oldest, had even suggested that since a year had passed since their mother's death then it was time for her to stop wallowing in self-pity.

She wasn't wallowing. She *had* decided what to do with the rest of her life. Momma's death had been hard and she had been the primary caregiver. All four sisters thought their mother would live forever. She had initially moved back home when Momma had fell and put in for a leave of absence from her job as a financial advisor. But momma had broken a hip and never really recovered. So Cicely quit her job on the west coast and moved back to the city where she'd been born. Buffalo New York. It was a culture shock. The pace was much slower than

L.A., but now she found deep down she was better suited to the life her hometown provided.

Of the four sisters she was the only one not married or have children. They all agreed it was logical she be the one to return Buffalo. They all had families to take care of. No one ever gave it thought to move their mother out of her home. Long before their mother's death, it had been discussed that Cicely would get the house. No one had objected then.

Maybe they did think this intervention was for her own good, highly unlikely.

Cicely continued sitting on the step. *"God" she wished she had a cigarette.* That was ridiculous. Forty years old and nervous about confronting her sisters. She hadn't smoked since moving back home. Momma would have never tolerated it. Broken hip or not, she would have beaten Cicely's ass.

In the beginning things were fine. But during her rehab Momma lost her snap. Her memory began to wander and her mind wasn't as sharp. The sisters didn't need a doctor to tell them their mother was in the beginning stages of dementia. Progression was slow at the start but it eventually reached a point Cicely didn't feel comfortable leaving her mother alone while she went to work. The job didn't pay nearly as much as the one she'd left in California, but it kept her busy. She had counseled low-income families so they could buy homes. Now a year after her mother's death it was time she put her plans into actions.

When their father had died nineteen years before their mother, the sisters had each received a tidy sum of money. Mr.

Macklin had been career military. Did his twenty then started a new career. He made sure his daughters were all college educated. Granted most of the investments were numerous insurance policies, but he left his wife of fifty-plus-years comfortably off. Buying the big two story, four bedroom house had been his idea, with the plan to fill it with children. It had taken a while before that happened.

Madeline was three when they bought the house, was almost four when Bernice came along. He was still in the military then and would be gone a lot. Momma was stern while he was away, but she always deferred to Daddy.

Madeline was stern like Momma, and she never deferred to anybody but Daddy either.

"Maddy," Daddy would say in that deep chocolate voice of his and all of her ice would melt. No one could call her Maddy except Daddy. "Maddy," he'd say, "don't give your mother a hard time." Occasionally she would tolerate their mother calling her "Maddy."

Mr. Macklin was out of the military when Cicely was born. Madeline was a hormone raging thirteen-year old. Maybe that's why she always felt Madeline hated her. Cicely thought, as she stood up from the step and stretched. She and Simone, born four years after her, had a "nine to five Daddy".

Moving down to the landing she stared out of the window. The glass was sparkling clean. Glancing down at her watch she saw there was still three hours before Madeline and Bernice arrived. Still time to put curtains up to the window, but she knew she wouldn't. Bernice and Madeline would just have to get over the window being bare.

"But people can look in," Bernice would say.

'Only, if they look up!' she thought. Besides, she liked the sunlight coming in. The house next door didn't have a real second floor. The Mackling house sat on a corner lot and the distance of the side yard separated the two properties. For someone to see in the window clearly they would have to use binoculars. And if they wanted to see that bad let them look. It wasn't that she was an exhibitionist, but dammit, she thought she looked good for forty. Never having had kids her stomach was flat and her C cup breasts still perky.

Yes, Bernice had caught her walking around naked once, but that had been in her own apartment and she had forgotten Bernice had come to visit. She didn't walk around nude in front of people, but Bernice couldn't wait to tell Momma and Madeline. But their Daddy while still alive had said when the last girl moved out, he was going to chase their mother around the house naked. Momma had just laughed, but Cicely had seen the twinkle of anticipation in her eyes. Unfortunately Daddy died when Simone was sixteen. They never got to do that.

Well, how did she know? It wasn't like they never had the house to themselves.

Nope, no curtains on this window. That decision made, she looked at her reflection. No wrinkles there. Not even the burden of caring for her mother had put wrinkles on her smooth milk chocolate complexion. Of course she moisturized religiously. She could easily pass for early thirties. She had donned a tank top and cutoff jeans while cleaning. Her arms were still firm. She raised her arm flexed her bicep and smiled she had guns. She struck a body builder pose in the reflection. Nice calves and thighs, round butt. She ran religiously weather permitting. Five-six, not skinny, something a man could hold on to.

Well that wiped the smile off her face. No man. She leaned in to look at her face closer. She wasn't what she would consider beautiful, maybe cute. A forty-year old shouldn't be considering herself cute, she thought. Now Momma was tall and beautiful. Regal, Madeline took after their mother. Bernice was like Cicely only rounder. Simone was the only one yellow like their father with a slim build.

Continuing her perusal Cicely noted her top lip was a smidge larger than her bottom one. Her nose was just a nose. Not wide, not patriarchal like Momma's and Madeline's. She could never look down her nose like they did. Her eyes were her best feature. Not light enough to be called hazel, but just light enough so they could not be called dark brown and naturally arched eyebrows. When she deigned to put on make-up she looked damn good.

Her hair; that was another matter. Not silky like Simone's. Not long and thick like Madeline's. She and Bernice got the short stick when it came to hair.

Caring for momma had caused her coarse hair to start turning grey. She normally kept it permed. But after the funeral and everyone had returned home she had it all cut off. What had started off as a very short natural, was now about three inches of dreadlocks carefully dyed her own natural dark brown color. She was comfortable enough now not to keep it covered with a scarf all the time, which she did now because of the cleaning. Madeline was going to have a cow when she saw it. Good. Maybe that would put the matter of the house on the back burner for a while.

She continued down the stairs, thinking 'Better hide that vibrator before nosy Bernice finds it'. She'd do it before they got here.

Directly in front of her was the front entrance with a strong wooden door with a window at the top half that opened to a small entry hall in front of the outer door that was wood with thick glass making up most of the door. Framing both doors was leaded glass from floor to ceiling. To the right through an archway was the living room. Complete with the fake fireplace found in many older homes. To the left was the formal dining-room, which had become their mother's bedroom when it became too difficult for her to navigate the stairs. Now it was returned to its original intent. Triple windows lined both rooms across the front of the house. And a porch stretched across the front of the house with the entry in the middle.

She turned left going through the dining room to the kitchen in the rear of the house. The sisters had gotten the kitchen redone as a Christmas present for their mother. How momma had loved the antique white cabinets that lined the wall without windows. Even after all these years Cicely still ran her hand over the black granite counter top when she entered the kitchen. The contractor had made a pass through between the kitchen and dining room, so even when momma was sick Cicely could keep up a conversation with her mother as she fixed their meals. To the left was a big bay window letting in plenty of light. Momma had grown herbs in the window space and she was considering carrying on the tradition. The kitchen table sat right under the window. All year round the view was nice. Even in the winter when the side yard was covered in snow.

Cicely headed straight for the fridge, stood there with the door open like a little kid. It wasn't like something was going to jump up and say, "eat me." She hadn't gotten groceries. Figured they could do take out tonight from Lee's barbeque. Even Madeline wouldn't turn down Lee's famous barbeque. Then tomorrow they could all go shopping for their one week stay. She was at the point where she was watching what she spent. She was not going to take on the expense of feeding her sisters. Dipping into her savings was not an option. Not to feed them anyway.

Her hand reached for a yogurt that she hoped had not expired. The fridge was practically bare. Before she could grab a spoon the cordless phone on the counter rang.

"Maybe they aren't coming," was her first thought before seeing on caller ID it was her BFF. Her girlfriend had never left town. She had married, was raising two beautiful twin girls and probably had wed the last good man in town. But they picked up their friendship without a hitch. Anita and her teenaged daughters had been invaluable when Cicely was caring for her mother.

"They there yet?" Anita asked before Cicely could even say hello.

"No. I told you their flight isn't due until late this afternoon. Simone is driving in for some reason."

"She don't want to be seen in your eight year old hoopty. Miss 'I-got-it-all'."

Cicely laughed and after verifying the yogurt was still good grabbed a spoon and began to eat.

"You know she always wants the best."

Anita snorted. "And don't care who pays for it."

"Don't talk about my baby sister like that," laughed Cicely, because it was partly true.

Simone expected the best. She wasn't mean hearted. She liked fine things and worked hard to get them. When hand me downs came her way, she took them apart and put them back together so no one ever knew they were second hand.

Her husband provided well for her and their thirteen year old daughter. But Simone worked. She wasn't a slacker. Went to school for fashion design and currently worked as a buyer for a major department store chain. But she came off as snooty.

Daddy would sometimes chastise her. "Girl you needn't act like you're better than everybody."

Maybe if Daddy had lived until she was full grown, Simone would have been different. In some ways she was stuck at sixteen.

"You want me to come over for moral support?" Anita asked.

"No, I'll be fine."

"Ok 'I'll be fine'. Then why all you've been talking about is them?"

"Because they want to take my house. Wait a minute, someone is at the door."

Cicely strolled through the dining room and stopped, "Oh my God!"

"What?"

"They're here. Madeline and Bernice are here."

"Told you. I'm coming over."

"Don't you dare. I don't believe it!"

"Believe they're early?"

"No, no, not that. Madeline has these big fat cornrows going around her head like a crown."

"Take a picture with your cell and send it to me."

"I gotta go."

Bernice was tapping impatiently on the outer door. "You know we can see you Cicely. Open the door."

"Don't forget the picture!"

Cicely hit the end button and opened the first door leading to the small hall. The second door leading outside was locked, but Bernice was busy shaking the knob.

"I have to pee!"

She almost hit Cicely with the door she rushed in so fast, going straight to the downstairs powder room.

"Well hello to you," Cicely said to Bernice's back.

Madeline strolled in just carrying an overnight bag, leaving plies of luggage on the porch.

"Like your hair." Cicely said.

"Like yours," Madeline shot back. She stopped in the archway of the dining room. Even though everything was as it had been, she could still see her mother laying in a hospital bed. Tears filled her eyes and began running down her face.

Cicely saw her body slump. Her eyes began tearing up. This was the first visit home without their mother being there. Without even thinking about it, she enveloped her oldest sister in a hug. "Oh, Maddy," she soothed.

Madeline audibly sniffed. "You're only allowed that one time," hearing her sister call her by the pet name only her father used.

"I miss her too."

They were still embraced when Bernice returned from the bathroom.

"Since when did you two get so touchy, feely?" she said

passing by to get the luggage.

Madeline gave her a final squeeze before letting go. "I don't know what's wrong with me lately, or her." She said glancing at Bernice.

'Menopause,' Cicely wanted to say. But didn't dare say it out loud.

"You two could help you know," Bernice said dragging in a couple of bags.

Two more sat on the porch. Four bags? How many times a day did they plan on changing clothes?

Madeline was headed up the stairs carrying one large bag. Better head her off, thought Cicely. "I'm sleeping in Momma's room," Cicely said picking up a bag.

"Like I wouldn't know that," snapped Madeline. "I told Bernice as much while we were on the plane.

"Back to normal," muttered Cicely. But it had felt good having her sister's arms around her. Almost like Momma's.

Momma and Daddy's room was the biggest. It took up the whole front of the house. Plenty of sunlight entered the front windows. Once she got used to hearing the traffic go pass the house at night, she was fine. One side of the room was the bed and dressers. The other side she had created a seating area, with a love seat and coffee table. It was the only room besides the living room that had a television. Bernice would balk at that, but too bad. If she wanted to watch late night TV she could do it downstairs.

Madeline went straight to her old room. It was in the rear of the house. Half the size of the one Cicely now occupied. It looked out over the detached garage. When she became a teenager she wanted to be as far away from her parents as possible. Especially when finding out a baby was on the way. Still it was a nice sized room, had a small closet that was now empty.

Madeline looked at the bag Cicely was carrying. "That's Bernice's."

Cicely looked down. Of course it was Bernice's. It didn't match the bag Madeline had. "I'll just put it in her room."

"And then would you bring up my other bags please."

She almost said "yes ma'am before she caught herself.

She met Bernice struggling up the stairs with the remaining bags and took one from her without a word.

Bernice's room was next to Madeline's. It looked out over the side street. Directly below her room was the enclosed sun porch. When they were little, in the summer Daddy would let them sleep out there. Even Madeline would sometimes, though she would say she was too old for such childishness, but her room was too hot so she might as well join them. Daddy would join them in sleeping bags on the floor. They'd have popcorn, tell stores and for a special treat sometimes Daddy would set up the projector and show home movies when Madeline and Bernice were little girls and Momma was young and beautiful.

Cicely wondered where that film and projector were now. She'd have to look in the attic and see if they were still there. It might be fun to watch them. The ones of her and Simone would be on video. She should get them all converted to DVD. That would make nice Christmas gifts.

"Looks nice," said Bernice looking around the room.

"I've missed you," said Cicely wrapping her arm around the plumper, older version of herself. She felt impervious stiffening before Bernice hugged her back. Cicely pulled away, her hand on Bernice's shoulders. "Is everything alright?"

She managed a smile before answering. "Sure, everything's fine. Madeline had me up before dawn. Saying she had booked us on an earlier flight. Everything just seemed to happen so fast these past few weeks. School let out." Bernice was a teacher. "Jeanine, graduating from high school. Oh, she said to thank you for the lovely gift."

Cicely held up her hand. "Stop. She has to thank me herself. Write me a thank you note."

That brought a genuine smile to Bernice's face. "Any way I'm just tired, rundown. Louis and I will soon have two kids in college. And Gerry's thinking about going back for graduate school, it could be three." He was her oldest child.

Uh, oh, thought Cicely. Here it comes, the pitch for her to sell the house. She wasn't ready for that conversation yet. "Why don't you lie down and take a quick nap," she said backing out of the room, closing the door, not waiting to see if

Bernice answered.

She made her way back downstairs and found Madeline sitting at the kitchen table waiting for water to boil to make tea.

"How can you drink tea when it's hot outside?"

"It cools you off. Besides you don't have anything else to drink but water," Madeline said staring out the window.

"I thought you liked water." Cicely answered becoming a bit perturbed.

But Madeline didn't seem to notice. "Are you going to grow herbs like momma?"

"I'm thinking about it," she said sliding into a chair across from her sister. Madeline's eyes were still moist. "I really do like your hair. What made you get cornrows?"

"Preston. My husband said we were letting ourselves become old before our time. Me wearing the same hairstyle I've been wearing forever. Him…"

Cicely interrupted her. "Don't tell me Preston is sporting and Afro, dreads?"

"No," laughed Madeline. "But he got some nice looking facial hair going on. He's always had a mustache, but now he has a nice goatee and soul patch."

"Soul Patch?" squeaked Cicely. She didn't think her sister even knew what a soul patch was.

"Oh yeah. And we take a Zumba class together. The man got some moves," Madeline said with a sly smile on her face.

This was the older sister she'd always wanted. But Madeline looked so much like momma it was almost like eavesdropping on your parents' sex life. Cicely was beginning to think, this woman just "looks" like my sister.

"Preston says, we can't be fuddy-duddy grandparents."

"Grandparents?"

"I'm going to be a grandmother. Lydia is pregnant, baby due around your birthday, early December."

So many thoughts went through Cicely's mind in a matter of seconds. First, her twenty-six year old niece was having a child, and "she" didn't have one. Second her twenty-six year old niece was married. Third, they wanted to use "her" home to secure the future for a child no one knew yet. She felt a mild ache in her chest and stood up. "Congratulations," she said hoping Madeline wouldn't hear the hitch in her voice.

"Are you alright?"

"Yeah I'm alright. Just can't help but think this would be Momma's first great grandchild."

"Maybe Momma's sending us this baby."

Not if it meant me losing the house, thought Cicely, but kept it to herself. She retrieved the whistling pot and poured the water into Madeline's waiting cup. "You want to go get some groceries while Bernice is napping? That way someone will be here if Simone shows up." asked Cicely, even though she really didn't want to be alone with her older sister. But she could just disappear at the checkout and Madeline would get stuck with the bill.

"Sure. I'll start a list while I drink my tea."

Cicely looked down at herself. "I'll change clothes. Oh, I thought we could all go out for ribs later."

"Sounds like a plan. Get some money from Bernice. Never mind," she waved that away. "We'll just split the bill four ways after Simone gets here."

Cicely bound up the stairs to grab a quick shower and change. Would wonders never cease? Madeline wanted to split the bill. Wait a minute, she thought. That was unfair of her to think her sisters would expect her to foot the cost of their visit. Madeline had never used people unfairly. None of her sisters had. Well maybe Simone sometimes. But even when Cicely lived alone and was making money hand over fist, when her sisters came out for a visit, they insisted on paying their own way. She had to argue with them to allow her to treat them. And each of them was well aware of how much she had given up returning home.

"Cicely!" called Madeline, "Hurry up. It looks like it might rain."

The sun was rapidly disappearing behind a bank of dark clouds.

"Ok, ok," said Cicely leaning over the rail. "I'll tell Bernice we're going. Do you want an umbrella?"

"No. I have this," she said holding up a rain scarf.

"Oh my goodness," laughed Cicely. "They still make those things?" She hadn't seen an old fashion plastic rain scarf in years.

"Would you rather see me in a plastic jheri curl cap out in public?"

"Definitely not. I hate it when I see young black women, men too, in those things, making it a fashion statement. How they expect someone to think the best of them when they don't looked their best? Who are they saving looking good for?"

"Yes, like when they wear that greasy head scarf," replied Madeline.

They continued the conversation about the lack of class the younger generation had as they left the house through the enclosed porch.

Bernice heard the muted voices of her sister through the open window. Maybe she should have gone with them. Now she was in this big house alone. When she'd first lain down it was sunny. Now it was definitely overcast, making the room gloomy. She sat up on the side of the bed letting her feet rest lightly on the cool hardwood floor. She would get up and double check if her younger sister had locked all the doors.

Not that the neighborhood was bad, it was she just wasn't used to being alone in the house, any house. Maybe she should take one of the antianxiety pills her doctor had prescribed.

Louis, her husband, had encouraged her to make this trip. "It might help you to get away," he said.

He meant well, but she'd come as much for herself as she did him. He needed a break also. She knew her crying jags sometimes un-nerved him, especially when he'd had to pick her up from school when she'd had a mini breakdown. Had scared her seventh grade students shitless when she'd began sobbing uncontrollably in front of the class. The school really didn't want her to come back in the fall.

She stood, walked out of the bedroom barefooted, intending to go downstairs to check the locks. Down the hall Cicely had left her bedroom door ajar and it seemed to beckon to Bernice.

Standing in the doorway she noticed Cicely really hadn't changed that much. The room was in shadows now that the sun was behind clouds, but it was calming. On the dresser was the wedding picture of Momma and Daddy. Each of the sisters had one. Momma seated in her white tea length dress with a short head veil, Daddy, in his military uniform standing slightly behind her. Rather than have her hands folded in her lap, momma had one of daddy's hands clasp tightly in both hers held to her heart. And they were smiling at each other. Not at the camera. The photographer must have been ahead of his time to let them pose like that. Or Daddy insisted he wanted everyone to see how much he loved his wife.

Bernice didn't realize she had entered the room until her fingers brushed the glass covering the picture. She looked at herself in the mirror. The dim light didn't hide the fact she had packed on the pounds. Her face showed it. She needed to take better care of herself but it was too much effort. Her shoulder length coarse hair was shot through with grey, made her look old. She wanted to care but didn't.

She glanced around the room. On the bed was a summer quilt handmade by their grandmother. Each of the sisters had one. Grandmother had died before Cicely and Simone were born, but some compulsion had her make four quilts, one for each of her granddaughters. Bernice crossed the room and sat on the bed. She lovingly ran her hand across the patchwork quilt. Ironically it was the wedding ring pattern and Cicely was the only one who had never married. The quilt smelled faintly of lavender. Cicely must have stored it with lavender cut from the bushes growing next to the house. Their momma had done the same thing. She laid down and wrapped herself in the quilt. The anxiety that had been building seemed to drain away. She took a deep breath, inhaling the scent of lavender.

"Oh Momma," she sighed. "I miss you so much. I need you." She was drifting off to sleep, but felt the mattress sag as if a person had sat down. A light feathery touch on her forehead and Bernice felt a calm she hadn't felt in months. The tension she had been holding unconsciously in her muscles melted away. And, as the rain fell outside, Bernice slept.

Sitting in her SUV, Simone peered at the house through the sheets of rain. It looked unwelcoming. She had blown her horn several times, but no one even looked out the windows. She considered waking her daughter Olivia, and making her run through the rain to ring the doorbell, but she'd paid too much to get that girls hair done to get it wet.

It was five in the afternoon. Maybe Cicely had gone to the airport to pick up their older sisters. She was tired. She had never driven that distance alone before. She and Olivia had left Chicago during the wee hours of the morning. Luckily the heavy rain hadn't started until they were almost to their destination. But now it looked like no one was home, some homecoming. Simone turned in the driver's seat to look at the rear of the vehicle. Trying to see if there was something she could easily grab so she wouldn't get soaked before she made it to the porch. It was piled high with everything she could squeeze back there. Giving up hope she opened the door and braced herself to get soaked. Reaching for her Gucci handbag to protect her hair, she glanced briefly at Olivia before making the mad dash to the porch.

Her Gucci driving shoes were ruined, she thought as she bound up the porch stairs. The rain wasn't cold, the grass warm and green. She could have run from the car barefoot. When they were kids Momma would have had a fit. Her girls were not country born. Ladies did not run around outside with no shoes, which she and Cicely promptly did. Maybe it was more Madeline's rule than Momma's. She remembered Momma being shoeless while she hung sheets outside in the summer. Momma said the grass felt cool and soft against her feet. Momma would tell stories how teenage Madeline would be mortified and would volunteer to hang the sheets. It was bad enough Momma didn't use the dryer.

"Maddy," Momma would chide, "Sheets smell so much better when the sun hits them.

Secretly, Simone thought this was Momma's way of getting Madeline to do the laundry. Bernice said only if Madeline did the laundry would it be guaranteed the underwear did not end up on the clothesline outside. Once Momma starting hanging clothes on the line, there was no stopping her. Well Simone knew for a fact that Madeline now hung her sheets outside during the summer months and sometimes even in the winter. Claiming you could never get that fragrance with fabric softener. Personally Simone thought sheets done at a professional laundry were the best. Her husband thought it was a waste of money. But what did he know?

She removed her waterlogged shoes and peered into the living room window. Crossing the porch, she cupped her hands around her face to look in the dining room window. She could see straight through to the kitchen. Nothing, not even a light on against the early darkness brought on by the storm.

Pulling away from the window Simone noticed she had left smudges on the sparkling window. She looked at the wide porch for the first time. Cicely had taken the time to place flowerpots all around the porch adding color.

The old wicker furniture had been repainted white and the pillow reupholstered in bright lime green. She would have gone with something sleeker, more modern. But the old stuff fit the character of the house. Maybe she could talk Cicely into getting something a little bit more up to date.

Her husband had courted her on this front porch. Such an old-fashioned word, court. Evan, she still liked the name. Evan. It sounded like the name of a man going somewhere. He had promised her the moon and the stars. And she had promised him he could get in her pants. And eventually she had let him. Right there in the deep shadows of the front porch. Tall, dark and muscular, she had noticed him before he had even noticed her. Put herself in a position where he couldn't help but notice her. Then ignored him. Oh, how she had made him work to get in her pants.

It was late when he'd brought her home from a movie one evening. She didn't even remember what the movie was. She bet Evan did. He was a romantic. She did remember his fumbling though. You would have thought she'd been his first. Later she found out, she was. He never found out he wasn't hers.

Oh, but once they found their rhythm he was the best she'd ever had. With Evan she knew why God created sex. It was a year before the got married. It was a wonder she hadn't been pregnant, because they'd fucked like rabbits every chance they got.

A lot of sex happened on this front porch and the enclosed sun porch too. Once, Madeline had almost caught them.

Madeline and her family had been visiting Momma. Her children were still young. Anyway, Evan already had her panties off. They'd pulled a metal lawn chair to the darkest corner of the porch. Come to think of it, maybe she'd never had panties on that night and had teased him about it all evening.

Madeline called herself a smoker at that time, but all she really did was puff. She'd come outside to sneak a cigarette, because you did not smoke in Momma's house.

Evan was sitting in the chair pants open and had just slipped on a condom. She was about to straddle him when she heard the inner door open. She quickly turned her back to him and sat on his lap. Unfortunately she missed the mark and Evan let out a strangled groan.

Madeline stepped out the outer door with the cigarette between her lips, ready to light it. She must have heard Evan, because she looked directly in their direction like

she had night vision. The only illumination was from indoors. She hadn't bothered to switch on the porch light, lest she reveal her bad habit to the neighbors.

"Oh," Madeline said, blinking rapidly. "I didn't know you were back." The cigarette disappeared so fast, Simone almost laughed out loud.

But she could feel Evan's erection quickly dissipating. "Just got here. Why don't you come sit with us? It's a nice night."

Evan frantically whispered in her ear, "What are you doing?"

She moved as if to stand up, and Evan roughly pulled her to sit on his lap.

But Madeline had already back stepped into the doorway. "No, no. I'll just leave you some privacy."

Simone didn't think she'd ever seen Madeline with a cigarette again. Needless to say Evan was useless the rest of the night. Even when she assured him Madeline didn't have a clue what they were doing. Madeline was too concerned about not seeming to be perfect. After that incident they went to a motel or if finances didn't allow, the back seat of Evan's car.

The rain seemed to be letting up a little as she rang the doorbell for good measure. She heard the SUV door open and turned to find her daughter, foot out the door.

"Stay there," she yelled. "Don't you dare get your hair wet."

"I got the umbrella. It was behind the seat."

Simone swore under her breath. She'd forgotten she always kept an umbrella in the pouch behind the passenger seat for times like this. She waved at Olivia to come on. She turned, looked at the front door. No one had come in response to the ring. "Come on," she waved again.

Olivia was slim like her, long dark hair. Simone had the stylist flat iron it, so it was straight, hanging half way down Olivia's back. Boobs were just now becoming noticeable.

They weren't close like she had been with her own mother. And she knew her job was partly the reason. As a store buyer she traveled a lot and sometimes wasn't home when the important things happened. Evan had been the one to drive to the store and get sanitary napkins because all Simone had in the house were tampons. He was the one that instructed Olivia to never flush a napkin down the toilet. When Olivia had cramps, she called her Dad for the heating pad, not Simone. But hell, Simone called Evan too when cramps hit her.

Daughter and Dad were close, especially this past year since Evan's high paying job had ended. He was essentially a house Dad.

That was part of their problem. He had gotten a very good severance package, but it wasn't enough as far as she was concerned. The news his job was over was waiting for them when they'd returned home from Momma's funeral. Talk about kicking a person when they were down.

Being the sensible person he was Evan had cut up all the credit cards. He insisted they live off her salary and his unemployment benefits. And now the benefits were about to run out. And no good job prospects were on the horizon.

Evan wasn't a deadbeat. He had invested wisely with Cicely's help and his 401k was still intact, but he wouldn't touch it. Instead he had put her big beautiful house on the market. "Downsizing," he said. "We don't need all this house." He had always wanted more children, but she was the one to say no.

It would sell really fast. In a good neighborhood, it had actually increased in value. Olivia would be starting high school in the fall, so it wasn't like she would be totally uprooted. That was just the tip of her and Evan's problems. But she had to have a good tale to tell her sisters.

"I'm hungry," Olivia said as soon as her feet hit the

porch.

"No one's home, sweetie. We'll wait twenty minutes; if no one shows up I'll take you to get something. Maybe some of that great barbeque we had the last time we were here."

"K," was all the girl said before plopping down on the wicker sofa.

One word answers were all Simone ever got from her. That was normal for her age said 'Bernice the teacher'.

She knew Olivia was angry with her right now, making her come on this trip. But a daughter belonged with her mother. Olivia better get used to it.

They sat side by side silently.

CHAPTER 2

It was pouring rain when they left the grocery store. Madeline looked dignified with her old lady rain scarf and Cicely felt the rain soaking through her baseball cap. They laughed at each other sitting in the car.

"Think we got enough food?" asked Cicely.

"If not, Bernice and Simone can come next time," said Madeline shaking off her rain scarf and patting her thick braids. "We should stop and get dinner," she continued. "No one is going to want to come back out in this weather."

Cicely pulled out her cell and hit one number.

"You have them on speed dial!" laughed Madeline.

"Who doesn't?"

She ordered enough for a feast. Ribs, potato salad, cole slaw, and for dessert a whole sweet potato pie.

"Girl, do you know how long I've been dieting?"

Cicely turned the ignition key and glanced at her. "For what? Look at you. With the new do, you look young and smokin' hot. You must be giving Preston a run for his money."

"Thank you, but I have been dieting for the last six months to get ready for our trip. Why do you think I brought all that luggage? When I leave here I am meeting my husband at

Disney World. Couldn't expect that man to know what to pack for himself."

"Disney World! But I thought…"

"Thought what?"

"Nothing," said Cicely pretending to concentrate on driving through the rain.

"Cicely, we've been enjoying each other's company, you thought what?"

"That you all came to gang up on me to sell the house."

"Sell the house! Why would we want you to sell where we grew up?"

"You're having a new grandbaby. That cost money."

"Key word 'grandbaby', not my baby. They are established enough to have a child."

"Bernice will have two kids in college."

"Her problem, not yours. Momma left the house to you. We don't have a problem with that. She knew you were the caretaker. Your doll babies were the only ones that kept their hair and clothes. And we expect you to take care of the family home. Besides how are you going to foster kids without a home? "Then, "LOOK OUT!" shouted Madeline bracing her hand against the dash.

Cicely had come dangerously close to running a red light. She slammed on the brakes causing the car to skid part way into the intersection on the wet asphalt. She looked in the rearview mirror and cautiously backed up. "How did you know that?"

Madeline glared at her, "You almost got us killed."

"There are no cars coming Madeline. How did you know about the foster kids?"

"Light's green," Madeline stated.

Cicely looked both ways and pulled off slowly. "Please Madeline you have to tell me. I've been stressing ever since you called. Wondering, why come now? All I could think is, after everyone thought it over, had decided Momma had made a mistake giving me the house."

"It's the anniversary of Momma's passing Cicely. I suggested to everyone we come for that. I thought it would be especially hard for you."

"Oh," said Cicely quietly.

"As to the other, who do you think they call as part of a background check? Family, that's who. When they called me, I thought what a wonderful thing for you."

Cicely turned her head to look at her oldest sister.

"Keep your eyes on the road please," said Madeline.

"What did you tell them?"

"I lied," smiled Madeline. "I said you would make a good foster parent."

Even Cicely knew that was a joke. "Thank you."

""You took such good care of Momma. I don't know if any of us can thank you enough."

"She was my mother too."

"But I don't know if we appreciated just how much you did or how much you gave up to do it. You put your life on hold Baby Girl."

"No one's called me that since Daddy died."

"I know. You were his favorite."

"No, I was not."

"You were a math geek just like him."

Cicely countered, "And all I heard from Daddy was I should look to Momma and you as role models. He admired you."

"He said that to me when I got my nursing degree."

"Every time he talked to his friends all we heard was, our Maddy got her BA in nursing. Our Maddy gave us our first grandchild. Our Maddy got her masters in nursing. I got so I would grit my teeth every time I heard 'our Maddy',"

"And all the time you were growing up and I came home to visit, you two had your heads together," countered Madeline.

Cicely laughed, "He was helping me with math and later with investments."

"He was a smart man," said Madeline.

"Daddy should have gone to college."

Madeline nodded solemnly. "Yes he should have. He would have out shone us all."

The sister's rode in silence, both with their own thoughts. Unintentionally Daddy had created friction between the two of them. But it didn't lessen their love for each other.

"When the agency called me," Madeline said finally breaking the silence, "I called Bernice and told her we should come help you get the house together before they came to inspect. Preston wanted to come, but I said we are the Macklin sisters. We can get anything accomplished. Two birds with one stone. Remembrance of Momma and help you start the next chapter.

"Cecily, why are you doing this? I mean not that you won't be good at it. I know you will, but I thought you enjoyed what you did."

"I did. I do. And I don't plan on stopping. I've already lined up employment. I want to be a role model; children need to see an adult strive for something. But you were right when you said I was a caregiver. Caring for Momma filled something in me I didn't know was empty. I have a lot to offer a child, children if they let me have more than one. I have a huge old house that needs filling."

"Why didn't you talk to me about it?" Madeline interrupted. "I was angry and a little hurt you didn't"

She sounded indignant to Cicely. "A little hurt?" she questioned.

"Ok, Cicely, a lot hurt. What was your reasoning for not talking to me?"

"I didn't want you to call me stupid!"

"Cicely Louise Macklin, when have I ever called anything you did stupid?"

She didn't hesitate a second before she shot back, "When I dyed my hair blonde."

The sisters stared each other full in the face. Then both laughed hysterically.

"You're right, that was a stupid idea," In her early twenties Cicely had made the mistake of coloring her hair golden blonde. Not a good look with her brown complexion. Before the week was done she was back to her non-descript brown.

"I was afraid Madeline. Afraid you would put a voice to all my doubts. How was I going to take a complete stranger under my roof? A child that I had no idea what or who they came from. Besides Momma, I'd never been responsible for any human being but myself."

"You did ok with that," said Madeline.

"Humph," was all Cicely said. They'd reached their destination. Cicely pulled into the gravel parking lot and chose a spot next to the building. Before she could get out the car, Madeline put her hand on Cicely's arm.

"Wait, I want to tell you something…" She paused as if deciding if she really wanted to say anything. "Cicely, if you say one word about what I am telling you, I will deny it. And I will make you wish you had never been born."

Madeline never made empty threats. Cicely waited

patiently for her to continue.

"I was pregnant when I got married."

"No, you weren't," said Cicely. "Emmanuel was born over a year after you married."

"I had a miscarriage about two weeks after the ceremony."

"What does that have to do with…"

"Just shut up and listen. The baby was not Preston's."

Cicely could not stop herself, "Did he know?"

"Of course he knew. And before you ask, Momma knew. I don't believe Daddy ever did. Momma encouraged me to tell Preston. She was a better judge of character than I was. And to be honest, if I hadn't got pregnant I might have never told him I'd slept with someone else. I didn't set out to hurt Preston."

Madeline sat quietly, staring out the windshield. Cicely had turned the engine off and they could hear the raindrops hitting the car roof. Madeline watched as a drop made a trail down the glass. It still wasn't really dark. It would be a few hours before true night came, but the heavy rain clouds cast a pall over the day.

"It was a mistake," she began. "I loved Preston and if that person walked down the street right now I probably wouldn't recognize him. It was a one night stand with a guy that thought he was all that. And me thinking I was all that because he wanted me."

"Did you tell him you'd gotten pregnant?"

"No, I wouldn't give him that satisfaction. I wasn't going to let him know how naïve I was. He wanted to be able to say he popped that cherry but I put a stop to that. I told him Preston had already taken care of that issue."

Cicely could feel the heat of a blush creeping up her face. If she were the color of Daddy or Simone, she would look like an over ripe tomato about now. Gawd, this must be what a hot flash feels like. She wanted to cover her ears.

"It wasn't even that good. Tell me," Madeline said looking at her, "why do cute guys think they are so good in bed?"

It was obvious Madeline really expected an answer. But Cicely was tongue-tied. All she could do was shrug her shoulders.

"I mean it took Preston and me a while before we perfected the bedroom moves. And that was after we married."

Cicely felt she'd never be able to look her brother-in-law in the face again. Let alone talk to him.

Madeline wave a hand through the air, "That's beside the point. I'm getting off track here. Momma knew I had missed my period. She probably knew I was pregnant before I did. It hurt so bad to admit to her the baby wasn't Preston's. I was just going to break things off. It was about four weeks before the wedding when I realized it. I was just going to cancel the wedding. But Momma made me talk to Preston.

"My husband-to-be told me he loved me. He was in love with me. Not because I was perfect, but because I wasn't. He knew I wouldn't be an easy person to live with, but he didn't want easy. He wanted me. And If I came with a little something extra then that was a blessing. Cicely he didn't care where it came from. For all he cared it could have been an immaculate conception. His words, not mine. The only way this wedding would not take place would be if I could say irrevocably I did not love him.

"But I did love him and that he was willing to accept my child made me love him more. When I lost the baby he genuinely grieved with me. I had lost "our baby", not some err in judgment I had made.

"So Cicely, I would not be the one to tell you taking in a child not knowing their pedigree is stupid. Not when I have a man that was willing to open his heart to the unknown."

"You know I had a crush on Preston," Cicely finally said.

"Yes," Madeline replied staidly. "That's another reason I married him. The damn fool would have waited around until you were old enough if I had turned him down, skipped right pass Bernice."

"Madeline," Cicely said horrified.

"Joking, baby girl. We need to spend more time with each other so you know when I'm kidding."

"Maddy, he never brought it up? Threw it in your face? Even when you had one of your knockdown, drag out, arguments?"

"Never. Not to say we both don't fight dirty at any given time. But that was off limits."

"Maybe we could clone him," smiled Cicely loving her brother-in-law even more. He and Madeline had been married over thirty years.

Both sisters stifled a scream when someone tapped on the driver's side window.

"Simone!" cried Cicely.

"Unlock the door," said Simone. She slid into the back seat. "Olivia and I have been waiting at the house for you," she complained. "We had to sit on the porch in the rain because we couldn't get in."

"Why not?" asked Madeline. "Bernice is there."

"Obviously Bernice didn't let us in, or we wouldn't be here."

"Where is Olivia?" interjected Cicely, "You didn't leave her at the house did you?"

"No, I did not," said Simone rolling her eyes at Cicely as if to say, 'I'm not a moron.'

"She's in the car," She said pointing behind them. "She spotted you when I pulled up. Olivia is hungry so after we waited for you, 'forever', I brought her here to get something."

"Just as well," said Madeline. "There's nothing to eat at the house. By the way you owe us for groceries."

Cicely gave Madeline the side eye. It was if they had not just shared a very intimate moment. "Bernice was taking a nap when we left."

"Well, all I know is Bernice would not get up off her fat behind and let us in."

"You know what, Simone? That was not called for."

"What?" asked Simone feigning innocence.

"Name calling." Cicely simply said.

"She's not here to hear it."

"I *don't* want to hear it," said Cicely. Before she could say more the backseat passenger door opened and Olivia jumped in.

"Hi Aunt Madeline, Auntie Cicely," she smiled. "Where's Aunt Bernice?"

"At home, too busy sleeping to open the door for us," answered her mother before either of her Aunts could.

Madeline half turned in her seat to take Olivia's hand. "Don't mind your mother. She's just cranky."

That gained another smile from Olivia.

Simone looked at her daughter. Seeing her smile was a rare occurrence these days. And Madeline was the one that had made her smile.

"Hi Livie," said Cicely. "It's good to see you. I didn't know you were coming with your mother." Even in the dim light she could see a sad look come over her niece's face.

Simone must have seen it too because she quickly said, "Mother-daughter time. You know Olivia is a daddy's girl so I have to steal my time when I can." She reached out and ran her hand down Olivia's sleek hair.

Well, sitting in a parking lot, in the rain was not the place to hear the whole story, thought Cicely. One heart to heart a day was enough for her. She looked at Simone, "Madeline and I got the groceries. Why don't you go in and get the order. It should be enough for everyone. And we'll just meet back at the house."

Simone started to complain, after all she had just driven hundreds of miles, but thought better of it, "Name?"

"Macklin!" said Cicely and Madeline in unison.

"Come on Olivia, I have to get my purse out of the car," she said opening the door.

"We'll take her with us," Madeline said. "She can help take the bags in the house."

"And who will help me?"

"We'll meet you at the door Simone. Better yet we'll wake Bernice," replied Cicely.

Olivia handed her mother the dripping umbrella and settled back fastening her seat belt.

Cicely rolled the window down as Simone walked away and yelled. "Stop and get some wine." She heard Madeline chuckle beside her.

CHAPTER 3

The sisters and Olivia consumed their feast in the dining room. It was awkward at first. Memories of Momma lingered. But soon they were laughing and sipping wine as Cicely told the story of how she thought they were coming to take the house away. She explained how she had qualified to take in foster children and would soon be starting a part-time job as a financial consultant. Flexible hours and could even work from home if she wanted. The home inspection Madeline mentioned had taken place earlier that week. A surprise visit, passed with flying colors.

Bernice admitted she had fallen asleep in Cicely's room. But she looked so much more relaxed than before, Cicely didn't take umbrage. Simone and Olivia would be sharing Cicely and Simone's old room. It was the only bedroom with two beds, right next door to the room Cicely now occupied.

"Ok Simone," said Cicely tilting her wine glass toward her sister, sitting across from her. "I know why Madeline brought her closet with her. She doesn't trust Preston to pack."

At that, Madeline stood up, "I forgot to let Preston know we arrived ok."

"Taken care of," said Bernice, a little tipsy from the wine. "Called him and Louis when I woke up."

Madeline dropped back down in the chair and reached for the almost empty wine bottle to pour more into her glass.

"Simone," Cicely began again. "Why do you have everything but the kitchen sink in your vehicle?" They hadn't begun to unload it yet, but Cicely had noticed when she helped Simone bring the food in, the SUV was as full as it could get with luggage and cardboard boxes.

"Um," replied Simone looking at her hands, fingers intertwined on the table. "We're going to stay with you a little while. Evan lost his job."

Cicely didn't initially hear Olivia speak. She was busy running logistics in her head. Evan and Simone would share a room. Olivia would have her own room. Of course Cicely would occupy one room, which would leave an empty bedroom for a foster child. This could work. Because there was no way she would turn away family.

"Go watch TV," Cicely heard Simone tell Olivia.

"Wait a minute," Cicely looked at her niece. "What did you say?"

"My Daddy hasn't worked in a year. Daddy was fired right after Grandmother died. I heard them fighting about it."

"He was not fired," interjected Simone, "He was downsized. And I told you to leave the room Olivia."

Olivia opened her mouth to protest, but one look at her mother's face made her re-think that action. She turned and stomped her way into the living room. No sister said a word until they heard the volume of the television rise.

"A year Simone," said Cicely, "Really?" She was now standing and carefully set her wine glass on the table. "How many secrets does this family have?"

Only Madeline saw Bernice's eyes widen. She watched Bernice gulp the rest of her wine, then turned her attention back to Cicely and Simone.

"It wasn't a secret," countered Simone. "It was my family business."

Cicely spread her arms, "What are we?"

"We're not destitute. We didn't need any help."

"And yet, here you are at my house." Cicely said dropping her hands to her sides. "When is Evan coming?"

"Evan is selling the house."

"Oh, your beautiful home," murmured Bernice.

"Exactly," said Simone glancing in her direction. Hoping she'd find someone in her corner.

"So Evan is coming when the deal is done?" pushed Cicely.

Simone inhaled deeply, "Evan is not coming."

Still not fully comprehending what she was hearing Cicely said, "Oh, you and Olivia will go back when he finds a new place to live?"

"I've left Evan," Simone said barely above a whisper.

Madeline rested her elbows on the table and pinched the area above her nose between her thumb and forefinger. "I knew Cicely had lied when she told Momma she hadn't dropped you on your head when you were a baby."

Cicely threw her a dirty look before returning her attention to Simone. "You left your husband because he is selling your house?"

"No. Even I know that is shallow. It's more than that."

"Simone, we're your sisters. We're automatically on your side."

"Until we learn the facts," threw in Madeline.

Which earned her another dirty look from Cicely. "Explain it to us," she said to Simone softening her tone.

"It's complicated," she whispered.

"Well I would hope so," said Madeline.

"Please Madeline," said Cicely sitting back down. "Let her tell us."

Everyone was quiet now. Madeline watched as Cicely gently nodded her head in sympathy as Simone told her tale. Occasionally Cicely would cover Simone's folded hands with one of her own. Yes. If Cicely could get even a semblance of truth out of Simone she would make an excellent foster mother.

They listened silently as Simone described the past year of what she felt was injustices toward her.

"He wanted to know every penny I spent."

"You were down to one income," chided Madeline.

"He still had something coming in," said Simone pointedly. "You know my job. I still have to look good for my job. He said I traveled too much. I wasn't traveling any more than I had when he was working. He wasn't there for me anymore."

Bernice stood.

"What?" asked Simone.

"I'm going to check on Olivia. I don't want to hear any more."

"Run away like you always do," said Simone.

Bernice laid her palms on the table and leaned toward Simone. "Looks like you were the one that ran away. I'm going to see about your child." And she left the room.

"It's a two way street," Madeline said softly. "You have to be there for him too. You love your job, it defines you. He lost part of himself when his job was gone. Evan always put you first. It's his turn"

Cicely remained silent. She had no experience with marriage. She just knew her parents supported each other.

"What did you do?" asked Madeline.

"He followed me. He followed me on one of my business trips. He said it was to surprise me."

No one said a word waiting for her to continue.

Bernice found Olivia sitting in the dark, with only the TV

for light. She was sitting on the floor with her back against the sofa. Her knees were pulled to her chest, her arms wrapped around them with her forehead resting on her knees. Olivia looked up when Bernice entered.

The older woman could see her niece had been crying. She sat on the floor next to Olivia and put her arms around her. The child buried her face in her Aunt's chest and sobbed quietly.

Bernice let her cry and rubbed her hand up and down her back like you would soothe a baby.

"My Daddy told her to take her things and get out." Her words were muffled because she still had her face buried in Bernice's bosom.

Bernice glanced around and was grateful to see a box of tissues within arm's length. She pulled a few from the box and gave them to Olivia to blow her nose.

"They had a big fight," she said. She stretched her legs out and kept her eyes on her feet. "I could hear them in my room. I think sometimes they forgot I was home. They fight a lot since Daddy doesn't work anymore. But he does work sometimes.

"Mommy said Daddy had no right to follow her. But Aunt Bernice," she said looking up at her aunt, "It was to surprise her. He told me. I got to spend the night at my girlfriend's house.

"A second honeymoon he said. But he came home the next day, Daddy was so mad."

"Angry," Bernice corrected her without thinking.

"When he picked me up," Olivia finished.

Bernice could imagine what Evan discovered.

"I didn't want to come with mommy. I asked Daddy could I stay with him. He said no." She looked at Bernice tears running down her face. "Does that mean my Daddy doesn't love me any more either?"

"Oh no," said Bernice, squeezing her tight, making a mental note to call Evan. "Your Daddy will always love you."

"It was completely innocent," continued Simone. "The guy in my room was a co-worker. We were having room service."

"Bet that wasn't all you were doing," murmured Madeline.

"I was in the bathroom," said Simone ignoring her. "Just changing, getting out of my suit. He answered the door thinking it was our dinner. It was Evan."

"Whoa," let out Cicely.

"You had a man in your hotel room while you changed?" asked Madeline saying idiot under her breath.

"I know this person," snapped Simone.

"You were dressed when you came out, right?" queried Cicely.

"I was in my robe."

"What did you expect Evan to think?" said Cicely.

"To at least give me the benefit of the doubt."

"Evan doesn't jump to conclusions Simone," said Madeline.

Simone sighed and looked from side to side, not seeing her sisters. "You don't understand."

"Oh Simone," said Cicely lowering her head to hold it between her hands.

"It wasn't intentional. He just made me feel like Evan used to. Whenever I came to town on a buying trip he would flirt. He knew I was married and nothing would come of it."

"Until you flirted back," said Madeline with pursed lips.

"It had only happened once before. And I wasn't sure it was going to happen this time. I felt so guilty the first time."

"But not guilty enough to keep him out of your room. Or have dinner with him," interjected Cicely.

"The first time I came home with the intention of making things better between Evan and me. Honestly, I did." Tears were beginning to run down her cheeks.

"You could have called me," Madeline said sympathetically.

"You are so judgmental," whispered Simone.

Cicely and Madeline shared a look.

"We were growing further and further apart. We didn't want the same things any more. It was happening long before he lost his job. Momma died. Then Evan was downsized, one thing on top of another. But I wasn't going to leave him under those circumstances. Everyone would think I left my husband because he wasn't pulling his weight financially. So I was holding on the best I could. I just took a little happiness where I could. What was wrong with that?"

They all turned at the sound of Bernice clearing her throat. She stood in the archway holding Olivia's hand. Olivia's eyes and nose were red.

"Are we still going to church tomorrow?" she asked. "Because Olivia's clothes are still in the truck."

Madeline said yes.

Simone said no.

"We are going to church," stated Madeline. "Momma's pastor is expecting us."

Simone shook her head no. "I'm not going. You can take Olivia."

Madeline stood. Found her purse and gave her rain scarf to Olivia. "Help your Aunties get some of the things out of the truck. We can finish unloading it tomorrow after church. Maybe it won't be raining then."

When the side door opened she turned to Simone still seated at the table. "You will go to church."

"Why? Because I committed a sin? Because I broke a commandment?"

"Stop thinking about yourself. It's the anniversary of Momma's funeral. That church loved Momma."

"I loved Momma. I know she would be ashamed of me. Olivia can represent me. I'm not going. I don't need to sit in church to feel any worse than I do"

"Not about you. The congregation expects us all to be there. You will attend if I have to drag you there screaming and hollering. And you know I will Simone."

They could hear the footsteps as the group brought in luggage and boxes, setting them on the sun porch.

Simone stood and faced her sister. "Yes I know you would. You always get your way Madeline."

Madeline looked at her with scorn. "So do you Simone. But I don't hurt anyone in the process. You didn't want to be married any longer and you found a way to get out of it. A very messy way."

It was still early evening but after unloading the vehicle everyone retreated to their room. Bernice claimed Olivia. "My bed is big enough," she said, daring Simone to say anything.

Madeline unpacked and went back downstairs to iron what she would wear to church. She wondered if Cicely had saved Momma's church hats. Then touched her cornrows. No, she couldn't wear a hat.

Simone's words came back to her.

Yes, she did get her way most of the time. But it was usually because she persuaded people to see it her way. She didn't leave hurt feeling in in her wake. She didn't consider herself inflexible. Her position as administrator proved that. How many times did the nurses come to her with a more efficient way to do things? And she changed the policy.

Or spoiled, which is what she generally thought of people who had to have their way all the time. She and Simone were nothing alike, Madeline thought, shaking her head.

As she prepared her clothing for Sunday, Madeline thought of the big claw foot tub waiting for her upstairs. Oh, she remembered Momma had a fit when Daddy wanted to rip it out and replace with a modern tub and shower. He ended up ripping out the built in linen closet instead and putting a shower stall in its place. No way would it ever be a two-person shower, but Daddy had his shower. It turned out to be a godsend, because as Momma got older she could no longer step up to get into the deep tub. After Momma recovered from her hip surgery and Madeline came to visit, she and Cicely would help their mother take a bath in her beloved claw foot tub.

Madeline was looking forward to sinking up to her chin in the water without the worry of getting her hair wet. She gathered everything she needed for a long soothing bath, then went back to retrieve her cell phone. She would call Preston while she bathed. In a week they would meet in Disney World. Maybe she could get his motor running before they got there.

Cicely immediately changed into her pajamas, thin cotton shorts and a man's sleeveless undershirt. It was still raining and a good breeze was coming through the bedroom windows. The sheer curtains were gently billowing. She propped herself up on pillows and reached for the phone to call her friend Anita.

"What happened to my picture?" asked Anita, with no hello. Caller ID had struck again.

"You'll see it in person tomorrow. You are still coming to church?"

"The twins and I will be at your Momma's church right on time. Other half can't come. They enlisted him to do something at our church. He said to tell you, sorry."

"I forgive him."

"Aren't you in a good mood? I would have thought you'd be a wreak since Mrs. Hell on wheels rolled in."

Cicely went on to explain it had all been a misunderstanding. How they had all encouraged her in her endeavor to foster children. Her sisters had actually come to help, with the exception of Simone.

"Evan kicked her out. She and Olivia will be staying here for a while."

"Get out!"

"Just act like you don't know when you see her tomorrow."

"I can do that. Now tell all."

She was just hanging up when there was a tap on the door.

Bernice waited until Olivia had fallen asleep before she ventured from the room to find her cell. They had talked about everything but, Olivia's mother and father. Bernice had never heard her talk that much, so she knew it was nerves. Olivia liked kittens. She'd never known her niece was a cat person. Personally she would never have a pet. Too much work.

She could hear girlish giggles and splashing coming from behind the closed bathroom door. That's all Madeline had talked about during the flight there, soaking in the big tub. She wondered if Madeline had remembered to take a glass of wine in with her. Bernice would do that same thing before she returned home.

No noise came from Simone's room but she heard Cicely say good-bye to someone before she raised her hand to knock.

Bernice opened the door but came no further than the doorway. "Did I leave my cell in here?"

Cicely reached over to the nightstand and picked up a phone attached to a lanyard. "You must have taken it off when you napped. It was wrapped in the covers." Cicely patted the bed, "Come sit with me for a while."

"No, I don't want Olivia to wake up and no one is there."

"That bad, huh?"

"Yes." Bernice stepped in and closed the door. "She thinks her Daddy doesn't love her anymore. I need my phone to call Evan."

"Use the house phone," said Cicely passing it to her.

"Sure," said Bernice taking the phone, then handing it back. "Can you dial? I don't know the number by heart."

Cicely dialed the number and gave it back to Bernice.

"Hello Evan? It's Bernice. Do not hang up the phone. I am not calling about Simone."

Cicely couldn't make out the words but could hear his anger coming through the phone.

"It's about your daughter. " She paused, waiting for Evan to speak. "Yes, they made it fine."

"Put it on speaker," whispered Cicely.

Bernice held the phone away from her ear puzzled and Cicely hit the speaker button.

"I've been trying to reach them all day. Simone must have turned her phone off. She purposely left Olivia's cell here."

"She was probably rushed," said Bernice making excuses.

"Simone knew over a month ago I wanted her out," he sounded bitter. Not mellow and smooth like usual. "So I guess she's poured out her heart to her sisters about how bad Evan is. How Evan did this and Evan did that." His voice was rising with every word.

"Evan," Bernice said in her teacher voice. "Evan, listen to me."

They could hear him breathing on the other end, trying to regain control.

Cicely looked at her sister and mouthed the word "Wow". She had forgotten the 'teacher voice'. It could put fear into the hearts of seventh grade boys.

"Eventually you and Simone have to talk," continued Bernice. "I am not calling to facilitate that conversation. I didn't call to pass judgment on you or Simone."

"Sorry," he said properly contrite. They could imagine Evan bowing his head.

"Whatever happened between you and my sister has made Olivia think you don't love her."

"That's not true," he said, his voice starting to rise.

"Evan," repeated Bernice in the voice. "I know that. But she is a child. When you refused to let her stay with you, it was like a smack down to her."

"Circumstances…," he began, but Bernice interrupted him.

"Not important. You need to talk to her and reassure her of your love."

"May I speak to her now?"

"She's asleep. It's been a rough day. Call her tomorrow. We will be attending church."

He barked out a laugh, "Simone going to church."

"Evan if you can't listen I will hang up this phone." She waited to be sure he would. "Call about two o'clock. If we aren't here keep calling. We might go to the grave site."

"I'm sorry Bernice. I'd forgotten the occasion."

"Understandable."

"Could I have your cell number? That way I can be sure to reach Olivia. Simone won't let me speak to her."

"No. Call this number, the house phone. I won't let my niece think I'm in a conspiracy with her father against her mother. Good or bad Simone is our sister. We'll make sure Olivia gets the call." She gave him the number. It was Momma's number still. The same telephone number she'd had forever. Bernice would never forget that. "And Evan, when you talk to her, make a plan of how often you will speak with her. And keep that promise."

"Yes Bernice. And thank you."

"Evan, I'm sorry about what has happened. I love you both. But I just want to be sure you both keep Olivia first.

"I appreciate that Bernice."

"Well, we'll talk tomorrow." Bernice wasted no time clicking off.

Cicely immediately stood and embraced her sister tightly. "You rock Bernice."

Bernice smiled. "I do, don't I?"

She moved to open the door. "Cicely I think it's wonderful what you are planning to do. But what happens after you put your heart into this, fall in love with these children and they leave and forget all about you."

"I won't forget them. I'll have memories. And if I have to, I'll pretend I made a difference in their life."

Bernice nodded, "Goodnight Cicely, love you."

"Love you too Bernice."

CHAPTER 4

After washing all the important parts and brushing her teeth, Madeline knocked on all the bedroom doors, before heading downstairs to start coffee. She would have her usual tea. Everyone had given her a response they were awake, even a groan from Simone.

A look out the bare window on the landing revealed it was still raining. That eliminated the trip to the cemetery today.

Past history indicated Cicely would be the next person up. She would give Simone an additional nudge to make sure she was moving in the right direction.

Madeline prepared her tea and took the cup upstairs to dress. Passing the bathroom she heard the shower stop running. It was like lining up dominoes. She had pushed the first tile, Cicely. It was Cicely's turn to push the next one. So on and so on, until everyone was up and dressed.

An hour and a half later the sisters were in the kitchen ready to leave.

"Why am I the only one not getting something to eat?" whined Simone. She had on black linen high waist crop pants. A white silk tank and a black linen bolero jacket, her outfit completed by impossibly high black pumps. They didn't know how she'd done it, but her hair fell to her shoulders in a mass of soft waves.

"Because you took too long to get ready," said Cicely eating the last of a half bagel she'd shared with Madeline. She picked up her black patent leather clutch that matched her black strappy high-heeled sandals. Her sleeveless lemon colored sheath had a thin black patent belt. Headed toward the side door, Cicely pick up a black pashmina thrown across the back of a kitchen chair. Her hair was held back with a black patent headband.

Olivia had shared her bagel with her Aunt Bernice. In her opinion Aunt Bernice looked very pretty today. She wore a navy blue dress with white polka dots. The silky dress had a full skirt that floated around her when she walked. It had tiny white buttons going down the back that Olivia had fastened for her. The sleeves reminded Olivia of butterflies, because they fluttered around Aunt Bernice's arms almost to her elbows. On her head she wore one of grandmother's hats, a wide brim navy straw hat, with a band of navy with white polka dots like the dress. She carried a white bag and wore white sling back peep toe pumps with a bow.

"It's raining," said Madeline to no one particular. To Bernice she said, "You're going to ruin Momma's hat."

"I have an umbrella." Unable to sleep Bernice had ventured up to the attic to look for memories. Unexpectedly she found a hat to match what she'd planned on wearing to church.

Mild shock greeted all the sisters when they saw what Madeline was wearing. A straight skirt that fell to her calves, an unstructured jacket, which covered her hips, and a black silk tank. What was different was the material. The fabric was African mud cloth. It was ivory muslin with a black design. Her necklace and earrings were made of tiny black seeds braided into an intricate design. With her cornrows, she looked every bit the modern African Queen.

Madeline looked at Olivia with approval. She was dressed appropriately for a thirteen-year old girl. On her feet were plain black flats. She had on black leggings with a short fuchsia colored full skirt. A white T-shirt and a black bolero jacket like her mother's but trimmed with fuchsia embroidery. Her hair was pulled into a ponytail with a fuchsia colored scrunchie.

"We'll take my car," said Simone grabbing her keys from the counter.

"Can you drive in those things?" asked Madeline looking at Simone's stilettos.

"I can run in these things if I have too," answered Simone.

They left the house with Madeline in the lead like a momma duck, each holding an umbrella over their do. Madeline rode shotgun as expected and the other three filled the back seat. Cicely briefly questioned the wisdom of wearing sandals, but figured her feet were no worse for the wear.

The morning announcements were being read when they entered the vestibule of the Morningstar Full Gospel Baptist

Church. At some point in its history the building may have belonged to another denomination. It had high ceilings and a balcony in the back. In an effort to help cool the building a number of ceiling fans had been installed, which also helped distribute heat in the winter months. Numerous stained glass windows lined both sides of the building. It had no center aisle. There was a wide row of pews in the center and narrow rows on each side. An aisle ran between the windows and the pews. Directly in front of the center pews was the pulpit. To the right was the musicians pit and to the left was the choir stand. The wall behind the pulpit was bare except for a large wooden cross.

The elderly usher greeted them as if each were her own long lost children returning to the fold. She passed them a copy of the church bulletin and to Simone's mortification, led them to the front of the church past filled seats and sat them in the rows directly behind the pew occupied by the Mothers of the church, removing the reserved sign as she went back to her post.

Simone leaned across Bernice, Cicely and Olivia to whisper to Madeline, "Did you know about this?"

Madeline just smiled and nodded.

Cicely received a poke to her back as soon as she sat on the cushioned pew. She turned to see her friend Anita with her daughters.

"You're late," smiled Anita.

She took her friends hand and gave it a squeeze. "Too early, if you ask me." The choir had not yet marched in. She gave a finger wave to the girls.

Anita spoke to each of the sisters in turn. And gave Madeline a thumb up for her hairstyle.

They all stood as the organist began to play for the procession of the minister, the assistant ministers and the choir. They remained standing as the morning scripture was read and a prayer said.

When the mornings musical selections were sang, only Bernice seemed to get into the spirit by standing and clapping to the music. The elderly Mothers of the church seemed to nod their approval at her actions.

Finally the minister stepped to the pulpit. "As you long time members know, it's been a year since Mother Macklin left us to be with the Heavenly Father. Today her daughters are here." He waved his hand toward them. "Please stand sisters."

This was just what Cicely had been afraid of. Their mother had been in good standing at the church until her death. Many months before her death she had been unable to attend but church members visited her on a regular basis. The sisters stood and smiled at the crowd behind them. She couldn't look at Anita or she would have burst out laughing. They had talked about just this thing. The old minister was not above putting people on display if he thought it was in his best interest.

He continued as they sat. "We all miss Mother Macklin, and her daughters have traveled here for this auspicious occasion. Sister Cicely still resides in our community and we would like to see more of you."

Talk about bold. Cicely did not attend church regularly but when she did, it was at Anita's church. She preferred the youthful reverend and their relaxed atmosphere. While Morningstar expounded a come-as-you are philosophy, the senior minister was garbed in his elegant pastoral robes. She noted the choir had differed to the summer months and were only dressed in their Sunday best not the heavy choir robes. She had come to maybe four or five services at Morningstar since her mother's passing. After today she didn't know if she would be returning.

"Didn't mean to call you out Sister Cicely," he said showing his dentures. "We know your mother trained you well. Your mother was very well loved."

A bout of applause broke out at his statement.

"Mother Macklin had a generous heart. No one needed for anything if she knew of their lacking. If she felt you were doing something wrong, she would tell you."

You should know, thought Cicely. Her mother had pulled him to the side many a time, never in public, always in private.

"Your mother and I both came here as young people. Whatever needed to be done to help the church she did it. I thought she was going to outlast me. "

Cicely covered her face with her hands. She hoped he wasn't going to preach the eulogy all over again. She and her sisters had agreed Momma's funeral service was to be short. But the leader of the church had felt otherwise and drawn it out. Only a signal from the Funeral Director had made him wind it down. Gravediggers are on a schedule. She felt Anita's hand pat her gently on the back. Cicely knew her friend did not think she was about to burst into tears.

"The bible says 'Honor your Mother', and that's what this congregation wants to do," his voice had start taking on the drone of a southern Baptist preacher. "That's not to say every member that achieves the longevity that Mother Macklin did will receive the same honor. We all agreed she was special. Many of you came to me and said we must do something to show our appreciation."

So that was the reason they were here, thought Cicely. Momma's friends in the church had insisted he acknowledge their Mother.

"I was of the same mind," he droned on. "But was at a loss of what to do. I could stand here all day and list what Mother Macklin did for this church. Brothers and Sisters of the church, Deacons and Deaconess of the church, Mothers of the church, this is what I have been instructed to do." He lifted his hand to indicate a Deacon now standing near one of the stained glass windows. They hadn't noticed the cloth covering the wall beneath the window when they'd been seated.

The Deacon pulled the cloth away and there was a plaque. It had a likeness of Momma etched on it. Under that were the words, 'In memory of Mother Zenobia Marie Macklin, beloved member of the Morningstar Full Gospel Baptist Church'. And the dates she was a member, which spanned fifty years. As the Deacon read the plaque the entire congregation stood and applauded.

Daddy was a member too, but Momma had been the driving force behind their membership. Now Cicely could feel tears rolling down her cheeks. She couldn't look at her sisters because she knew they were moved by the gesture also. One of the Mothers in the row before them produced a box of tissues and urged the sisters to take them. "The old fart wasn't supposed to do this until after the service," she murmured to them. "Your Momma would have had his head for not following the program."

That brought smiles to their faces, because they knew she was right.

Madeline stood, dabbing at her eyes. All eyes looked at the Pastor; the congregation knew he wasn't expecting this.

"Please sit," she encouraged. "My sisters and I appreciate this honor you have given our mother. She loved this church."

The Deacon who had read the plaque hurried over to pass her the microphone so she could be heard, gaining a look of disapproval from the senior Pastor.

"She knew most of you by your first name. And it would make her heart swell with the love for the respect you have shown her. You have overwhelmed us with this gesture. This is a very emotional time for us. It's only been a year since we lost our Momma. She was everything to us. And we still grieve. So I'm sure you will all understand if we have to take a moment to ourselves. Pastor, please continue."

Madeline signaled to her sisters and niece to follow her out of the Sanctuary to the vestibule. Anita and her daughters struggled pass the other parishioners on their row to follow.

"Excuse us, excuse us. We are very close family friends. We'll just see that they are alright," she said.

Madeline continued through the vestibule into the drizzling rain. She stood there under her umbrella laughing at what they'd just done.

"I'll never be able to come back to this church," said Cicely. Suppressing her own laughter.

"Oh, you didn't want to come back anyway," said Anita.

"I wanted a picture of the plaque," sulked Bernice.

"I'll get us pictures," said Madeline. "Us with the plaque, without that old man showing his teeth."

Olivia giggled.

"Don't do that Olivia. It really wasn't very nice what we did," said Cicely.

"I know Auntie, I couldn't help it."

"Well what next?" asked Simone. "I'm hungry. Let's go get something to eat."

"No," said Bernice tugging at her undergarments. "I've

got to get home and get out of this girdle."

"You have a girdle on?" questioned Cicely.

"Not a girdle. One of those things that holds your fat in. It's killing me."

"Spanx." said all the women in unison.

"Then I guess its home," said Madeline. "We can cook something there. Won't you join us Anita?" She asked heading for the car before someone came out to check on them.

"Well since we didn't get a chance to stand when they asked for visitors, I guess we'll head to our church to hear the message." She said looking at her watch.

She and Cicely shared an awkward hug under the umbrellas. "I'm sorry," offered Cicely. "I didn't know this was going to happen."

"Are you kidding?" said Anita over her shoulder as she and her girls walked away. "I would not have missed this for the world. Other half is going to be sorry he missed it. Oh, have Olivia take a picture of the four of you. Y'all Macklin girls looking good today."

Olivia reminded them of the picture when they reached the house. She had them stand in front of the fireplace and took picture after picture with her Auntie Cicely's digital camera. Cicely promised to have copies for each of them before the end of the week.

After changing into comfortable clothing, they converged

in the kitchen. Cicely pulled out the old waffle maker and instructed Olivia how to make the batter while she cut up fresh strawberries. Finishing the strawberries she helped cut up vegetables for the omelets Madeline was making. Bernice was busy with the microwave cooking enough bacon for the five of them. Simone's contribution was a big bottle of champagne.

"Hope there's orange juice. Mimosa's for everyone."

"Oooo, mommy can I have some?" pleaded Olivia.

"Just a sip Sweetie. And only while we eat."

"Mostly orange juice," warned Bernice.

"I'm not trying to raise an alcoholic Bernice." Simone chastised.

It became a moot point because Olivia didn't like the taste, and preferred plain orange juice. But she insisted the breakfast they had prepared was every bit as good as a restaurant one, even though she had to help clean the kitchen afterwards. After asking to be excused she left her mother and aunts sipping mimosas on the sun porch while she went upstairs to watch TV in her Auntie Cicely's room.

The rain was not hard but coming down steadily. The sun porch had what people called Florida windows. They consisted of slats of glass that when closed were weather tight. In the summer you rolled them open to reveal the screens. Got the breeze, without the bugs. Everything looked super green outside in the rain. You could see water rushing down the street and heard it gurgling into the gutter at the corner. As soon as the rain stopped everyone in the neighborhood would have out their lawn mower.

The furniture on the sun porch hadn't been kept up as nice as that on the front porch. Some of it has been around since before their Daddy had died, his old recliner that no one had the heart to give away had made its way to the porch. Simone had claimed that seat and sat with her legs folded under her. Madeline sat in Momma's old wooden rocking chair. Some of the spindles were missing in the back, and it creaked every time she rocked. But somehow that sound along with the rain was comforting.

Mismatched tables were scattered around the porch. Cicely and Bernice shared a seat on an ugly floral patterned sofa. When momma had gotten new furniture the couch had made it no further than its current spot. Even though the day was overcast, no one had bothered to turn on the porch light.

The conversation was light. They mentioned people they had seen at church but hadn't gotten a chance to speak to because of their dramatic exit. Madeline shared how it felt becoming a grandmother for the first time. How much she and Preston were looking forward to visiting Disney World.

Cicely voiced her concerns about being a foster mother. With her sisters rushing to reassure her, she would do a good job.

At exactly two o'clock the phone rang. Cicely went into the kitchen to answer it. They heard her calling to Olivia.

"Who is that calling Olivia?" asked Simone rising from

her seat. "Her friends don't have this number."

Bernice stood also. "Her Daddy."

"He has no right…." Simone snarled ready to leave the room.

Before she could, Bernice grabbed her tightly by the arm.

Simone tried jerking her arm free, but Bernice held her tighter. By morning she would probably have the outline of Bernice's hand on her arm.

"Unless you can tell me without lying, that Evan put his hands on you or Olivia, he has every right to talk to his daughter," said Bernice.

Simone reminded Madeline of a guppy the way her mouth kept opening and closing.

"You and Evan hate each other right now. I got that. But you will not turn that child against her father. Be an adult in this mess you created. Because, if you cut her off from her father right now, she will learn to hate you. Same for Evan.

"And who's going to tell him that?"

"If he hasn't got the message already, I will," said Bernice

"You've talked to Evan? Behind my back?"

"Yes I have. And I wasn't going behind your back. I talked to him about Olivia and that was it. I wouldn't let him tell me anything about your and his situation. I don't want to know. I just want Olivia to come out of this whole mess okay." Bernice let Simone jerk her arm free.

"I'll be in my room," she said brushing past Cicely as she came back onto the porch.

"She's in my room talking to her Daddy," said Cicely to Bernice, staying close to the wall so Simone wouldn't run her down. "Is she going to interfere?" she asked pointing at a retreating Simone.

"No," said Bernice, sitting back down. "I need to tell you something. My secret."

Cicely saw the serious look on Bernice's face and sat close to her sister on the sofa. "Do you want me to get Simone back here?"

"No. Let her have her temper tantrum. She'll find out eventually but she doesn't have to be here now."

It seemed like minutes went by before she spoke again.

"I have early onset dementia." She said it flatly. No emotion in her voice.

Madeline's glass shattered as it hit the floor. "Alzheimer's?" Working in her field Madeline knew how devastating the disease could be. "But you're only fifty"

"I don't want to use that word. I refuse to give that word power."

Cicely took her hand and spoke. "How long have you known?'

"Since right after Christmas."

"And you didn't tell us," said Cicely unbelieving.

"Cicely if you had known would you have left me alone in the house yesterday?"

Cicely bowed her head and shook it no.

"And Madeline, if you had known would you have left me standing in the middle of the airport with our baggage while you went to pee?"

Madeline could not look at Bernice.

"I'm not ready to be treated like an invalid. While I'm still me, I want to be treated like me. Louis encouraged me to tell you, but the time never seemed to be right. Then this whole thing with Simone made me realize I didn't want to keep you in the dark any more. I need you as my support system, before I slip away. Cicely reminded me that even if I forget you, you would never forget me as I was."

She went on to explain she was currently on medication that helped slow the progression of her dementia. Telling about her breakdown in front of the class was an embarrassment to her. Her mind had gone completely blank and that was what had driven her to see a doctor.

"You wear your cell phone around your neck," said Cicely.

"So I don't lose it,"

"Everyone loses their cell phone," said Madeline coming to sit on the other side of her sister. Her eyes filled with unspilled tears.

"Everything is pretty stable for now. I finished the school year, but they don't want me to come back. But I have to figure out something to do. I can't sit at home waiting for it to happen. It could be months, years before I am unable to function."

They all knew years would be stretching it. Especially, with Bernice being diagnosed so early. But no one would speak negativity into the atmosphere.

"Burnie," said Madeline calling her by her childhood name. "Have you gotten a second opinion? So many things can mimic dementia. Even some medications can cause erroneous symptoms."

Bernice laughed. "Louis has dragged me to every kind of specialist you can think of. And I'll keep going to them. We pray a lot and every day we thank Him."

She told them she had been unable to convince her daughter, Jeanine to go with her original plan to go away to school. Jeanine would go to school locally. Her only concession would be to live on campus. "Mostly I forget little things, nothing major. Louis doesn't want to let me leave the house alone. But for now I'm fine. I have to push him out the door to go to work. I do have a medical alert bracelet, so if I become confused someone can help me. The thing is right now I am still able to tell something's not right. As it progresses I won't realize something is wrong."

All three of them were crying now.

"There is one thing I need you to do for me Madeline," she turned to Cicely and patted her hand. "I'm not leaving you out Cicely. But Madeline lives the closest and will be better able to judge. Do not let Earl become a martyr. Don't let my children become martyrs. When you think things are overwhelming them make sure they don't try to keep caring for me at home."

"And you Cicely, Louis is still young. Don't let some young thang come along and turn his head. And he does need to remarry or hook up. Despite what our children say."

Cicely put her sister in a bear hug. "No one will be able to match you Bernice."

"I know that," she said swiping away tears. "I just don't want him to be lonely or get taken for his money."

Madeline laughed, "Yes Louis with the big bucks."

They all knew Louis could make the eagle scream.

"Burnie," said Madeline all excited. "We still have time to make good memories. You and Louis come to Disney World with Preston and me."

"I don't know," said Bernice shaking her head.

"That's a great idea," said Cicely, grasping both their hands.

"Did you bring a bathing suit?" asked Madeline.

"Of course not. Look at me."

"We can go shopping. Either here, or in Florida. Here

would be cheaper though," said Madeline. You could almost see the thoughts running through her head.

"Madeline, it's too late to make those kinds of arrangements," said Bernice still shaking her head.

"No, it's not," said Madeline standing and pulling Bernice with her. "We're going to go upstairs right now and call Preston and get Louis on a three way"

"That sounds kinky," said Cicely feeling the mood lightening.

"You have a dirty mind little sister," chided Madeline pulling Bernice along.

You could look at Bernice's face and see the excitement building in her. If it was doable, Madeline would be the one to get it done.

Cicely rose to clean up the glass Madeline had broken and headed to her room. She heard a noise in the downstairs bathroom and opened the door to find Simone sitting on the closed toilet crying quietly. "You heard?" she asked.

Simone stood and wrapped her arms around Cicely's neck. "I hid to hear what you all would say about me. But it wasn't about me. What do I say to her? I've been so mean."

"For now you say nothing. She wants to be treated no differently." In their position Cicely could not help looking at Simone's hair closely. "Simone, what did you do to your hair?"

Simone pulled away, sniffed and tossed her hair. "Hair piece. How did you think I looked so good this morning," she said smugly.

Cicely pulled her back into an embrace. "Girl, I love you."

"I love you too," said Simone squeezing her back.

They both went upstairs. Simone fetched Olivia from Cicely's room, saying they were going for ice cream even if it was raining. Cicely wondered if Simone would try to pump Olivia about what her Daddy had to say, but she wasn't going to worry about that now. Madeline and Bernice had confiscated her laptop to continue making plans for their joint vacation. Neither sister had ever taken a vacation that had not entailed visiting family. So this would be a real treat considering the circumstances.

Cicely tried watching television, but that wasn't working for her. She could not help but think about what the future would hold for them when Bernice's illness became apparent. She buried her face in her pillow and sobbed. First Simone's announcement that she and Evan were no longer together and then Bernice revealing she had a devastating disease. Her last thought before falling asleep was it comes in threes.

She awoke to laughter coming from downstairs. It was still raining so it was hard for her to judge how long she had slept. A glance at the bedside clock said it was just a little after five. She shuffled to the bathroom to wash her face. Making sure no trace of her hard crying remained. Her little locks were sticking up all over her head. Served her right for falling asleep without tying her head up. She tried smoothing them down, then gave up. It was what it was.

They were all on the floor in the living room when she came down. Photo albums spread across the floor.

Simone was leaning over Olivia's shoulder pointing to a picture, "And this is your Aunt Madeline when she was five."

Madeline took the book to see, "How would you know? You weren't even born yet."

Cicely knew which photograph they were talking about. Madeline hated that picture. She had been tall for a five year old. Very short shorts revealed long legs and knobby knees. She had her hands on her hips and a scowl on her face. Her hair was a wild halo about her head. Even she couldn't remember when the picture had been taken. They just speculated Momma had just washed her hair and Daddy had pulled the camera out. Madeline was not fond of candid shots.

"Did anyone think of dinner?" asked Cicely.

"Mommy and *I*," Olivia said, looking at Bernice, indicating she had corrected her before, "bought pizza. From that place you all like. It has all the main food groups on it."

"Okay," said Cicely going into the kitchen to get a slice, "All of you are going running with me in the morning. Rain or shine. I will not suffer alone after eating all this unhealthy food."

CHAPTER 5

Cicely woke just as it was starting to lighten up outside. But the rain had stopped and the birds were busy making noise. She liked this time of morning during the summer months, when everything was still. Occasionally she would hear a car go pass with a swish, meaning the streets were still wet. Maybe the rain had been Momma crying from heaven because of all her daughters were going through. Maybe no rain, meant things were going to get better. It comforted her to think Momma still watched over them with Daddy at her side.

She slid out of bed to her knees on the bedside. She thanked God for His goodness and continued blessings. She prayed and threw in all the things Momma always did. Thank you for waking me up this morning in my right mind. She paused and briefly wondered how many more right minds Bernice was going to wake up to. Out loud she said, "Devil get out of my thoughts." Then, continued to pray out loud. Momma always said voice your prayers. God already knows your thoughts, so speak to Him with the voice He gave you. Don't let the devil use your tongue. He'll creep into your thoughts easy enough.

That done she decided to wash a load of towels. With all the women in the house, keeping clean towels was going to be a chore. She gathered the towels and her dirty underwear and headed to the basement. The door to the basement was between the kitchen and the sun porch. She flipped the light on and started down the stairs with the laundry basket, then realized the basement floor seemed to be moving.

She peered closer and saw the basement was flooded. "Shit, shit, shit," she said. There was at least a foot of water lapping at the bottom of the stairs. Cicely sat down on the stairs ready to shed some tears. Why had this happened now?

She stomped up the stairs not caring whom she woke up. She stood at Madeline's door and knocked. "Madeline," she called.

Madeline answered the door in a white cotton sleeveless nightgown and a sleep cap on. "What? What?"

"The basement's flooded."

"What do you want me to do it about it?"

Bernice's door opened a crack. "Call one of those rotor rooter places, or a plumber. Call a plumber."

"I don't know any plumbers," snapped Cicely.

By this time Simone and Olivia were standing in the hall. "What's the matter?" asked Simone. "You're waking up everyone."

"The basements flooded." Madeline told her. "I guess we need a plumber."

Olivia went back into the bedroom and came out with a piece of paper in her hand and tried giving it to her Auntie

Cicely.

Cicely took it without looking. Waving it while she talked. "Why did this have to happen now?"

Olivia took her hand and pointed to the ad on the back of the church bulletin. Plumbing Service, 24hrs a day. Mention this ad and get ten percent off most services.

Cicely kissed her niece on the forehead. At least someone had read the church bulletin. "Thank you sweetie," and went downstairs to the kitchen to call.

It seemed to take forever before anyone answered. She was about to hang up when a male voice answered. "Walter's Crew Plumbing. How can I help you?"

She paused. His voice was deep and smooth, came from deep in his chest, not just from his throat. The kind of voice, that even if an ugly man had it, it would draw women to him. He sounded like her Daddy.

"Hello?" he said.

She finally found her voice and explained where she lived and why she was calling.

"Has your basement flooded before?" he asked.

She turned to her older sisters and repeated the question.

"Years ago," said Madeline. "You were a baby."

"You're talking about almost forty years ago," she said to Madeline not realizing she was also talking into the phone and the person on the other end could hear everything.

"Do you have many trees on your property?" He asked.

After answering him yes, she had to repeat to her sisters everything he was saying.

"Put him on speaker," said Bernice using the same tactic Cicely had used when she had been speaking to Evan.

Cicely really didn't want to put him on speaker. She didn't want to have to share his voice with her sisters. But she did it to make things simpler. He was asking questions about the electrical box and appliances.

"It's almost six now," he said.

Cicely looked at her sisters. None of them seemed to notice the timbre of his voice but her.

"I can't be there for at least another hour and a half. A lot of people in your area are having the same issue because of the rain."

"Call someone else," volunteered Madeline.

"Ma'am," he said.

Simone snickered because he had called Cicely ma'am.

"He wasn't talking to me," whispered Cicely to her baby sister and pointed to Madeline.

"Ma'am," he said again. "You're welcome to call someone else."

Cicely could feel his voice in her belly.

"But I don't know how successful you'll be. Look, this is what I'll do. You call someone else but I'll still come by in an hour and a half. If I don't see you have someone, I'll stop."

"We'll do that," said Cicely, but she really wanted to see who went with that voice.

Walter was bone tired. The steady rain had created some extra business for him and his crew, one other licensed plumber, an apprentice and two helpers. He'd gone to bed at ten, fell asleep at midnight and was up at two am because of emergency calls. Walter's Crew Plumbing really didn't need to do emergency calls any more, but, when he and his aunt's husband had started the business those kinds of calls were their bread and butter. Now the business mostly subsisted on new builds and bathroom remodels.

But Walter would go by the house with all the women. He was curious. It sounded like the household he was raised in. His mother was unmarried and seventeen when she'd had him. He'd been named after his mother's brother who hadn't made it past two months old. His formative years were spent with his mother, her two sisters, and his grandmother. And his grandfather, who didn't hesitate to put a foot up his behind if he even thought about disrespecting any of the women. He thought his grandfather would still put a foot up his behind if Walter behaved badly toward any woman even at thirty-one years old.

It was nearly two hours later when he pulled up to the house in his pickup truck. He liked the look of the house. It was older but well kept. Probably still had the original radiators for heat. Something else plumbers took care of. There were some large old growth trees that could have accounted for the flooded basement, but he had to get things drained before he would know. There was no indication another plumber had come before him, so he got out the truck and headed up the front walk.

Simone was watching him through the dining room window. He didn't walk. He had a swagger. Not like a young punk. But the swagger of a man who knew exactly what he wanted and how he was going to get it. Made her think of the cowboy movies her Daddy used to watch, the sheriff, walking down the street with a gun at his hip. Damn, if he didn't look like that black guy they had killed off that CSI television show. What was his name? Gary something.

He was brown skinned, but with a reddish undertone, over six feet tall. He wore his hair in a short wild afro. It was a funny sandy colored brown. His mouth looked very kissable, even from this distance. She would have to wait until he got up close before she could see what color his eyes were. Simone was betting green. He needed a shave. But maybe that was his style. She preferred clean-shaven herself.

Couldn't really tell his build, he had on those damn overalls. Well at least they wouldn't have to look at a plumbers crack. But that might be a crack worth seeing, smiled Simone. His sleeveless T-shirt did show his well-sculpted arms. Plumbers must do some kind of physical labor to have arms that looked like that, she thought.

Simone was so busy looking Cicely beat her to the door

when the bell rang.

She reached the door just as Cicely was telling him to go to the sun porch to enter the house. "What color were his eyes?" asked Simone breathlessly.

"I don't know," said Cicely. "I wasn't going to let him traipse through the house with those big rubber boots on." But she had noticed. They were hazel with green flecks. And he was younger than she'd thought. But his voice sounded even better in person.

Walter stood in the dog trot between the sun porch and the kitchen. He was facing the kitchen where the four women and young girl were sitting. With the exception of the teenager he could tell they were sisters. The light skinned one gave him a look that said she was interested if he was. The one he assumed to be the oldest looked to be around his mothers' age, maybe a little older. But they were all damn good-looking women. Mentally he gave himself a kick. His mother would not appreciate him calling clients damn good-looking women. His grandfather might though and they would laugh about it. Nothing disrespectful about calling a woman good- looking.

He was explaining to Cicely, because he'd been told she was the homeowner, there was nothing he could do until the water was gone. He'd started the sump pump and it was working fine. It was not raw sewage coming in the house so she didn't have to worry about that. He had to leave because he had an appointment to keep. He would be back. The sump pump was staying so what choice did he have but to come back. If the water emptied before he got back it would automatically stop. And she didn't have to pay anything until he returned.

Walter did have an appointment. Besides the plumbing business he had a side thing going with his mother. She was a real estate agent and in the past year they had started flipping houses. His mother had a good eye when it came to run down property that still had life. She had her own crew when it came to gutting a house and putting it back together. The plumbing part strictly reserved for Walter and his crew. But she bought no property without input from Walter. She had never married but never turned her son into a momma's boy. He had his life and she had hers. Walter had just enough time to get home, shower and shave before meeting his mother at the latest property she hoped to acquire.

Cicely was left home alone to wait for the plumber to return. Madeline had accomplished what she wanted, getting Bernice and Louis to accompany her and Preston to Florida. So they had gone shopping. Simone insisted on leading the expedition because her store had a location in the area. She would just flash her ID and big discounts would be had. Olivia went along because she was starting to discover fashion.

First Cicely sat on the basements steps watching the water level go down. That got boring pretty quickly. She started to call Anita to tell her what was happening, then realized her friend was at work and couldn't talk freely. There was no one else she wanted to call. There was nothing to stop her from thinking about Walter.

Who knew a plumber could look so good? She was expecting an older man. His voice, over the phone, conveyed a more mature man. When did young men start becoming plumbers? It could be a dirty job. Most young men didn't like getting their hands dirty. But Walter's hands had been clean. Nails cut short, no doubt to keep dirt from accumulating under them. He hadn't objected when she'd sent him around the side of the house. He knew his clothes were grungy. But what could you expect when he had come from another job to her house. Bet his wife had a time keeping his clothes clean. But there had been no wedding ring had there? Were plumbers allowed to wear rings? Couldn't they get caught on the equipment they used?

Cicely stopped her musing. He was too young and she was too old, for him anyway. She wasn't looking for a relationship. That ship had sailed, but a nice stable man would be nice. Someone her own age, or older. It didn't hurt to look though. Didn't men say that all the time? She wasn't dead yet. And Walter was a nice piece of eye candy.

The sump pump had stopped by the time he returned. The meeting with his mother had gone bust. The broker for the property had wanted too much money. His mother figured in a few months the broker would call begging them to buy. He'd told his mother about the house he was currently working on. She knew the house and loved the old property. She'd vaguely known the elderly woman that owned it and had watched to see if the property would be listed when she'd heard the woman had died. It was good to hear it was staying in the family. It would have broken her heart if the lovely old house had fallen into disrepair.

Cicely was watching when he got back. This time he was in a big panel truck with the name of his company on the side. She watched as he unloaded two industrial sized fans. That was a good idea. She hadn't thought about how the basement was going to dry out. He was no longer in overalls, but clean dark work pants with a short sleeve shirt to match. The shirt did nothing to hide his arms and she could see the tendons tighten as he lugged the fans to her door. Now if he would only turn around so she could see his butt.

Her wish was granted. Walter jogged back to his truck to get something he had forgotten. He leaned over into the truck before pulling the door down. If Cicely could have whistled she would have. What a nice rear end.

The only audience Walter had when he entered the house this time was Cicely. By the quiet, he guessed everyone had taken off leaving her to deal with him. She had on shorts and he knew if she were going in the basement she should put on long pants. But he didn't want to suggest that. He liked looking at her legs. She had runner's legs. Muscled thighs and calves that a man could picture wrapped… "Whoa, Walter," he thought. Where did that come from?

He needed to take his mother's advice and date more. Actually, his mother had said he needed a one night stand every once in a while. She wasn't pressuring him to make her a grandmother any time soon, or a mother-in-law. Still, looking at his grandparents, he could picture himself married one day. They had a solid relationship that he hoped he could replicate.

Cicely did follow him to the basement so she could see the damage for herself. She had slipped on a pair of rain boots. He had watched her slip them on. He thought she had nice feet. Her toenails were painted bright red. He liked when women painted their toenails, even more than when they had nicely manicured fingernails. Probably had something to do with growing up around a bunch of women. He also watched when she came down the stairs. She didn't have a bra on and her breasts jiggled beneath the t-shirt. Not bounced but jiggled. Walter liked that jiggle and felt himself becoming aroused.

Damn, his mother was right. He quickly ran through some names in his head and just as quickly dismissed them. He put the fans in place and started to disassemble the sump pump to distract himself.

"We aren't going to need that again?" Cicely asked watching him.

He couldn't look at her when he answered. He kept winding the electrical cord around his arm. "No, it's not supposed to rain again this week. And I'll set you up with one if it's needed."

Walter explained to her he had a piece of equipment, a small camera actually, that he could run through the lines to see what was blocking them. After telling her all the reasons the basement could have flooded and what could be done about it he was ready to go. He'd be back when she decided what she wanted done. He had checked out the hot water tank to make sure it was still lit. Told her it was a good thing the washer and dryer had been sitting on a platforms. The boiler for the radiators was above the floodwater so that wouldn't be an issue when the cold weather came. He even offered to come back and bleed the radiator lines when the time came.

Walter also told her to keep the fans running all night with the basement windows cracked open. To make sure the basement door was locked in case anyone was stupid enough to try to come through a window and come into the upstairs. She might want to consider glass block windows. What he didn't tell her was the fans were not a normal part of his service. He had rented the fans on his own and brought them over.

"Oh, I have to pay you," said Cicely jogging up the stairs to get her checkbook.

That was almost Walter's undoing. He took the stairs slowly to give himself time to recover and waited for her on the sun porch.

She had the church bulletin in her hand when she returned. "Ten percent discount?" She asked with her head kind of tilted to the side.

"Sure," he said glad his Uncle had suggested putting advertisements in church bulletins. "No problem." He gave her a price and his name Walter Moore.

Walter went home and took yet another shower. He

debated calling his grandfather and settled on his mother. He could have just walked next door. They shared a duplex. The first piece of property they had owned together. In another year or so they would sell it and make a good profit. His buddy's teased him about living with his mother but they knew the situation and they knew his mother. His friends thought his mother was cool. They kept separate households and very rarely shared a meal. Thankfully the bedrooms did not share a common wall. His mother was known to have a gentlemen caller every once in a while. She probably had a more active personal life than he did.

"Ma," he said when she answered. "How do you feel about me seeing an older woman?"

"Does she still have her own teeth?" she asked.

"Yes ma'am."

"Then what are you calling me for Walter," she said and hung up on him.

He laughed, a sound Cicely would love when she heard it. The phone rang before he could put it down. It was his mother.

"On second thought Walter, having no teeth might be a good thing for you." She said and hung up again.

He laughed again. His mother had no shame.

Cicely didn't realize until after Walter left, she had no bra on. She wasn't one not to wear a bra just to get a man's attention. No wonder he'd kept staring at her.

CHAPTER 6

She hired him so the basement wouldn't flood again. It took Walter three days to finish the job with a helper, a fourth day for cleanup. During that time Cicely avoided him unless he specifically sought her out. He'd make up something about the job just to talk to her. Bernice would bring him cold drinks. Madeline would bring him a sandwich. Simone would sit on the stairs and just watch what he was doing, and trying to get a conversation going. He had figured out she was estranged from her husband because when Olivia got a phone call from her father she was ecstatic and Simone became very pissy.

He knew, the one day they visited the cemetery because the house was unnaturally quiet when they returned. Now, he knew for certain Cicely was a runner. When he'd arrive to start work she would be leaving, going for a run before the sun got too hot. She would be gone for about an hour or more, so she was serious about what she did. He would speak, and Cicely would wave and take off.

The last day he waited to come over just so he could be sure she would be there. No way could she avoid giving him the final payment for the repairs he'd done. He'd worked up enough nerve to at least ask her out for coffee.

He was outside loading his truck when a strange car pulled up, rental, by the looks of it. A white guy got out and walked up the stairs onto the front porch. He had on a dark suit, his tie loosened at the neck. The man was tall his dark hair sprinkled with gray.

Walter walked to the side of the porch and called out to him, "May I help you?"

The man peered at him through the bannisters, "No, I don't think so," and rang the bell.

From his position, Walter couldn't see who answered the door. Whoever it was had not let him in, so it had to be Olivia. He did hear someone pounding up the stairs inside the house.

Olivia ran up the stairs calling, "Auntie Cicely, there's a white man here to see you"

Cicely stood in her bedroom doorway. She was staying hidden until she had to pay Walter. "Did he say who he was?" She wasn't in the mood for some salesman.

"He said to tell you it was Darren."

She walked down the stairs to the nosy looks of her sisters. Ready to have her back if she needed it. She wanted anything but that right now. Someone had let him in and he was waiting at the bottom of the stairs for her.

He wrapped her in his arms. She turned her face before he could plant a kiss on her lips. "I've missed you Cicely," he said.

Over his shoulder she could see Walter standing in the doorway and she put her hand on Darren's chest and gave a little push to give herself some space.

"We have to talk," she said softly. But knew her sisters were straining to hear what she said. "Wait for me on the porch." Cicely turned to go back upstairs to change, her sisters following her.

They gave her no privacy while she changed into a white full cotton skirt with a wide brown belt at the waist. She yanked a white cotton eyelet sleeveless blouse out of the closet while they pounded her with questions.

"Who is that?" asked Simone.

"Someone in her life I guess she doesn't want us to know about," Madeline said answering for her.

Cicely stopped putting on the chunky heeled sandals she was slipping on to look at Madeline, "He from the west coast okay. I haven't seen him since I moved back home."

"So you say," quipped Simone.

Cicely didn't say anything, just continued fastening her shoes.

"Oh, my God! Cicely, you were having an affair with a married man." Simone said leaping to conclusions. Anything to make Cicely look bad. "Talk about the pot calling the kettle black," she added smugly.

"Why is he here?" asked Madeline.

"I don't know," said Cicely. "But I'm not going to have that conversation now." She grabbed her purse and left the room.

Walter was sitting on the wicker sofa with Olivia when she made her appearance outside. Darren was standing on the sidewalk. No friendly chatter between the men.

"Let's go for a ride," she said walking past Darren to his rental car. There was no place private for them to talk here.

Walter watched her hips sway in that skirt and cursed to himself. Saw the man put a proprietary hand at her waist as they walked to the car. She stood while he opened the door. Now he knew why she wasn't interested in him.

They had only driven two blocks when Cicely asked him to pull over. "Why are you here? We haven't seen or talked to each other in five years."

"I'm divorced now. You said if I was free…"

"That was years ago Darren. Did you think I've been pining away for you all this time? I was taking care of my mother," she said angrily.

"No. But I thought you were developing feeling for me before you found out I was married. Now that obstacle isn't here."

"Obstacle? The idea you would even try to hook up with me and you were married was enough to make me never want to be with you. How did you find me anyway?"

"We had some acquaintances in common. I just casually asked about you. People love to talk. They told me your mother had died and you were alone. No one ever knew we were romantically involved."

"We were never romantically involved Darren. A few dates. A couple of kisses. That's all it ever was."

"It was more than that to me."

"Five years is an awful long time to hold a torch. Flying cross country... Oh, you had business here," she said realization coming to her. "And you thought I'll go see Cicely. Maybe she'll buy the BS I'm selling now."

"Yes I had business here," he said thoughtfully. "But you're short-changing yourself. Cicely you had a very strong impact on me. Let's go have something to eat and talk about this."

"There is nothing to talk about."

"Cicely I think you are being unreasonable."

"What's unreasonable? It's not like you professed some undying love for me. I told you I couldn't see you anymore because you were married and you walked away like it was nothing."

"I was being respectful to your wishes."

"And not your wife. You think you are so smooth Darren."

"What do you mean by that?" he asked, becoming a little red around the collar.

"I know people too. And you're right, they do love to talk. No sooner than I kicked you to the curb you found another black woman to go out with. One that didn't care you were married. That's the new it thing isn't it? White guy having a good looking black woman on his arm?"

"Kicked me to the curb? Is that what this small town has done to you? I thought you were more sophisticated than that. Or is the young kid at your house more your taste now? I thought cougars were a west coast thing," he said smugly.

Cicely unfastened her seat belt and opened the door. "You shouldn't have gone there Darren. You wasted your time coming to see me. And yes I did kick you to the curb. That's universal. I should have made it clearer I wouldn't give a man who would cheat on his wife the time of day. And I certainly won't become the woman you sleep with whenever you're in town. Do us both a favor and forget where I live." She slammed the car door and took her time strolling away.

She smiled to herself when he burned rubber pulling away and hoped the GPS in the rental car broke and he got lost.

Walter saw her coming down the street. He was determined to stay until she got back. He did have to get paid after all. He didn't let her get to the front stairs before he confronted her. He was invading her space. "So that's why you won't give me the time of day. I'm too dark"

She looked him up and down. "Don't tell me you've never lifted the skirt of a white girl."

He came right back at her. "Once, when I was five. I wanted to see if little white girls had the same thing in their panties that little black girls did. My mother had to come to school for that one."

She couldn't believe what she had heard and burst out laughing. It was a big belly laugh, the kind that she hadn't had for a while.

First Walter smiled. Then he laughed with her. Any anger he had drained away. "I want to take you for some ice cream. Let me take you for some ice cream," he said.

She had to look up at him. He was clean-shaven today. And Darren was right, he was young. But his laugh stirred feelings in her belly.

"Why?" she asked.

Walter took a step back. No woman had ever asked him why before. There was usually some mutual attraction, which he was pretty sure he had with Cicely. He knew she had some reservations about something. He just wasn't quite sure what they were. Even though he'd made that dumb remark about race, he was pretty sure that wasn't it. Was this what it was going to be like if he pursued this woman? Would she question everything?

He moved back into her space.

"Because it's hot. To celebrate your basement won't flood again. Because do you really want to spend the rest of the day explaining your white friend to your sisters. Or..." he said holding up one finger, "We both like ice cream. Choose one."

She was uncomfortable with him standing so close, but wouldn't let him know it. And he was right. She did not want to face her sisters at the moment.

Cicely hadn't given an answer though.

"You sit on the porch; they don't even have to know you came back. I'll go change and come back for you," Walter said. "You don't have to go in"

"Better yet," said Cicely sashaying toward his pickup. "I'll ride with you and wait."

It only took Walter a few steps to catch up with her. "The A/C's not working in the truck. I don't know if you want to ride with me," and gestured at the sweat marks at his armpits.

"We can keep the windows down," said Cicely sliding into the passenger seat, not waiting for him to open the door, belatedly wondering if her white skirt would survive. She knew he was sweaty. But he didn't stink. There was a pure masculine odor about him. Maybe in a matter of time it would become funky, but at this moment he just smelled like Walter.

It took Walter all of ten minutes to reach his house. Though it was only minutes away, his neighborhood was in transition. And that was being kind. Several vacant lots dotted the area and on the block he lived, a few houses were boarded up. His was an older two-story side-by-side duplex. However the area was being developed. Directly across the street from him were two newly built single-family homes.

He invited her in where it was cooler, but Cicely turned him down. This was just ice cream, she kept repeating as her cell phone kept ringing. She looked, saw it was one of her sisters and let it go to voice mail. Finally she texted Simone. 'Tell everyone to stop calling. Can't talk now. Will see you later.' Hoping that would give her a little reprieve.

She texted her best friend to let her know Darren had shown up. When she returned home she would tell Anita all about that drama. Now her friend texted back "OMG."

Cicely hadn't noticed, but after about fifteen minutes of waiting a woman had approached the truck. She had put her hands on the lowered window and said, "Hi." Startling Cicely.

"I didn't mean to scare you," the woman said when Cicely jumped.

Cicely couldn't determine how old the woman was. She looked to be about her age. Her permed hair was short and sleeked back from her face. She was shorter than Cicely and a pair of glasses hung around her neck by a chain.

The woman didn't give Cicely a chance to protest as she opened the door and pulled Cicely out by her hand. "He shouldn't have left you sitting in this dirty truck, especially as hot as it is. At least you didn't ruin your skirt," noticing how nice Cicely was dressed.

"No, really I'm fine," Cicely was saying as the woman pulled her along.

The duplex didn't have a porch, just a few steps leading to the front door. The woman had produced a key and led them in. It took a few moments for her eyesight to adjust to the dim room after being in the bright summer sun. By then Walter was coming down the stairs beginning to button his shirt.

Yes, he had pecs, thought Cicely, just lightly covered in fine hairs. A dark line of hair ran from his navel to the waistband of his thigh hugging jeans. No hard six pack, but a flat belly also covered in fine hairs and an innie. If she had been a cartoon character her tongue would have rolled out of her head. She had a hard time dragging her eyes to his face.

"You met my mother," he said knowing full well he had enlisted his mother to get Cicely out of the truck, once he knew she was home.

"No, she hasn't," said the woman turning to Cicely with her hand extended. "I'm Janice."

Cicely shook her hand and said her own name. She had been ogling Walter in front of his mother. That dampened any impure thoughts she was having. Now that her eyes had fully adjusted she could see the resemblance. The woman was lighter than Walter, but they had the same hazel/green eyes. She looked really young, especially dressed like she was in flip-flops, black capris and a white tank. Pretty much the same thing Cicely wore when she was home.

"Walter," Janice said as she was leaving. "If you're going out take your car. It's too hot to drive someone around in that truck. Besides it's dirty."

"Yes, Janice," he said closing the door behind her. He didn't know what payback his mother would require for doing him the favor of getting Cicely into his apartment.

"You call your mother by her first name," said Cicely, not moving from the spot she was standing.

"Only when I want to irritate her," he said as he finished buttoning his shirt. He was smiling but knew Cicely was becoming pissed.

"How old are you Walter? Your mother doesn't look like she's old enough…"

He became serious. Now he knew the source of her reluctance to give him the time of day. "I'm thirty-one years old. My mother was seventeen and still in high school when I was born. My father is not in the picture, has not been in the picture since his family learned of my conception. Used to be the girl got shipped away. In this case the boy got shipped away. I'm not angry I grew up without a father. My mother, with her parents and my aunts and later their husbands did a pretty good job. I have my own business and know enough not to make a baby then abandon it. I have no baby momma drama."

"Walter," said Cicely holding her arm up, like a crossing guard stopping a car. "I'm..."

"It don't matter to me how old you are Cicely." Her name just rolled off his tongue.

"I'm forty and I have a birthday coming in December."

"And I had one in May. I didn't picture you as a person that bent to convention. Can we just get to know each other? Be friends? Whatever you want. I want to get to know you Cicely."

"I don't know Walter."

"Then let's just go get ice cream," he said opening the door.

CHAPTER 7

It was after ten pm when Cicely entered the house barefooted. She was hoping to get to her room before being accosted. No such luck. A voice called out to her from the living room, where Madeline sat in the dark watching TV. So Madeline had been the one elected to interrogate her. Cicely sat down in an armchair away from Madeline.

"So they picked you as the inquisitor," said Cicely. It was like being caught by Momma for sneaking in after curfew.

"No one picked anybody Cicely. You're grown. Just like Simone."

Inside Cicely flinched.

"You've been gone a long time. We got worried."

"I haven't been with Darren all this time. I was with Walter," she let slip. In the darkness, she could picture Madeline's one eyebrow go up.

"You're two consenting adults," shrugged Madeline. She hadn't missed the interest Walter had shown in Cicely. And smiled to herself, the idea of it was driving Simone crazy.

"Not with him **that way**," huffed Cicely. But she'd thought of it. It was kind of hard to be in Walter's presence and not think about it. They'd gotten something to eat at one of the chain restaurants and took a walk through the city park. And then went for ice cream, hardly what you'd call a hot date. He'd talked about how he'd become a plumber. And she explained how she'd ended up back in Buffalo after almost a decade away.

"So which one did you let down gently?" asked Madeline.

"There's no one to let down. Walter was helping me escape the inquisition and Darren was a mistake I almost made. I ended it as soon as I found out he was married. It never went anywhere."

"If that's true, why did he show up here?"

"Ego. He's divorced now, so he says. And I was the one that got away."

"So Simone's speculation was wrong?"

"Dead wrong," she said. Then asked, "You all knew I was with Walter?"

"Nope. Only me," shrugged Madeline.

"And you didn't tell anyone. So they kept calling me."

"No didn't tell anyone," shrugged Madeline again.

They sat in silence for a while before Cicely spoke. "I didn't know he was married in the beginning."

"But you knew he was white," quipped Madeline.

Finally Cicely spoke again, "Are you going to bust my balls for that? I didn't pick you for a closet racist Madeline."

"First of all you don't have a pair or you would have said something before now."

"That I dated a white guy a couple of times? What's the big deal about that?"

"So it was it just a novelty for you?"

"If circumstances had been different I might have come to care for him. But I don't play in another woman's sandbox."

"Glad to hear that."

Cicely knew she meant one adulteress in the family was enough.

Madeline stood.

"Madeline," said Cicely before her sister could retire for the evening. "Does it really bother you that much that I dated a white guy?"

"When I was younger I would have said no. But as I get older the mixing of races does bother me. Black men with White women even more. It's like a slap in the face to our Momma and Daddy." Madeline answered. "Momma…"

"Madeline, do not invoke Momma."

"Fine," said Madeline throwing up her hands. "No one expects you to live a life of celibacy just be more selective."

"I suppose that warning includes Walter?"

Madeline began walking up the stairs. "Don't use Walter to scratch that itch."

Cicely followed her and stood at the bottom of the stairs. "You just said I'm not expected to be celibate. He's a grown man."

"Walter likes you. But I don't see him as the type to take a woman to bed lightly. And you aren't that person either. "

"Aren't you going to say he's too young for me?" demanded Cicely.

"He's a grown man. Isn't that what you said?" Madeline went to her room.

Cicely sat on the bottom step, her shoes dangling in her hand. She didn't know what to do about Walter. She had to admit she was attracted to him but, in her mind he was too young for her. His mother was barely older than she was. He should be out finding a woman his own age, marry and have children.

She stood, turned the television off and made sure the doors were locked. As she walked up the stairs she thought, "Guess *I'll use the vibrator to scratch that itch*."

Next morning Walter stood looking at his reflection in his bathroom mirror, trying to decide whether to shave or not, decided no, to save time. They were starting a new job this morning on a new build and as a minority business it wouldn't look good to be late. He had taken more time on Cicely's house than necessary. Not like him.

He knew he had moved in on Cicely way too fast, again, typically, not him. But seeing her with that man had not felt good. When he'd seen her walking back, he'd actually felt something akin to relief.

Most of his life his mother and grandfather had

admonished him, do not follow the dick. Following the dick can get you into trouble. His mother, being a teenaged unwed parent had been very open about sex. She'd embarrassed the hell out of him by providing his first condom at fourteen. At least his grandfather had waited until he was fifteen. Him, he'd waited until he was seventeen. And even after using a condom was afraid a father or brother was going to come knocking on the door. He had reacted to Cicely way too quickly. Walter looked down at himself and said, "I'm not following you."

Which could be a problem. Because he still had to be paid.

Cicely had not slept well the night before, yet she got up to run. Hoping the action would help clear her thoughts.

There was no resolution about Walter. All she could think of was to avoid him. So she was pissed when she returned home to find he had stuffed the final bill in her mailbox.

Walter had played the avoidance card first.

CHAPTER 8

It was hard to believe a week had passed. Bernice and Madeline were in Florida enjoying Disney World with their husbands. Somehow before they'd left Madeline had managed to get them into the church and have pictures taken of them admiring the plaque. The photographer promised it would have a prominent place in the church bulletin.

Simone and Olivia had taken over Madeline and Bernice's rooms respectively. Cicely didn't know how Simone had done it, but this was now her home base. She got up Monday morning leaving Olivia in Cicely's care.

Olivia and Cicely looked at each other across the breakfast table.

"Well, what would you like to do today?" asked Cicely.

"Don't you have to go to work Auntie?"

"Mostly I work from home. Next week I have to go into the office. Then we're going to have to decide what to do with you."

"I'm old enough to stay home by myself," pouted Olivia.

"I know sweetie. It's just it would get lonely for you all day."

"If I was home with my Dad…"

Cicely reached over and covered Olivia's hand with her own as her niece's eyes filled with tears.

"What did you do with your dad?" Cicely asked.

"I don't know," said Olivia shrugging her shoulders, typical teenager. "We had fun."

"You grandfather died before you were born. But I know Dad's aren't always fun."

"Oh, he made me do chores. And keep my room clean."

"Boyfriend?" knowing Olivia wouldn't admit to liking any particular boy.

"My Dad says I'm way too young to have a boyfriend. But he did let me go to my friend's boy girl birthday party."

"It must be hard not talking to your friends." Cicely knew at that age she and her friends stayed on the phone constantly. Their conversation, mostly about boys.

"My Mommy did let me use her phone to call a couple of my friends."

"You can use the house phone too. I don't mind."

"Thank you, Auntie."

"Miss your Dad?"

"I really do Auntie Cicely," she said wiping at the tears with the butt of her hand. "He doesn't have anybody."

"He has you."

"No, I mean with him. Mommy has you. Daddy doesn't

have anyone."

Cicely didn't say anything. She and Simone spoke, but it had been strained. Simone preferred to believe the worst about her relationship with Darren. But Simone had to see how unhappy her daughter was.

Taking things into her own hands, she called Anita. The twins were working at their church run daycare for the summer. A paying job for them, halleluiah, said Anita. She would talk to them and see if Olivia could tag along on the days Cicely had to go into the office. In that setting they couldn't complain about a thirteen-year-old hanging with them. The rest of that week Cicely spent taking Olivia to the places she liked visiting when she was her age.

The fourth of July had passed. Simone had reconnected with some old friends and took Olivia to a cookout at one of their homes for the holiday. The first time she had really done anything with Olivia, where she finally met girls her own age that left her feeling a little bit less lonely.

Seeing Olivia wasn't as unhappy any more Cicely waited until almost the middle of July before she said anything to Simone. Olivia's new friends had invited her to the movies leaving the sisters alone.

Simone was sitting at the dining room table painting her nails when Cicely placed a registered letter in front of her. "I signed for it," she said.

Simone glanced at the thick envelope and continued what she was doing.

"Aren't you going to open it?"

Simone looked at her. "My nails are wet. If you are so curious, you open it."

Cicely grabbed the envelope slit it open and pulled out a sheaf of papers. Reading the letter enclosed with them she said, "Evan sold the house. He needs your notarized signature."

Simone said nothing. Finally she said, "It's Saturday. Where am I going to find a notary on Saturday, Cicely? He can wait until next week."

"I can do it. I have a notary stamp."

"Fine," snapped Simone. "And you can mail it to him too."

"Have you even talked to Evan?"

"No. What is there to talk to him about?"

"Your divorce, for one thing. I'm going to assume you still don't want to be married to him."

"You'd be right there. But until he gets employment, it's no way I'm talking divorce. I will not pay that man spousal support."

"Simone, what makes you think he would take anything from you?"

"He took my house," she said angrily.

"It was both your house. And he says right here in the

letter as soon as it closes he will send you your half. You need to talk about Olivia."

"I have Olivia."

"She is not a possession. Don't you see how unhappy she is? You are so busy with your life you don't have time for her. Grow up Simone."

"Like you Cicely? You're all grown up with a big empty house." Simone stood and made a wide gesture with her arms.

Cicely was silent. Simone was always the sister that went for the jugular when they fought. "You know my plans," she managed to say.

"Yes, take in children. Well where are they? No children, no man and no prospects of a man. I always thought Madeline was the prissy one. But it's you. Walter would have fucked you. I saw how he looked at you when he thought no one was looking. But I guess you were too proper to let a real man go at it. If it wasn't for Olivia and me you would be all alone."

Before she had known what she had done, Cicely slapped her across the face, leaving a bright red handprint. She was immediately sorry. Many times she and her sister had fought. But never had they become physical.

"Tell you what," said Simone, "I'll sign the damn papers. And *you and Evan* can decide what to do with *my* daughter, since I'm not grown up enough to do it. By the way, I leave for business on Tuesday, so whatever you decide, gets it done before I get back from my trip." She stopped in the kitchen for a towel and ice before going to her room.

Cicely wanted to ask her if she was seeing her lover, but didn't.

She waited until Olivia was in bed before she called Madeline and Bernice to tell them what she planned. They had a three way call going and Bernice asked, "Are you sure you want to do this? You don't even know if Evan is able to do this."

"He'll have to agree first, but even if she just spends the rest of the summer with Evan it will be better than it is now. Maybe by the time school starts Simone will have settled down."

"And when Simone snatches her back it will be worse," put in Madeline.

"If you could only see her,"

"I'm not saying you're wrong Cicely. But you may just be postponing the inevitable."

"I know. But when school starts Olivia will have more to occupy her. I'm sorry to bother you but you had to know what was going on." She didn't include the details of the slap. Or the horrible things Simone had said to her.

"I appreciate you keeping me in the loop," said Bernice.

"How are you doing Bernice?" Cicely asked.

"Don't worry about me. I'm stable. Just take care of Olivia. That will be one less thing to worry about."

"I will."

"Call after you talk to Evan," said Madeline.

Cicely promised to call. They said I love you all around and hung up.

The next morning Cicely felt emotionally drained but woke her niece and they attended Anita's church. Olivia now knew more people by going to the daycare. People complimented her on how well she worked with the little ones, but it still wasn't the same as being home with her friends. Even her new friends couldn't replace the friends back home. Cicely didn't say anything to Olivia about what she was planning. She wanted to make sure she and Evan were on the same page before getting Olivia's hopes up.

Cicely tried to concentrate on the message of the day, "Don't let anyone steal your joy," but it was difficult. She talked to her friend Anita after the service. Told her what was happening. But still didn't repeat the things Simone had said about Walter. Some things you just did not want to tell anyone.

Simone was waiting on the front porch when they returned from church. And immediately took Olivia and left. Maybe she thought she was hurting Cicely's feelings by taking Olivia, but it just gave Cicely the opportunity she needed to call Evan.

"How are you Evan?" she asked when he answered the phone.

"I just am Cicely. Did Simone get the papers?'

"Yes I'll be dropping them in the overnight mail

tomorrow."

"You? Why not Simone?" He thought about it then said, "Never mind."

"Have you moved out of the house yet?"

"I put everything I didn't need in storage. Sold some and got a small two bedroom apartment. You know, just in case," he finished.

"That's why I'm calling Evan. The just in case."

"Nothing's wrong with Olivia?" he asked his voice becoming anxious.

"Other than she misses you, no. But it's lonely for her here. She hardly knows anyone and with me working and Simone working it would just be better if she spent the rest of the summer with you."

"And Simone has agreed with this?"

"Not exactly. But maybe if Olivia is with you it will force some sort of dialogue between you and Simone."

"That will never happen," he said venomously.

"I didn't say reconciliation. You have to talk about a divorce, a separation whatever, you have to talk."

"Let me think about it Cicely. At least I'm home every night."

"Oh, you got a job," said Cicely getting excited for him.

"Nothing like I was doing before. But it's steady and it pays the bills. No weird hours. Olivia will be able to stay with friends while I'm at work. No chance this could become permanent is it Cicely?"

"I don't know Evan. Maybe you and Simone will reach a point where you can at least talk about joint custody. Will you ever forgive her?"

"Don't know if I can. I knew what she was like when we married, but I never thought she would cheat on me. Walk out on me maybe."

Cicely could hear the smile in his voice. "You're joking about it Evan," she said.

"Yeah, the first time. You've given me hope Cicely, saying I should have my daughter."

"It has to be this week Evan. Simone's leaving for business on Tuesday. And if it's going to happen it has to happen while she's gone. I don't want a big scene with Olivia around. I hate to rush you but call me tomorrow. Either way, call me."

"I will Cicely. Thanks. I miss Olivia so much."

Evan returned her call Monday evening. He had booked Olivia on a flight home. When Simone left for her business trip, unbeknownst to her Olivia's flight was leaving two hours later. Olivia was proud that her Dad and Auntie Cicely thought she was old enough to fly alone.

Cicely took the time to pack what wouldn't fit in a suitcase to ship Evan's new address. What she did find odd was, not once did Simone call to see how Olivia was faring without her. But Cicely prepared herself for the fight she knew was coming when Simone returned the following Monday.

When Cicely came home from her day at the office, Simone's bags were packed and sitting in the foyer.

"I've saved you the trouble of telling me to get out," said Simone before Cicely could even put her bags down.

"You don't have to leave Simone. It was better for Olivia to spend some time with her Dad. She can come back when school starts," said Cicely tired of the fight before it even got started.

"So you and my husband decided I could have her back in the fall. Didn't know you and Evan were like that."

Before she could stop herself the devil took her tongue and Cicely said, "You didn't want him."

Simone clamped her lips together and started carrying luggage out. When she came for the last bag she spoke. It had taken her that long to think of something to say. She knew Cicely would never betray her with Evan but she wanted to hurt her so bad. She wanted Cicely to hurt like she was hurting. There was no doubt in her mind that Cicely was looking out for Olivia's best interest. But she felt all her sisters were abandoning her. And now Olivia was gone. Momma would have understood her. If Momma hadn't been so ill the last year of her life, what had happened with Evan probably never would have happened. Momma had a way of reining her in. Making her see how destructive she was being. But she didn't have a mother any more. She had nothing but a good time in bed with a man other than her husband. She didn't even have a place to lay her head that night.

"Well that's what you do Cicely. Collect things that don't belong to you, husbands, children." And she walked out slamming the door making the glass rattle.

Cicely went to the kitchen, got a glass and a bottle of wine. She juggled both as she stripped while walking up the stairs. Stopped in the bathroom, to start bathwater and went to her bedroom to retrieve her IPod and finish undressing. When the bath was ready, fully foaming with bubbles, she turned the IPod to music that made her want to dance. She stepped into the tub careful not to spill her wine. She would not think about how alone she was.

CHAPTER 9

Two days after Simone moved she was showing a client out when the phone rang. "Ms. Macklin, we have two little girls for you. It's only a temporary situation. I know you were looking for something long term, but this is an emergency. We want to keep the sisters together. Their ages are four and seven. This isn't the first time they've been in foster care. I can give you more details, but I need to know you will take them."

Cicely didn't hesitate. She was finally getting a chance.

The social worker went on to explain the girls' mother was in jail and could not make bail. No family member wanted to take them because there could be behavioral problems.

"Behavioral problems?" questioned Cicely.

"The youngest is a bed wetter and doesn't talk as much as a child her age should."

Cicely would have to pull out the rubber sheets from when her mother was incontinent.

"There is no father in the picture," went on the woman.

Her thoughts went immediately to Walter. She had mailed the payment but heard nothing from him.

"As I said she cannot make bail, but when she comes before the judge she will most likely get time served. That's according to her public defender. "

"Can I ask what for?"

"Misdemeanor drug charge."

"And she gets her kids back just like that?" asked Cicely incredulously.

"That's the way it works Ms. Macklin. She hasn't shown to be a bad mother in the past."

Or nobody noticed, thought Cicely. "What time can I expect them?"

"Sometime around six."

Cicely looked at the clock. It was five o'clock now.

"Unfortunately they had to spend the night at juvenile hall. Their mother was arrested late last night and it was the only thing the police officers could do with them. The file ended up on my desk a little while ago or I would have called you sooner."

"No problem," said Cicely. "I'll take them. Their names?"

"Shanequa and Tamequa."

Poor babies, thought Cicely. Saddled with names like that. She knew the reasoning of black people not wanting to give their children slave names but she'd wished they considered the origins of the names they were labeling their children with.

"The social worker who brings them will have a file with more details. And some papers you have to sign. Hopefully you won't have to keep them very long."

"This is what I signed up for," said Cicely before hanging up.

She figured she had just enough time to change the sheets on one of the twin beds before the children arrived. Then time to search for something to feed them if they hadn't eaten before leaving the juvenile hall. This is what she wanted but she felt so unprepared.

At exactly six o'clock the bell rang. She still hadn't found anything for them to eat but peanut butter and jelly. Not the best meal when coming to a place you'd never been before. Maybe it was though. Most kids liked peanut butter and jelly.

Both girls hair was done in cornrows from front to back close to the skull. They ended in multicolored beads. Someone had loved these girls enough to keep their hair neatly done. Ok, Cicely knew how to do that. She had practiced enough on Simone's hair until her baby sister had insisted on having a perm. They were thin, but not underfed. The oldest held her sister's hand tightly. The youngest had the thumb of her free hand stuck firmly in her mouth. Both girls had on shorts and rubber flip-flops with ugly flowers, someone had painted their toenails. Their tops matched. Bright pink ruffled belly shirts.

The two women left the children standing in the foyer while they completed the paperwork in the dining room.

Cicely saw two backpacks. "Is that all they have?"

"I'm afraid so. That's all that was gathered last night."

"Can we get into where they lived to get more clothes?

Or at least a toy or two."

"Only the police or a family member can do that. And I don't think that will happen," answered the young woman. "But this is only supposed to be short term, so if you spend anything, keep your receipts and you can be reimbursed for anything not over and above what is allowed."

Cicely drew in a breath. This was not starting well.

The children had not moved when the women returned to the foyer, also not a good sign in Cicely's eyes. Young children were supposed to fidget, an inconvenience at times, but a fact. She locked the door behind the woman then squatted to be at the girls' level.

"My name is Cicely," she said. "You may call me Miss Cicely or Miss CC. What are your names?"

The oldest spoke right up. "My name is Shanequa Brown."

"Do you have a middle name?" Cicely asked. She really didn't want to call this child Shanequa.

The child gave her a puzzled look.

Cicely put a hand on her own chest and said, "My full name is Cicely Louise Macklin. Louise is my middle name."

"You mean when my momma get mad at me name," said Shanequa. "You don't have to know that name. We won't be here long enough for you to use that name. My momma will be to get us."

Cicely could have looked in the file, but if she wouldn't tell her, Shanequa would not answer to it.

She turned to the younger one, "What's your name?"

She looked at her sister before answering. As if looking for approval. Without removing the thumb from her mouth she answered.

Cicely could not understand a word she said. She reached and pulled the thumb from her mouth. It came out with a resounding pop, revealing a space where her top front teeth should be. Kind of young to be missing her front teeth, thought Cicely. Someone had neglected dental care

"Say again."

"Tamequa." Her name came out with a lisp because of the missing teeth.

Cicely stood. Their names were their names. It was nothing she could do about it.

"Are you hungry? I have peanut butter and jelly."

The little one started to nod yes, when the older girl gave her arm a little jerk before answered. "No, we ate already."

Cicely noticed the little one wanted to answer yes, so she guided them toward the kitchen. "Well I already made them so you might as well help me eat them."

Cicely sat at the kitchen table with them sharing the sandwiches. Thinking what a terrible foster mother she was. The only thing she had to drink with peanut butter and jelly appropriate for kids was water.

After washing the sticky from their face and hands Cicely took them upstairs. It was nearly seven. What made children take so long to eat? She showed them the bathroom and even though it would be a couple of hours before it got dark, she plugged in the bathroom night light as not to forget later.

"You live here all by yourself?" asked Shanequa seeing all the doors that led to other rooms.

"Yes, I do," replied Cicely. "My sisters grew up and moved away." She didn't want to mention her dead mother for fear the child would ask if her mother had died in the house, which in fact she had.

Cicely showed them the bedroom next to hers. The one she and Simone shared while growing up.

"Why ain't you got a man?" Another question from Shanequa. "You don't look bad. Or you one of those funny ladies that like ladies? My momma say they has them in jail and she have to be careful because she pretty."

OMG! Cicely didn't know which statement to answer first.

She was saved from saying anything, because Shanequa had already moved on to the next thing.

"My momma say a woman need a man to take care of her. That why you takin' in kids cause you ain't got no man to take care of you?"

"Shanequa," Cicely spoke to get her attention and to shut

her up. "What grade will you be in when school starts?"

The little girl puffed out her thin chest. "I'll be in third grade. I am very bright."

Cicely looked at her. She probably was very bright. Already she was slipping in and out of the ghetto dialect, most likely picked up from her mother.

"I was very bright at your age too," said Cicely. "It was easy for me. I bet it's easy for you too."

Shanequa nodded yes.

"It was so easy for me, I finished high school and went to college. Now smart people like you and me and maybe even your little sister, we don't have to wait around for anyone to take care of us. I like men. Men are nice. But when I can take care of myself, I don't have to pick the first man that comes along. I can pick the best man."

Cicely could see the girl's mind working behind her eyes.

Finally she said, "But you ain't got no man, Miss CeeCee."

Mentally Cicely was pulling her dreads out. Why was she having this conversation with a child?

They spent time unpacking the backpacks and putting clothes away in the dresser drawers. Cicely wouldn't have them living out of a bag no matter how short the stay. During that time Tamequa hardly spoke and never removed her thumb from her mouth. While Shanequa asked what seemed like a million questions about Cicely's sisters. One being did they have a man?

Their wardrobe was sparse. No toys or books to speak of. Cicely decided in the morning they would get groceries and then to Walmart for clothing, and a toy for each girl. Before bedtime she went up to the attic to find a children's book. It had been years since a child had lived or even visited under this roof. But this was a family that never threw books away.

Cicely sat on the floor between the twin beds. Tomorrow she would bring momma's old rocker upstairs. She made sure Tamequa used the bathroom before putting her in the bed with the rubber sheet.

"There's no TV in here," said Shanequa.

"No, I'm going to read you a story. Hasn't anyone ever read to you?"

"In school they read stories. This ain't school."

"Isn't school," said Cicely, the Bernice in her coming out, before starting to read. She read until they fell asleep.

Cicely couldn't get into a deep sleep. She kept waking up and resisting the urge to check on the girls least she wake them. The doors to their respective bedrooms remained open in case of a crisis. And she had left the hall light on. Around one o'clock she stopped resisting and went to check.

Both girls were sound asleep in Tamequa's bed. Guess they had no problem sleeping in strange places. They were all arms and legs entangled in the covers. This was new to her. Cicely didn't know how she should feel. She was more than a babysitter. She was a paid caregiver that was her job description.

But it didn't even begin to give her any guidelines as to how she should feel.

This is what she'd wanted. To care for children that had no place to go. But she'd requested an older child, someone who would be with her for a while. Not shuffled in and out.

How was she supposed to feel? Because in the end how she felt would determine how she'd treat these children. Madeline said she was a natural caregiver. These girls may only be with her a few short weeks. How could she prove herself in that short time? Could she do no harm in that time frame or ruin them for life?

Not ready to return to bed, Cicely sat on the bed Shanequa had vacated. No sooner than she'd sat down she stood. Her butt was wet.

Shanequa was the bed wetter, not the little one. Some social workers they were. They had labeled the wrong child a bed wetter.

Cicely strode to her bedroom to get clean pajama bottoms before heading to the bathroom to clean up. She knew something the social workers didn't. It kinda made her feel better about herself.

No matter how short of time she had these girls, they would know she cared.

The first order of business the next morning was to strip the soiled bed. Shanequa helped strip the bed all the while pleading for Cicely not to give her sister a whipping for peeing in the bed.

"Why would I spank her?" asked Cicely. Wondering if Tamequa often took punishment for her older sister.

The child was almost in tears as she explained. Her mother said Tamequa was old enough to know not to pee in the bed. And should be punished when it happened.

Cicely looked at Tamequa. She sat on the dry bed sucking her thumb. Cicely knew this was not the first time Shanequa had blamed her for the wet bed. She did not even voice an "It wasn't me."

Cicely bundled up the bedclothes in her arms to take to the basement. "No one is getting a whipping. Sometimes people pee in the bed. It's was an accident. We have to find a way to help her so it doesn't happen again." But Cicely had no idea what that would be.

She bathed the girls together to save time, scrutinizing their little bodies for any signs of abuse. If they were with her past a week, she would take their hair down, wash it, and rebraid. After a quick breakfast, still no milk, she let them stay in her room to watch TV while she showered and dressed.

Cicely wasn't used to this. She left the bathroom door open in case one of them needed her. After stepping out of the shower she realized she hadn't brought her underwear into the bathroom. Was it okay if the girls saw her naked? When she was their age she saw her mother in various stages of undress. It hadn't scarred her. In the end she wrapped a towel around her and retrieved her underwear and clothing and got dressed elsewhere.

Cicely had never taken a child to a major grocery store before. She was sure at some point or another she had taken one of her nieces or nephews to the corner store for something. Held their hands while they crossed the street. Kept a firm grip on their little hands while they were in the store. But nothing prepared her for this.

She immediately grabbed the shopping cart made for parents with kids, not realizing how unyielding it could be. A plastic car with seats for two children and a full sized grocery cart attached in front. Cicely lost count of the number of times she abandoned the cart and children, to get something she had forgotten in the previous aisle. What if someone had taken them? Some foster mother she was.

You heard horror stories about children throwing temper tantrums in the grocery store. Cicely had seen them. But Shanequa and Tamequa were very well behaved. Cicely was the one going a little berserk, less sugar, healthier snacks, more fresh fruit and vegetables. She'd forgotten to read if either of girls had any food allergies. And damn near forgot to buy milk.

Cicely was exhausted when they returned home. She'd stopped by the dollar store to get crayons and coloring books. Of course she couldn't just run in like she normally would. She was responsible for two little human beings. She had to take them into the store with her. She picked Tamequa up and slung her on her hip, and with her free hand held onto Shanequa. Neither girl asked for anything extra. She'd have to compliment their mother on the girls' public behavior.

They were in the checkout line when the woman behind them looked at Cicely and said, "Your daughter is too old to suck her thumb. It will ruin her teeth."

Cicely released Shanequa's hand and removed Tamequa's thumb from her mouth and told her to smile at the lady.

"She has no teeth, so we are using her thumb to plug the hole until she gets some."

The woman looked at Cicely her eyes rapidly blinking. "Humph, try and help some people," she said and turned away.

The girls tried to help Cicely put the groceries away, passing her things as she filled the cabinets and refrigerator making it difficult to finish the job quickly. When they finished Cicely decided it was lunchtime, then nap time, more for her than them. She made bologna sandwiches and gave them carrot sticks. It was funny watching Tamequa eat little carrots with no front teeth. After their nap they would still go to Walmart.

Cicely didn't know if the girls slept or not. They all went to her room, where she turned the TV on and went to sleep.

Walmart was better than the grocery store. She got a regular cart and sat Tamequa in it. She picked out a dress for each of them and additional underwear, some cute sandals and cheap sneakers. She had lucked out. Summer would be over soon and everything was marked down. School clothes were displayed, but she knew she wouldn't have the girls by then. Tamequa picked out a stuffed panda bear for her toy. It had a secret compartment she could put her jammies in. Shanequa went for the Barbie doll with a couple of changes of clothes. She tried to interest them in toy dishes saying they could play tea party. But the girls had clearly never played tea party before. Cicely bought them anyway. And a couple of board games they could play together.

Walter saw her standing in the checkout two lines over from his. She had on some black legging things that hugged her thighs and calves. Her top was bright yellow and sleeveless, some sort of tent thing that hit at mid-thigh. Her arms were just like he remembered them. He smiled, her toes were painted bright blue. It had been over a month since he'd last seen her. Yep, the attraction was still there. Then he noticed she had young children with her. So, what the oldest sister had told him had happened. She had her foster children.

Shanequa tugged on Cicely's top to get her attention. "That man is staring at us."

Cicely turned to see Walter slowly coming toward her. They say when you are attracted to someone, your pupils dilate when you see them. Cicely was sure her pupils were as wide as if someone had put drops in them.

"Hi," he said in that easy way of his.

She remembered his voice. Deep from the chest. She knew she should say something, but the words wouldn't come.

Luckily for her Shanequa spoke up.

"We don't know you." The little girl looked up at Walter.

"Cicely knows me," he said. He knelt down to her level and stuck out his hand. "I'm Walter, what's your name?"

She took his hand and shook it vigorously. "My name is Shanequa."

Walter looked at Cicely and raised his eyebrow. She just shrugged.

He stood and took Tamequa's hand. "And what's your name?"

She needed no prompting to take her thumb out her mouth and spoke clearer than Cicely had heard her speak in the day and a half they'd been with her. Walter did have charm.

He continued speaking to the girls. "You're buying clothes. I'm buying underwear." He held up the package of boxers in his hand.

Now Cicely knew what kind of underwear he wore and would imagine him wearing only that.

"So you are staying at Cicely's house?" he asked Shanequa.

"Yes, our momma is in jail."

Cicely would have to talk to her about blurting out certain things in public. "It's short term," she said to Walter.

He knew she wanted something more lasting.

The line moved quickly and he just took the place in line behind Cicely and the girls.

After she paid, she turned to tell him good-bye, but Walter wasn't quite ready to let her go yet.

"Let me take you and the girls to Mickey D's for dinner," he said.

Cicely was all set to say no. One look at the girls told her it wasn't a treat they got often. So she agreed.

Walter followed them to her car to see where she parked then came back in his truck. Cicely pulled out and he trailed them to McDonalds. She wasn't going to put anything into this. Walter was nice and it was nice of him to do this for the girls.

At McDonalds' Shanequa would not give up her seat next to her sister in the booth, so Cicely and Walter were forced to sit next to each other. Cicely tried not to make it obvious she didn't want his jean encased thigh to touch hers.

He made it seem easy keeping the girls engaged in conversation as they ate their happy meals. But he was very obvious of Cicely next to him. The meal was over way too soon for him.

Walter walked them to the car like it had been a real date. He watched Cicely buckle the girls in the back seat. She stood with the drivers' door open standing between the door and the car. Walter peeked in the back to say good-by to the girls again. "Cicely, I know its short term, but you need to get booster seats for them. Maybe a car seat for the little one."

"Shit," said Cicely. She hadn't thought of that. They had been driving around all day. She was lucky they hadn't been stopped.

Walter stepped closer, into her space as he was wont to do. He leaned in as if he was about to kiss her. She got the little flip in the bottom of her stomach. He whispered in her ear. He might as well have kissed her, the reaction his breath on her neck caused. If she had not had on a bra he would have seen her nipples harden. Then she heard what he was saying.

"Cee," he said, cutting her name to one syllable, but making it seem longer. "You really shouldn't swear in front of the children."

He stepped back, allowing her room to breathe again.

Cicely stared at the base of his throat and could see his pulse. If his pulse was any indication, Walter wasn't as unaffected as he pretended. His heart was beating as rapidly as hers.

Her eyes moved to his face. From her angle his eyes looked half closed, bedroom eyes.

She laughed.

What she did next took Walter off guard. Unable to resist flirting with him she placed her hand flat on his chest. Right at his sternum, and let it linger and said, "Very funny Walter." Removed her hand, got into the car and drove off.

When Cicely looked in the rear view mirror, he was still standing there. She laughed again.

Walter didn't know how long he'd stood there. Apparently the blood had left his brain. A little old white woman was standing next to him talking. "Are you all right son? Are you having a heart attack?"

He was rubbing his chest absentmindedly. Walter was pretty sure if he looked, her brand would be on his chest. No he wasn't all right, but he wasn't sure what to do about it.

The next day Cicely found out she could get some wage paying work done with children in the house. After she'd fed them breakfast and helped them dress, they sat quietly at the dining room table and colored while she did a brief teleconference with her employer on the laptop. The good thing about Skype was she only had to look decent from the waist up. On the bottom, she had on her cutoff jeans and flip-flops like the girls. And as soon as the conference was over, off came the bra and on went the tank top.

But she knew she couldn't keep the girls inside twenty-four seven. Any work assignments she had to do she could take care of after they went to bed that night. So after lunch she took them on the front porch. It was too hot to stay indoors anyway. There were children on the block, Cicely just didn't know them. In the past occasionally one would ring the doorbell asking if she have any children that could come out and play. So she figured if she showed them children now the others would come by.

At first they just sat on the porch coloring. Then Cicely remembered she had bought sidewalk chalk. She left them for a quick minute then came out and drew a hopscotch board on the front walk leading up to the porch. It used to be fun for her and her Simone. Maybe it would be fun for them.

It wasn't long before two little girls approached. They looked to be about eight or nine years old. The bravest one asked Cicely, "Can they come play with us by our house?" The little girl pointed to a house about two doors down. "We need someone to help turn the jump rope. And we have to stay in front of the house."

So they had committed an infraction by walking to Cicely's house.

Shanequa looked at Cicely expectantly. And Cicely nodded yes. She could see the girls clearly from her front porch. Tamequa didn't want to go and it made Cicely feel nice the girl wanted to stay with her and not go with her sister. Still Tamequa wasn't talking much to Cicely, but she was becoming more vocal and not holding on to Shanequa's hand all the time.

She and Tamequa stayed on the porch and she listened to the little girl recite the alphabet and count to fifty with coaching. She took a book and let Tamequa point out the words she knew.

After a while a young woman from up the street came to introduce herself. She wanted to know where the strange child had come from. "I didn't know you had children," she said to Cicely.

"They are visiting," Cicely told her. She didn't think it was anybody's business they were foster kids. And she had admonished Shanequa for telling people her mother was in jail.

"It's good to see some more little girls in the neighborhood. It's over run by little boys," the woman said.

Cicely laughed and explained there had been four girls in the house when she was growing up. The neighborhood had been just the opposite. Full of girls.

The woman, who introduced herself as Jackie, had been living there for about two years, so didn't know Cicely's mother. Had heard how nice she had been from other neighbors.

Cicely understood. She hadn't been very friendly with the people living around her. Most of her time had been spent caring for her mother. Now it was up to her to get reacquainted with everyone. While they talked, Tamequa crawled into Cicely's lap and fell asleep. They talked for a few minutes longer then Jackie said she had to go start dinner, but the girls were welcome to come over anytime.

Cicely had to do the same thing, but she was reluctant to disturb Tamequa. It felt good to hold a warm body in her arms. She almost dozed herself listening to the sounds of the street. The sun was warm and children were laughing. Every once and a while a car drove down the street. An older woman waved to Cicely as she passed by walking her equally old dog. Across the way she watched a teenage couple walk down the street swinging their clasped hands between them. Simone crossed her mind and she promised herself she would call her sister that night. She couldn't stay angry with her.

It was becoming hot holding Tamequa against her chest. The child was beginning to perspire in the heat. Just as Cicely was about to wake her, Walter pulled up in his pick-up truck. She stood and shifted Tamequa to her hip.

Walter exited the truck and went to get something from the back. He pulled out a car seat and a booster. Cicely was walking down the front walk toward him. He liked the way she looked with the child on her hip. Plus the jiggle was back.

"You didn't have to do this Walter," she said when she reached him.

"I didn't buy them. I have lots of cousins, with lots of kids. Things tend to lie around until someone else needs them. You need them. When you're done just return them."

"Thank you," she said. Cicely had forgotten about safety seats for the girls. She was touched Walter had remembered.

"I'll put them in the car for you," he said starting toward the side of the house, where her car was in the driveway. "Is it unlocked?"

"I have to get the key."

By this time Tamequa was fully awake. She took her thumb out her mouth and said, "Hi Walter."

"I'll take her," he said, putting the safety seats down and holding his arms out for Tamequa.

The little girl had no qualms about going to Walter. Cicely felt a little pang of jealously that Tamequa would leave her so readily, but let her go so she could get the keys and Walter could leave.

In the time it took her to find her keys Shanequa had discovered Walter was there. She was asking him if he was there to take them to McDonalds again.

"No," he answered. He had to go back to work.

Walter had taken time from work to bring her the safety seats. "Thank you again Walter," Cicely said as he put the seat in the correct way and showed her how to strap the kids in.

"No, problem. I didn't know when you might have to take them somewhere. "

All three of them walked him to his truck.

"Cicely," he said stepping up into his truck, standing on the running board speaking over the roof of the cab. "If we get a good rain I would like to come by and check out the basement. It really hasn't rained since I finished the job."

"That'll be good Walter," she said.

The three of them waved to Walter as he drove off. And he had to remind himself to look at the road and not the jiggle.

After the girls were in bed Cicely remembered to call Simone, but the call went straight to voice mail. She left a message, "Simone we can't stay angry with each other forever. I love you. Call me."

She worked for a little while then watched TV before turning the light off and going to sleep.

She was awakened by a loud clap of thunder and

lightning brightened the room. She heard the scurry of little feet and opened her eyes to see two pair of eyes staring back at her. "Can we sleep with you?" asked Shanequa.

In answer Cicely pulled back the cover and moved over. She just hoped the bed would still be dry in the morning. Her last thought before falling back to sleep was, maybe she would get to see Walter again tomorrow.

CHAPTER 10

August was starting and the girls were still with Cicely. They had not seen Walter. The thunderstorm turned out to be just an overnight rain. In the morning everything was fresh, new looking, and dry, including the bed. Twice Cicely had gotten up to take each girl to the bathroom so they wouldn't wet her bed. She'd continued the practice even when they returned to their own beds in the following weeks.

During that time they also established a routine. Mornings Cicely allowed them to watch TV while she worked on her laptop. She declined any new clients coming to her residence at that time. Her exercise regime was shot to hell. She almost called Walter to see if any of his cousins could provide a stroller, so she could at least walk.

It was a while before it occurred to her to ask Jackie if she could watch them so she could get a run in. She scheduled it in the afternoon when the girls were usually outside playing.

She still had not talked to Simone. Evan had though. Cicely called to check on Olivia and Evan told her while it hadn't accomplished anything he and Simone had talked with only minor bloodshed. Simone had also talked to Madeline and Bernice to tell them what an awful person Cicely was. How she had gone behind Simone's back to talk with Evan. Neither sister let on to Simone they knew the whole story. They just let her rant, which you had to do sometimes to let the person get all the venom out of their system.

Madeline and Bernice didn't upset Cicely by telling her what their baby sister was saying about her. They just assured Cicely Simone was safe and had her own place not too far from where Cicely lived.

Louis was still insisting Bernice see different specialists. He wasn't convinced of her diagnosis. She had shown no sign of further deterioration. They had enjoyed the vacation with Madeline and Preston so much, they were already planning a cruise next year on faith. Her school was adamant she not return, so Bernice was speaking to her union rep to see what could be done about it.

Cicely did hit a hiccup with the girls when she noticed a foul order coming from their bedroom. It took some time before she discovered the backpack one of the girls had been hiding food in. Unfortunately it was the type of food that should have been refrigerated. A hot dog, half a peanut butter and jelly sandwich were among the things in the backpack. Cicely's first instinct was to confront the children. But as she walked down the stairs to clean out the backpack, she calmed down. It was obvious there was no new food in the backpack. The children had forgotten about it. She was sure Shanequa was the culprit. This wasn't their first time at the rodeo. Shanequa was trying to guarantee she and her sister would not go hungry. After cleaning the backpack she refilled it with non-perishable items. A couple of juice boxes, a bag of dried fruit and an unopened package of pepperoni.

She didn't want to tempt fate so Cicely didn't call child services. The girls were doing fine and so was she. Tamequa was sucking her thumb less, because she was talking more. Sometimes it seemed she competed with Shanequa for face time with Cicely.

Cicely would be content with the situation as long as Social Services was.

She had bought the girls dresses at Walmart and they'd never worn them, so she decided to take them to church. But first their hair had to be done. Their cornrows were starting to look a bit fuzzy, not as crisp. In the evening they sat on the front porch while Cicely removed Tamequa's braids. It wasn't until she'd washed Tamequa's hair that she realized how much hair the little girl had. She immediately called her own hair salon, a place that specialized in natural hair care, to see if they could squeeze Shanequa in while Cicely got her locks taken care of. Grey be gone.

Not to be undone by a little girl and her hair, Cicely starting braiding. They were both almost in tears when she stopped. She was only half done. Her vision had been a head full of braids about the width of Cicely's baby finger. The ends covered in beads. Tamequa's hair could be caught up in a ponytail or worn loose.

Cicely felt so bad. Completely disappointed in herself. How proud could she be reducing a four year old to tears? It wasn't Tamequa's fault she had so much hair. She didn't know what she could do to make it up to the little girl.

The best Cicely could do was hug and kiss Tamaqua as she put her to bed. Tell her she was sorry and hope the hair salon had time for one more head.

Cicely took pictures. Shanequa said they had been to a hair salon with their mother, but no one ever did their hair but their momma. It was fun watching the girls experience something new. The salon operators had the girls boosted up in chairs to make them adult height. And with more than one person working on each girl, Cicely's vision came to life in no time. Shanequa's and Tamequa's momma was missing out on so many memories.

CHAPTER 11

Ok, it was Cicely's fault they had left for church with no food in their bellies. She had underestimated how long it would take to get herself and two little girls ready for church.

It should not have been difficult. Dress the girls. Sit them on the sofa. Dress yourself. But these weren't the same two frightened little girls that stood unmoving in the foyer. Now Shanequa openly tormented her sister causing Cicely to stop whatever she was doing to referee. Finally Cicely took Tamequa into the bedroom with her while she dressed.

The little girl sat on the bed and watched Cicely, like Cicely used to watch her mother. As she stood at the dresser putting on simple gold hoop earrings and a chain necklace she watched Tamequa staring at her. Maybe she had made a mistake walking around in front of the girl in her underwear.

"What's wrong?" she asked, turning to look at Tamequa.

The four year old looked at her and said, "You pretty Miss CeeCee. You pretty like my momma."

Cicely quickly turned away. What better compliment could a child give someone? She dashed the tears away and turned back to Tamequa. "You're pretty too, sweetie," she said and kissed the child on the forehead.

She knew she was going to have to give them back, but

for now she would savor the feeling.

Her friend Anita was on usher duty so Cicely and the girls were sat near the aisle in case anyone had to visit the little girl's room. Not too close to the front but certainly not in the back.

Cicely decided to wear the same ensemble she had worn to her mother's church. The yellow sheath. But now the sun was shining and it made her feel good. Besides, no one at this church, but Anita, had seen it before.

She sat on the pew using herself as a buffer between the girls. No, Shanequa said she did not remember ever going to church.

They stood for the morning hymn. Tamequa couldn't see, so Cicely stood her on the pew and got a disapproving look from the woman in front of them. Which she ignored.

The praise dancers were next. Cicely didn't especially care for the praise dancers, but King David danced for God, so what could she say. The girls seemed to enjoy it, so they remained standing. Cicely sat and read the church bulletin. She kept her hand lightly on Tamequa's waist to guard against her falling off the pew.

She jerked to attention when she felt the girl move from her grasp. Cicely looked up to see Walter picking Tamequa up. He sat and let her stand between him and Cicely on the seat so she could continue watching the praise dancers.

Cicely looked annoyed. "Are you stalking us?" she

whispered, which earned her another evil eye from the lady in front, but a smile for Walter. She had attended Anita's church many times and had never seen Walter.

He smiled back at the woman before answering Cicely, which made her want to hit him.

"I brought my grandmother to church," he said trying to point without being too obvious to a much older woman near the front of the church.

She was watching them and when Cicely looked her way, she smiled and waved. She looked to be about the age Cicely's mother would have been, maybe a tad younger.

"It's our family's church home. My grandfather wasn't feeling well today so she asked me to bring her."

And Cicely was irrationally thinking, "Why didn't Anita know this was Walter's grandmother's church home. She could have warned me he might show up sometimes."

Walter was surprised when he'd escorted his grandmother to church and saw Cicely. He'd almost didn't come, but then decided it had been awhile since he'd been to any church, so he might as well go with his grandma. He would have walked right past if his grandmother had not pointed Tamequa out to him. The child was swaying to the music along with the praise dancers.

She just thought the child was cute, not that Walter knew her. She'd seen the frown the woman gave Walter before looking her way. She turned her attention to the praise dancers and thought, so this was the woman that had her grandson tied up in knots this summer.

Cicely had never seen Walter all dressed up. Her first thought was he cleans up nice, very nice, charcoal grey suit, white shirt with black stripes and a red tie. She peeped at his feet. He had on red socks. And before she could stop it, the thought of his boxer shorts popped into her head. Surely she was going to hell for thinking of Walter in boxer shorts while in church.

Every time the congregation was asked to stand, Walter surreptitiously looked at Cicely's legs. He was pretty sure a bolt of lightning would strike him where he stood.

The girls stayed interested in the service as long as music was playing. When the preacher started talking Tamequa made herself comfortable on Walters lap. Shanequa peered around Cicely to see Walter was occupied and raised Cicely's arm to slide beneath it. Walter saw Cicely pull the girl closer and kiss the top of her head. It made him feel warm in a good way.

Cicely kept taking side glances at Walter. He seemed genuinely interested in the sermon and it didn't bother him to hold the sleeping Tamequa. One arm held the little girl, his free hand resting on his thigh. She studied his hand. It was large, not overly large just fit his size. His nails were short and clean. The few times she'd seen him she'd noticed when he wasn't working his nails were clean. They looked like workers hands. His cuticles were a little rough around the edges and he could have used some lotion, but they were good hands. Cicely knew if she picked up his hand and turned it palm up, he would have some calluses. Walter worked for what he wanted.

She began to listen to what the young minister was saying. God put in your life what you needed. You may not always agree with Him, but if you waited and would just be still, it would be revealed you had everything you needed right in front of you. We needed to stop fighting what God knew was best. Our lives would be so much simpler if we accepted what was given to us. God loved us. We are His children. What parent doesn't want the best for his child?

Cicely watched Walter nod in agreement.

It was impossible for Cicely and the kids to make a quick exit after the benediction. Walter was slow about leaving the pew and the people on the other side of her also wouldn't cooperate. She was trapped so when Walter's grandmother approached she had nowhere to go.

"This is my grandma, Mrs. Moore," said Walter introducing them. "Grandma, this is Cicely and Shanequa and Tamequa."

Cicely had no choice but to hold her hand out the grasp the older woman's. Her hand was small and frail.

Walter had to bend slightly to hear his grandmother speak. "I have a ride home Walter. You can do whatever you want to do."

"I was going to take these ladies to eat, Grandma," he said.

Tamequa and Shanequa immediately said yes.

"You don't have to do that Walter," said Cicely.

"But we didn't have breakfast," pouted Shanequa.

"Let him take you," said his grandmother. 'I have friends taking me home. I did get him up early to bring to me church when his granddad didn't feel well. It was so good to meet you. The children are so cute." She patted Shanequa on the cheek.

"I'll meet you out front," said Walter. "I just want to walk her to the car. Make sure she's okay." And with that, he took off after his grandmother.

Anita magically appeared when Walter left, blocking Cicely from leaving the pew. "Who is that?"

"The plumber, "was all Cicely could manage.

"You didn't say he was so cute."

"And young. Don't forget young."

"He's not that young Cicely. I thought you were talking about a boy. He is definitely not a boy."

Cicely did not know what to say so she just said, "He's taking us out to eat."

"Then go eat. Don't let me stop you. Just call me when you get back. I want to hear all the details."

As far as Cicely was concerned there weren't going to be any details. They decided to take her car for breakfast so she wouldn't have to move the car seats. She didn't understand why Walter seemed to think it was important for them to all ride in the same vehicle, not comprehending he wanted to spend as much time in her company as he could. The girls wanted to go back to McDonalds, but Walter was more of a mind to take them to a better restaurant.

The four of them trooped into IHop. The waitress led them to a booth and produced booster seats for both girls. Cicely and Walter sat opposite each other.

The day was going to be a hot one. Walter had taken off his suit jacket and left it in her car. He didn't take his tie off but loosen it at the collar and rolled his sleeves up. As they waited for their food Cicely kept looking at his arms. He wasn't a hairy person, but she could see the fine hairs on his forearms. He didn't wear any jewelry just a gold tone watch on his right arm. She hadn't noticed before he was a lefty. He was helping Shanequa color her placemat.

Walter knew Cicely was looking at him with some interest. But he wasn't going to move too quickly like before. He wanted to be in this for the long haul and if that meant moving at a snail's pace then that's what it would be. He liked her in yellow and the dress she wore showed all her curves. He could wait.

The restaurant was crowded and from where they sat the foursome did not have a clear view of the entrance, but Simone saw them. So Cicely had gotten her family. As she watched, one of the children knocked their juice over and Walter seemed to take it in stride, grabbing napkins to mop up the mess. She was not ready to face her sister. Simone turned to her companion and said it was too crowded. That she'd rather go to a buffet and have a real meal with some alcohol involved.

Walter thought he'd glimpsed Simone but wasn't sure so didn't say anything. Cicely never saw her sister.

CHAPTER 12

The previous week was uneventful. After Cicely returned Walter to his car she didn't hear from him again. She didn't know what to think. Maybe he wasn't interested any more. She still hadn't heard from child services and couldn't help but have a nagging worry. The children had been with her for almost a month and she knew when they were gone it would break her heart.

This particular Sunday they were going to the yearly jazz festival in MLK Park. There was a stage for music with a make shift dance floor in front of it and an area near the big splash pool with a small carnival with rides for younger children. Vendors had set up tables all around the area to sell everything from food to jewelry. While the day had started off overcast now it was hot and humid.

Anita and her husband Ben, had set up a couple of canopies and every year invited the same people to join them. A long table was loaded with food and under the table sat a cooler full of beer and wine. Her husband had decided to become adventurous this year and brought a small propane grill to cook hot dogs and hamburgers. Cicely wished he had done ribs. Anita's husband could cook a mean rib that rivaled Lee's.

Cicely's contribution was potato salad and a fruit salad she had made the night before. She made quite a sight when she arrived with her rolling cooler and two large tote bags. More prepared for children this time, she packed extra clothing for the kids. Band-Aids, hand sanitizer and anything else she could think of. She'd made a quick trip to Walmart and bought the girls bathing suits to wear under their clothes, so they could go in the splash pool. The most Cicely would be getting wet would be her feet, not her white shorts and off the shoulder top. That meant towels. She almost left the house without bringing herself a folding chair.

Cicely hadn't come the year before because she was still grieving for her mother and didn't want to be around a lot of people. This year she would enjoy the festival. First thing, Shanequa and Tamequa begged to go on the rides. Wanting to be around some adults for a little while, Cicely bribed the twins to take them after making them promise to keep a close eye on the girls. And to be sure to check back in an hour's time. They didn't have to come back, just call or text to say everything was fine. She even made them set the alarm on their phones as not to forget, and to have the volume on the ringer as loud as it could go and to vibrate.

"You are a mother hen," Anita laughed at her. "My girls are certified babysitters. You don't have to worry about them."

"I know," said Cicely finally getting a paper cup with wine. "It's just, so much can happen."

"The perils of being a parent," said Anita. "Lighten up."

The festival was in full swing. People were coming and going from the tent. Conversation was lively the music good.

When she received a text everything was fine they were still having fun, Cicely relaxed and had a second glass of wine. She and Anita made a game out of talking about the people walking by. Wasn't that awful what that woman had on. That one should not have dressed so young. What made her think yellow hair looked good? Ooooo, wasn't he fine. Anita's husband was having a good laugh just listening to them.

"It's nobody's fault you two are forty and fine," he said. He and his buddies sat at the back of the tent. They weren't fooling anyone. Anita knew they were checking out the women, but it didn't bother her. They had a good relationship.

The girls were cranky when they got back. Cicely fed them, and then made a pallet for them to lie down, out of the way so they wouldn't get stepped on. It didn't take long for them to fall asleep. Anita nudged her. "Isn't that Walter?"

She looked to see Walter headed in their direction. He had not seen them yet. Anita was about to wave her hand to get his attention when Cicely stopped her.

There was a young woman hanging on to his arm. She was pleading with him about something, but they were both laughing. He gripped her hand and was playfully shaking it her face. Walter had on faded blue jeans, a soft blue chambray shirt with the sleeves rolled up pass his elbows, shirttails hanging out and it was unbuttoned half way down. Showing his sculpt chest.

Walter was laughing because his young cousin was begging him for money to buy a leather bag she wanted. Walter thought the guy wanted way too much money for it, saying it was genuine African leather. His cousin was still in college and if he gave her the money he knew would never see it again. "Ask your momma," he was saying. Knowing her mother would never give her the money. He'd slip his cousins money every once in a while but this was not going to be one of those times. She knew it too. She was laughing because the vendor has insinuated that she could get the money out of her old man, meaning Walter.

Cicely couldn't help but stare at the young woman. She had long legs and wore shorts that showed them off to an advantage. She was close to Walter's height and was thin. Cicely figured she outweighed the woman by about thirty pounds. She was light skinned and wore her hair in a short afro. Large hoop earrings accentuated her long neck.

Walter was still laughing when he spotted Cicely. If it was possible his smile got bigger. His cousin noticed. She also noticed the look Cicely was giving them, before she could fake indifference. This wasn't the first time she had been the recipient of an 'if looks could kill' look. Here was the woman Walter said wasn't interested. But he wanted her. BS. Maybe she didn't want to admit she wanted Walter, but the look on her face said she didn't want anyone else to have him either.

"Hi Cicely," he said, still holding his cousin's hand. He turned to speak to Anita and introduce himself and his cousin, when a voice called him from the back of the tent.

"Hey Walt, how you doing man?" Anita's husband stood to greet him.

Walter let go of his cousin's hand and continued to the back of the tent. The two men did the manly hug thing. Ben reached in the cooler and handed Walter a beer.

Cicely looked at Anita and mouthed, "They know each other?'

"Just like a man," said the young woman standing before Cicely. She stuck out her hand. "I'm Lisa, Walter's cousin."

Cicely took a closer look. She saw the resemblance now. The woman had the same funny colored hair as Walter and the same green/hazel colored eyes.

"Our mothers' are sisters," she said and stuck her hand out to Anita after she finished shaking Cicely's hand.

They must have gotten their odd coloring and height from their grandfather, thought Cicely. Both their grandmother and Walter's mother were short. She didn't think what Walter's father may have contributed, because Walter didn't.

The men were still engaged in conversation so Lisa spoke up, "Tell Walter I'm going back to our parents' tent. I'll see him later." Lisa couldn't wait to get back to the family to give them a four-one-one on Cicely.

Anita leaned closer to Cicely so no one under the canopy could hear her. "You thought that was his girlfriend."

"I did not," but knew her friend had seen right through her.

"Puleeze," said Anita drawing the word out.

"You didn't tell me Ben knew him."

"Because I didn't know. Ask him to stay."

"I will not. This isn't my tent."

"If you don't I will," said Anita trying to force her hand.

"Don't you dare!" said Cicely then she looked around to see if anyone had heard her.

"Ben," Anita shouted. "Ask him to stay." Both men turned to her when she yelled her husband's name so she waved. "Hi Walter, I'm his better half."

Walter raised his beer can in her direction and said, "No doubt."

Cicely said under her breath to her friend. "I am so going to stop speaking to you."

"No you won't," said Anita. "And make sure you name your first born after me."

"Just shut up," said Cicely shaking her head. "Just shut up."

Ben and Walter talked a few more minutes then he wandered back to the women. The band on stage was playing some pretty good dance music so Walter asked Cicely to come dance with him.

She shook her head, "No, I don't want to dance."

Walter looked at Anita, "She does dance, doesn't she?" he asked.

"Hell yes, she dances. Go with him Cicely."

"The girls might wake up."

"I'll watch the girls. Go dance."

Even Ben put in his two cents and told Walter to take her. If Anita had told Ben anything she had told her friend about Walter, she would kill her.

Walter held out his hand, but she stood without assistance. He took her hand anyway when she stood to lead the way through the crowd. They made stops along the way to speak with people Walter knew and he introduced her each time. Cicely saw people she'd known since high school, but wasn't about to stop and introduce Walter. Let them think whatever they wanted. When he let go of her hand it was only to place his hand on the small of her back to guide her through the throng of people to the dance floor. When they finally reached the dance floor a slow song was playing.

Cicely just stood there. "I'm not going to slow dance with you Walter," she said.

Before he could lean in and whisper in her ear, Cicely stepped back, her automatic response when he got too close. He was not going to throw her off balance again.

He smiled at her, "Your loss." He reclaimed her hand and led her to where all the vendor stalls were.

Cicely refused to let him buy anything for her, but he did purchase two inexpensive stretch bracelets for Shanequa and Tamequa. The girls were awake when they got back and were ecstatic to see Walter and he had brought them a gift. They were disappointed he would not go to the splash pad with them. He begged off saying he had to leave. Cicely was glad he'd left because when she stepped in the wade pool she slipped and sat on her butt in a couple of inches of water. She'd brought extra clothing for everyone but herself.

CHAPTER 13

Mother Nature was kind enough to allow the last tent to come down before allowing it to rain and it had been raining ever since. The girls had not been able to go outside for two days and it was beginning to take its toll. Cicely was in the kitchen trying to work on an assignment that was due the next morning. She had not worked on it over the weekend because of the festival. Her bad, she had left it for the last minute. Putting the girls on the sun porch to color, she thought she could get some work done before starting dinner in a couple of hours. Now she heard Tamequa crying and screaming at the top of her lungs.

When she went to the sun porch, Shanequa was standing over her sister, taunting her. "What is going on?" she asked trying to keep her voice calm. Tamequa had never cried this way before. "Are you hurt?"

Tamequa pointed at her sister, tears and snot running. "She broke my crayon."

"I'm sure she didn't do it on purpose."

"Yes I did," admitted Shanequa. "It's ugly. It's an ugly color. I don't like it."

"But it wasn't your crayon." Cicely had deliberately purchased each their own package of crayons to avoid any fights.

"It was ugly." Shanequa had now bent down to get in her

little sister's face. "Ugly, ugly, ugly."

This made Tamequa cry louder.

"You cannot go around breaking things that don't belong to you," said Cicely sternly. The screaming was beginning to get to her. She picked Tamequa up to take her into the kitchen to clean her face. "Tell your sister you are sorry and give her one of your crayons."

Shanequa followed them into the kitchen. "No I'm not."

Tamequa was still in Cicely's arms and she kicked out at her sister with her barefoot, catching her on the side of her head. Not hard enough to cause the howl Shanequa let out.

Shanequa grabbed Tamequa's foot as if to bite it. Cicely grabbed her by the forearm and jerked her away. "Don't you dare." Her voice was hard. It was then she heard the front doorbell. She didn't know how long someone had been ringing it. As she stomped to the front with one child on her hip and pulling the other by the arm, she thought, it better not be Walter to check on the basement. I am not in the mood for his cat and mouse games today.

It wasn't Walter at the door, but she didn't feel any relief. A well-dressed middle-aged black woman with a brief case was waiting to be let in. Her identification was hanging around her neck. It could only be social services. She hadn't heard anything in weeks and now they were at her door. Her belly filled with dread.

The woman looked at the trio before her. All three were

barefoot, the one in the woman's arms was sniffing to keep her nose from running, and the one standing next to the adult was holding her arm, her eyes were filling with tears. The adult looked like she was waiting for the axe to fall.

"Oh, looks like I came at a good time." She said introducing herself.

Cicely tried to manage a smile, but it looked more like a grimace.

"Ms. Macklin, I had three children and I remember what it was like when they couldn't go outside. Sometimes they just have a meltdown and take their mothers with them. I'm not here to judge you on any one thing. I have to talk to the girls and look at the arrangements you have for them and have a talk with you about their mother. So why don't you take a few minutes, clean their faces, soothe their hurts and while they show me where they sleep calm yourself. I'm not here to take them away," she added with a smile.

Cicely was able to give her a real smile then. She took them to the downstairs bathroom, where she sat on the closed toilet to compose herself before doing anything. Tamequa had popped her thumb in her mouth. Behavior Cicely had only seen lately when it was bedtime. She removed the thumb, had her blow her nose and proceeded to wash her face. Without prompting, Shanequa apologized to her sister and allowed Cicely to wash her face. Cicely looked at herself in the mirror and took a couple of cleansing breaths. She could feel her heartbeat slow. Taking their hands the three left the bathroom to meet with the social worker.

Cicely started to lead the way up the stairs when the woman stopped her. "The children can show me the way. I'll talk with them then meet with you."

She moved to the side to let them pass and she went into the kitchen to start the teakettle. Some of Madeline's tea would be good about now.

Shanequa took the woman's hand and pulled her along to show where they slept. She pointed out which bedroom was Cicely's. The door was open so the woman stuck her head in to look. The room was tidy, the bed made. On the nightstand was a well-worn bible. She let herself be pulled into the girls' room.

It was also tidy. In the middle of the room between the beds was a rocking chair. On the seat was a short stack of children's books. Tamequa crawled onto one bed and hugged the stuffed animal there. The woman knew the children had arrived with next to nothing, because Cicely had called to complain about it. The other bed had a Barbie doll in a state of undress. She noticed in one corner was an empty milk crate filled with toys a child might like to play with. Next she opened the door to the small closet. Two pairs of shoes for each girl were lined up on the floor. Sneakers and sandals. There was one dress for each girl. Now just being nosy, she pulled open a couple of dresser drawers and saw clothing for the children neatly folded.

She sat on the bed with Shanequa and asked, "What happen today?"

"She broke my crayon." Said Tamequa pulling her thumb out her mouth before speaking because Ms. CeeCee said people couldn't understand her if she spoke with her thumb in her mouth.

Shanequa puffed up, ready to lie, then said, "I said I was sorry. But she kicked me in the head." Having to get her story out.

"So that's why everyone was crying?" the woman asked.

"Hm hm," nodded Shanequa.

"Tell me what you've been doing while staying here."

Once Shanequa started talking she couldn't get the words out fast enough. They had friends up the street. Miss CeeCee had taken them to church and shopping. She and Tamequa liked church. They shopped for clothes and food, but Miss CeeCee din't like to shop for food at Walmart so they shopped at two places. They had went to McDonalds and IHop to eat. And Miss CeeCee let her make her own peanut butter and jelly sandwich. She read to them, like the teacher did in school. Sunday they'd went to a big picnic in the park.

Mrs. White knew which park, she and her husband had attended.

"What about your mother?"

"Our momma in…" started Tamequa

Shanequa stopped her with a "shush" before she could finish.

"What about your mother?" the woman asked again.

"Miss CeeCee said we shouldn't tell people," said Shanequa. "It ain't nobody's business."

"You can tell me," the woman cajoled. "I won't tell anyone."

Shanequa thought about it. "Our momma in jail. But you'd better not tell nobody. Miss CeeCee said when momma gets out we can be with her again. But right now, we get to stay with her."

The little girl clamped her lips shut, subject closed. She went to the dresser and brought back the bracelets to show the woman. "Walter gave us these. Ain't they pretty?"

"How old is Walter?"

"Old, like you and Miss CeeCee."

"Does Walter live here?" This was some information the woman didn't have. No one said anything about an unmarried male being in residence. "Or stay in Miss CeeCee's room sometimes?"

"No," the little girl smirked. "Miss CeeCee ain't got no man. She said she's smart and when you're smart you don't have to have a man to take care of you. When I grow up, I'm going to be smart."

The woman chuckled. She was sure Cicely hadn't said it like that.

Cicely was waiting for the water to boil, wondering what

was going on upstairs when the doorbell to the side door rang. She walked across the sun porch to the door and hesitated when she saw it was Walter. I had been raining for two days so she should have expected him. She opened the door, "Not now Walter, it's not a good time."

"Cicely," he said looking harried. "I have to check on the basement."

"The girls' social worker is here. I don't think it would be a good idea for her to see you here." She stood with one hand on the door, her other hand on the door jam, blocking his way.

"I'm a plumber. I think the social worker has probably seen a plumber before." He moved her arm and went directly to the basement.

Cicely stood there for a minute before returning to the kitchen. A little peeved he'd completely ignored what she'd said.

She was pouring herself a cup of tea when the children and social worker came into the kitchen. She offered the woman a cup, and she accepted, saying the day was perfect for a cup of tea.

"We can talk here in the kitchen," the woman said. "Is there someplace the children can go?"

Cicely ushered them onto the sun porch, with an admonishment not to break any more crayons.

"I'm impressed Ms. Macklin. And that is not an easy thing to do. You've made the children feel at home."

Cicely looked down at her cup of tea. "Thank you. I like having them here."

"Even today?" asked the woman with a smile on her face.

Cicely smiled too. "Even today."

"I'm glad you said that. The girls need to stay with you a little longer. "

Cicely had a big grin on the inside.

"Their mother is getting out shortly, but will be going directly to a halfway house. While some halfway houses do have accommodations for children this isn't one of them. She will have to wear an electronic ankle bracelet. And if she follows the rules she'll be released. Then once she finds a place to live she can petition to have her children back. Because the children are school age, she will be expected to find some kind of employment, even if it's only part time, to show she can be responsible. So, in my opinion, I believe the children will be with you a few more months. If you think you can handle that?"

"Yes," Cicely said, nodding her head vigorously.

"School will be starting shortly. I have all the records here," she said patting her briefcase. "I have Shanequa's school records and both girls' medical records and their pediatrician's name. All immunizations are up to date. Tamequa didn't attend school before, but I understand you have a neighborhood school that has a pretty good pre-k program, so if I were you I would enroll her."

Cicely interrupted her, "You said Tamequa didn't attend

school before, but she knows her alphabet and can count. She can even read a few words. She's very bright for a four year old."

The woman frowned. "Maybe my records are incomplete. As we told you, they have been in temporary foster care before. Something could have been left out." She began shuffling through her briefcase and pulled out a file folder and another sheet of paper that turned out to be a check. "This is the only time you will get a check handed to you. After this all funds will be loaded onto this benefits card." And handed Cicely an envelope containing the card. "The girls need school clothes and I know we didn't provide you with much when they came. I had to fight to get this check for you."

Cicely accepted both and said, "Thank you."

Walter checked to make sure no water was coming in and was on his way out of the basement. He heard the conversation and came no farther than the top step. He considered sneaking out unseen, but wanted to apologize to Cicely for being so short with her. They had taken his grandfather to the hospital before daylight that morning. He had worked most of the day and now he wanted to get back to the hospital. He decided to leave and call her later. They'd never had a phone conversation. It lifted his mood a little to think of them having a phone conversation. He left the basement and stepped through the doorway onto the sun porch.

"Walter," little happy voices greeted him.

The social worker had fastened her briefcase and was

about to leave when she heard the girls call Walters' name. She walked pass Cicely onto the sun porch.

Each girl had Walter by a leg. He looked pass the woman at Cicely, "The basement is dry." He said lamely.

"You don't stay in the basement, do you?" asked the woman, she had heard of stranger things.

"No, no," said Cicely. "He's the plumber." She moved to detach the girls from Walter's legs. "I had a water problem the last time it rained this much. So he came by to check while you were upstairs with the girls."

"This *is* the Walter that gave the girls bracelets?"

"Yeth," said Tamequa her lisp prominent. "He was at the picnic with Miss Anita."

The child had not lied, but she made it seem Walter was there with someone else. Out of the mouths of babes.

That was good enough for the social worker. She drove away thinking, why didn't her plumber look that good?

Walter didn't have anything to say. He knew he could have blown the interview for Cicely.

Cicely gave each girl a gentle swat on the behind to send them from the porch, telling them to go watch TV. She put her hands on her hips and faced Walter.

He knew the situation was serious and he deserved every blistering word she would throw at him. He was fully prepared to say he was sorry, but her appearance grabbed his attention.

He could never look at her enough.

Her toenails were painted a dark color, burgundy he thought. He'd once had a burgundy colored car, but couldn't tell by the lighting on the porch. His eyes moved up her smooth brown calves and thighs, left bare by her cutoff jeans wondering if she shaved her legs, but he didn't care one way or the other. Her belly was flat and Walter imagined she had more muscle definition than he did, because of her running. His eyes traveled to her breasts. Did not the woman wear a bra at home? He knew she wore one, because he'd checked it out, at the park, at church, at Walmart. He could see slight movement each time she breathed in and out. Her mouth captured his attention last and Walter wanted to kiss her.

No matter how hard he tried to fight it she always had an effect on him. She would flirt with him, exchange playful banter. And mostly put up with him because the kids had formed an attachment to him. Because of her own screwed up ideas about his age that's as far as she would let it go.

Walter spoke before Cicely. "I'm sorry I came at a time that wasn't good for you Cicely. But I promised I would come if it rained. It rained, so I came. I left a **paying** job to stop by here before I went to see my grandpa in the hospital. All you have to do is say, Thank you Walter."

He'd made her angrier. He recognized when the anger took over by the set of her mouth and the slight change in her stance.

It didn't change his feelings. If possible, it turned him on more.

"I gotta go," he said, turned and walked out the door.

Cicely stood at the open door, watched him walk through the rain, get in his truck and drive away.

She slammed the door so hard a pane of glass in the multi-paned door shattered. Shanequa and Tamequa came running at the sound of breaking glass. She stopped them at the doorway by holding her hand out. She didn't want them to stepping on glass. The medium sized shard of glass sticking out her left foot was enough.

It hurt like hell when she pulled it out and the bleeding wouldn't stop. Every time she took a step blood would ooze out. The cut was about an inches long and deep, so she duct taped a piece of plastic over the broken window pane, got the girls together and drove herself to an emergency care place with a bloody sock wrapped around her foot.

After they cleaned her wound and assured her she wouldn't bleed to death she remembered what Walter had said. His grandpa was in the hospital. It hadn't been that long ago he'd been too ill to bring his wife to church. When an x-ray confirmed no tendons had been cut but she did need stitches she called Anita to keep her mind off the needle.

"Walter's grandfather is in the hospital" she said.

"Are you asking me or telling me?" replied Anita.

"Telling. No asking."

"How would I know? You see Walter more than I do."

"His grandparents go to your church. They're members."

"I don't have a direct line to the sick and shut-in committee."

"See what you can find out."

The doctor picked that moment to interrupt her call to explain he'd given her five stitches and she would need a tetanus shot and antibiotics. The nurse would be in to give her the injection and tell her how to care for the wound. Because the girls were so well behaved while he cared for their mother, he gave them both suckers. No one bother to tell him Cicely wasn't their mother

"Where are you?" asked Anita overhearing the conversation.

"One of those emergency care places. I cut my foot."

"How did you cut your foot?"

"It's a long story." Not wanting to admit how stupid she'd acted in front of the girls.

"Tell you what," said Anita, "I'll make some phone calls about Walter's grandfather and when I call you back, you tell me the long story."

She stopped at McDonalds on the way home going to the drive-thru. Everyone had enough drama for the day.

She sat in bed with her foot elevated on a pillow so it wouldn't throb while she used her laptop to work on her assignment. Anita had verified Walter's grandfather was in the hospital. Mr. Moore was currently in CICU, but doing well, expecting to be moved to a semi-private room the next morning. He'd had a mild heart attack. Cicely went on-line and ordered an arrangement of live flowers, (because personally she hated cut flower arrangements, eventually you were left with something dead) to be delivered to the hospital and hoped Walter's grandmother remembered her.

Anita shared her joy at keeping the girls longer and commiserated with her as Cicely related her Walter/foot story. Inside Anita was laughing her ass off wondering how long it would take before the two hooked up.

Walter drove directly to the hospital to sit with family until his grandmother shooed them away with the exception of Walter. Saying it was too much like a deathwatch and no one was dying today. She knew Walter wouldn't leave because his grandpa was like his dad. So he sat with his mother and grandmother until the doctor came and assured them he was doing fine. After monitoring overnight in the CICU he would be moved to the cardiac floor barring any complications.

The doctor gave permission for each of them to visit five minutes, but no longer, his patient had to rest. Both women agreed to let Walter go first so he could see with his own eyes his grandpa would be fine.

"Walter," said his grandmother placing her had on his arm. "Do not go in there making a fuss. He's going to be alright."

"I'm not…."

"Walter, you're angry. Don't go in there telling him what he should and should not be doing. He already knows that. Just tell him you love him."

"He knows I love him"

"But it's nice to hear sometimes."

Walter's heart almost stopped when he entered the room, his grandfather was so still. He'd heard the steady beep of the machines, but it didn't register at first. He'd never seen his grandfather immobile before.

His grandfather opened his eyes and said, "Breathe boy."

Walter didn't even realize he was holding his breath and let it out in a rush. "You scared us," he said.

"Scared myself," said the old man beckoning Walter closer.

"Don't do it again," Walter said his voice cracking like he was thirteen all over again.

His grandfather pulled him into his embrace, which caused all the alarms to go off on the machines he was attached too. He said in Walters's ear, "You turned out good."

It took seconds for a nurse to appear in the doorway. Seeing the men in an embrace she knew some wire had probably came loose. "You shouldn't scare us like this Mr. Moore," she said efficiently putting everything to right.

"I told him that," said Walter trying to keep his tone

even. "I love you grandpa," he added.

Many people thought Walter was a younger version of his grandfather. Janice was relieved when her baby looked nothing like the boy that fathered him. When she looked at her son she wasn't reminded how young and foolish she'd been. How disappointed her parents were in her.

They loved Walter and when anything requiring a father came up, Walter's grandfather was there. Mr. Moore was a different generation and if his son had lived he would have never received the attention his grandson Walter received. Walter got a kinder, gentler grandpa. But still one that insisted he fight if picked on. After the age of nine, do not hit girls unless your life was in danger. When it was that time of month keep a low profile in the house. It was a couple of years before Walter caught on to what that time of month was.

His grandfather taught him to drive and gave him his first beer. Gave him his first real whuppin', with a belt. Walter couldn't remember the why, but he never forgot the whuppin'. Unfortunately he couldn't say it was his last.

When running from his mother because of some infraction he'd committed, it was his grandfather Walter hid behind. Grandmas were good but, Grandpa's were better. It was his grandfather that taught him to respect and appreciate women.

Grandpa was a wealth of information. No, your johnson would not fall off if you played with it, but don't make a habit of it or you **will** go blind. Self-discipline was good.

Walter did not miss having his father around. Janice asked him at sixteen did he want to know him, again at eighteen and finally at twenty-one. Each time Walter said no. At sixteen it was because he was pissed. By eighteen he felt it would disrespect his grandfather. At twenty-one he had spent some time at community college and was a plumbers apprentice under his uncle, so even after his grandfather said it wouldn't hurt his feeling nor would he commit manslaughter, Walter didn't care.

If the boy that was instrumental in creating him hadn't grown up enough to see what he'd spawned then Walter didn't want any parts of him.

So if he was the spitting image of the man lying in the hospital bed that was fine with Walter.

The nurse had finished re-plugging everything. Walter's grandfather said, "Send your momma and grandma in. Let's get it over with so I can get some rest."

Walter went straight home. Sitting at the hospital had drained him. It wasn't until he had taken a shower that he thought about Cicely. He wanted to call her but decided against it. Better to let her get over her mad first. If he called now, she would tell him not to come over her house again and hang up on him. In that order.

CHAPTER 14

Walter was in the middle of a job when his cell phone rang. He and his crew were running pipe in a new home. The rule was no one used their cell during work so he gave everyone a break so he could return the call. With his grandfather still in the hospital he wasn't taking any chances.

"Walter, what was that woman's name I met at your house this summer?" his mother asked.

There was only one woman his mother had met at his house recently but he couldn't understand why she was asking. "Cicely," he told her.

"I thought so," said his mother repeating the information to someone else.

"Why?"

"Mother asked is she the same one she met at church with the little girls?" She didn't answer his question, just asked him another one.

"Yes Grandma met her. Why are you asking?" He was getting tired of the question game. "Is everything okay with Grandpa?"

"Daddy's fine. That's all I wanted."

"Ma," he said getting a little impatient. She still hadn't answered his question. "Why are you asking about Cicely?"

"Oh, she sent your grandpa a beautiful potted plant and get well card. And your grandmother and I just wanted to make sure she was who we thought she was. Your grandma says to tell her thank you the next time you see her."

Mentally Walter took a knee and did a fist pump, like he had just scored the winning touchdown. Now he had a reason to see Cicely, besides the obvious one.

Sunday Walter escorted his mother and grandmother to church. As a matter of fact his aunts and uncles and most of his cousins also escorted his grandmother to church. No one kept it a secret they were blessed by still having the family patriarch among the living. He would be coming home in a couple of days and everyone was in church to say thank you for the blessing.

Walter looked, but Cicely wasn't there. He kept turning in the pew so much to see if she had arrived, his grandmother poked him in the ribs to be still. He saw Cicely's friend and after the service tried to catch her before she left with no success.

One of his cousins volunteered to take their grandmother to the hospital, so Walter went home. He stripped his bed and threw the sheets in the wash. Tried watching a pre-season football game, but his team was so bad he went outside and washed his car. That made his work truck look bad, so he rinsed that off. He procrastinated as long as he could. He would have to talk to Cicely face to face.

When he pulled in front of the house Cicely was sitting on the front porch. She had on some long dress thing that women wore in the summer. It was black and white striped, sleeveless with a scooped neck. It looked to hit her around the ankles. He couldn't really tell from the car. He took a breath and picked up the pizza he had brought hoping the girls liked cheese. He'd gotten half cheese and half pepperoni, because his cousins' kids didn't like pepperoni, he figured Shanequa and Tamequa might play by the same program.

Cicely was sitting on the porch so she could keep an eye on the kids up the street. Soon the weather would change and it wouldn't be so pleasant to sit on the porch and listen to the kids play. She had the windows open and could hear the music drift from the stereo in the house. Some light jazz had her tapping her hand on her thigh and bobbing her head in beat to the music with her eyes closed. She had a glass of red wine and her injured foot elevated on an ottoman she had dragged from the living room. Hearing a car pull up she looked, but didn't recognize it, so let her eyes drift close. She had only seen Walters's car one other time earlier that summer and didn't hear him until he reached the top step of the porch.

The closer Walter got to the house he could hear the music. He watched the way she moved, yeah, she could dance and one of these days he would take her dancing. He stood for a minute holding the pizza watching her before making his presence known.

"You're allowed to drink in public?" He asked grinning.

"Walter," she gasped. She tried to get up, hide her injured foot, but it was too late. He had seen it.

"I didn't mean to startle you. And before you say

anything, I'm supposed to thank you for the flowers. My grandmother liked that they were living. And I apologize for being such an ass. I brought gifts," he said showing her the pizza.

"Yes you were. But you don't have to apologize. I get you were worried about your grandfather and I was acting like the world was going to end if the social worker saw you in the house. He's doing okay?" She stood to take the pizza and winched when she put the full weight on her foot.

"He's doing good. You sit down," he said. "I'll take it in; just tell me where to put it. And not where the sun don't shine." He smiled.

She instructed him to put it on the counter in the kitchen and if he liked, to help himself to a glass of wine. The glasses were in the cabinet next to the refrigerator.

Walter had never been past the kitchen and admired the natural wood of the house. He peered upstairs and wondered which bedroom was Cicely's. Walking through the dining room he stopped to admire the pictures on the wall of Cicely and her sisters at various ages, her sisters and their families. A portrait, of whom he assumed was their parents hung in the dining room. After depositing the pizza on the counter, he got a glass and grabbed the bottle to take outside.

"That's an open container," said Cicely pointing at the wine bottle.

"I won't tell," said Walter leaning against the rail in front of her.

Cicely pointed to a chair. "You can sit."

"I'm fine here." And he was. From his position he could just sit and look directly at her. He hadn't noticed the slit in her dress before and with her leg propped up the slit allowed him a clear view of her thigh. Her locks had grown longer since he'd first met her and he liked the look on her. He was fine leaning on the rail.

Where he chose to sit was fine with Cicely. She liked the view. He leaned against the railing with his feet crossed at the ankle. He had on men's flip-flops and she got a look at his feet, narrow feet, and toes not unnaturally long. No hairy toes, she did not like toes with dark hair, it grossed her out. He wasn't flat footed, she saw no crusty callouses. The nails were trim and neat. She did notice his feet were lighter than his hands. Guess he didn't wear sandals much. He did have nice feet though, so there was no reason for him not to wear them. He had his arms folded across his chest and holding the glass in his left hand.

"What did you do to your foot?" He asked.

"Broken glass, had to have several stitches," she said, hoping he would think she dropped a kitchen glass on her foot.

"Ouch," he said in sympathy. She hadn't changed her nail color and her nails were the color of the wine they were drinking.

Several moments went by and neither of them spoke. She noticed when Walter's head started nodding to the music.

"So you like jazz?" she asked.

"I do. My grandfather's influence. You should let me take you to hear some live."

"Walter…"

"Just a friend, Cicely. Just as a friend. You can pay your own way if it makes you feel any better."

"We'll see," she said, not wanting to ruin the atmosphere.

They enjoyed the music for about ten more minutes before the girls discovered he was there. "Walter," said Shanequa running up on the porch holding a clothesline they were using for a jump rope her friends following her. "Can you turn the rope for us? Tamequa is too little and Miss CeeCee's foot is hurt."

"I am not too little," said Tamequa stomping her foot, the last one to join the group on the porch because her legs weren't as long as the other girls.

"Sure," he said unwrapping himself.

"Walter, do you even know how to jump rope?" asked Cicely.

"How hard can it be?" He shrugged putting his wine glass down.

Cicely moved to sit on the top stair to have a better look of a grown man over six feet tall playing jump rope with a group of little girls. He made sure they let Tamequa have a turn jumping even if she was too short to turn. Cicely had been holding her cell phone in her hand absentmindedly; now whenever it was Walter's turn to jump she took pictures, careful not to let him see her.

They were in the kitchen waiting for the pizza to get warm. Walter had to admit jumping rope with little girls was not an easy thing to do. Of course he was hampered by not having on the proper footwear. Cicely called him on that, inviting him over when her foot healed and he could bring any shoes he wished.

Walter's demeanor was relaxed as he sprawled in a kitchen chair watching Cicely clean the girls face and hands. She had a short wooden stool next to the sink and stood each girl on it in turn to soap their arms and face.

"I didn't know girls got so dirty," he said.

"This is just a preview," said Cicely as she wiped the soap from Shanequa's face. "You should see the ring around the tub after their bath tonight."

No, thought Walter, he'd like to be the ring around the bathtub when Cicely bathed. But he stood and said, "Where are the dishes? I'll set the table so you don't keep walking around on that foot."

"I want to help," said Tamequa holding her arms out to Walter to be picked up so she could reach the plates.

"Walter," said Cicely as she helped Shanequa from the stool. "Why do you keep feeding us?"

He paused and looked at them. Tamequa, Shanequa and Cicely. "Maybe…. You look hungry to me."

Walter stood on the porch for a moment before going to his car. It was getting darker earlier and he could see the stars because of the cloudless sky. He had stayed until Cicely told the girls it was time to take their bath and go to bed. In the beginning he'd thought taking Cicely to bed would be enough. Friends with benefits. For the first time Walter felt his heart was in jeopardy and not just from Cicely.

By Thursday Cicely was ready to rip the stitches out herself, her foot itched so bad. She returned to the emergency center and they agreed, the wound was healed enough for the stitches to be removed.

She had checked with her neighbor, Jackie, and was anxious to start school shopping for the girls. Jackie's girls attended the same school Shanequa and Tamequa would go to and she let Cicely copy the list she'd received from the school. Cicely knew they wouldn't have everything, but she wanted to get as much as she could before school started. The school did have a dress code and a few stores in the area carried those items. Besides their uniforms the girls had to have socks, more underwear, which included undershirts for cooler weather and winter coats. Cicely knew having every child dress alike was important but she hated the idea of the girls having no individuality, so after reading the dress code very carefully, she bought the wildest socks she could find. Shoes had to be black, but nowhere did it say socks had to be a certain color.

Cicely still had not revealed the circumstances to Jackie why the girls were with her, but Jackie agreed as long as the girls were with Cicely they could take turns seeing the girls to school. They would alternate weeks. Cicely was going to make the girls walk weather permitting, the school wasn't that far. Jackie could use any mode of transportation she liked. The first day of school however, Cicely would take her girls.

The next day Cicely dressed the girls so they could go to school for early registration. She wanted them to see where they would be going each day and meet their teachers so they wouldn't feel like strangers the first day. She also wanted to speak to each teacher and explain the situation. The school population was diverse according to Jackie, so the students there would be from all types of families. Most likely the girls would not be the only foster kids attending that school.

Cicely wanted to make sure if there were any issues during the school day, they wouldn't hesitate to call her. It was no surprise to find Shanequa wouldn't be the only Shanequa in her class. Which was fine, as long as she wasn't called Shanequa B.

She went over the curriculum with the young woman that would have Tamequa, to make sure the little girl wouldn't become bored. Cicely explained what Tamequa knew and was pleased to see the woman start a folder with Tamequa's name and write down what Cicely was telling her. They had a very productive morning and the girls were looking forward to starting school, Cicely was the apprehensive one.

She'd promised Walter she would go visit his grandfather. According to Walter, the old man wanted to meet the woman that had sent him the nice plant. He'd been home two days and while she thought she should wait, she knew if she didn't do it right away it wouldn't get done. Better to get it out of the way. She didn't want to become too familiar with Walter's family. He'd introduced her to his friends at the park, without meaning to she was part of his circle. So after lunch she and the girls went to Walter's grandfather's house. She picked early in the afternoon trying to avoid Walter. Odds said he should still be at work and since it was a workday it was less likely she would run into any other family members.

If anyone had asked, she would have said the Sunday afternoon spent with Walter was very nice. No boundaries had been crossed. He seemed to accept the limits she had set.

Cicely parked in front of the house and did not get out. It was a one-way street so she was able to park so she wouldn't have to take the girls out on the traffic side. It was a quiet neighborhood from what she could tell. The street was tree lined, everyone kept their grass cut. She looked at the house. Unlike hers it was brick, one and a half stories, but older liked hers. The concrete porch only took up half the front of the house. The other section was windows on all three sides. Someone could look out the window on the porch side and see who was at the door. The houses on either side were almost identical.

She really didn't want to do this. It made her uneasy to meet the man Walter may or may not look like when he reached that age. There was no rationale to it, but she didn't want to meet him. She didn't even want to examine the feeling to find a reason for it. If she left now Walter would never know. She could make up some excuse, say it slipped her mind. Decision made, Cicely put her hand on the key to turn the ignition when Walter's truck pulled up behind her. It was too late to leave now.

Quickly she said to the girls, "We are not staying long, don't sit down, even if they ask you. If you are asked do you want anything to eat say no thank you. Got that?"

Walter opened her door just as she finished giving instructions. He took her hand to help her from the car and didn't release it. He closed the door and had her standing against the car. She had on black capris and a pretty blue floaty top that hit her at mid-thigh. He looked down, "How's the foot?" he asked.

"Stitches out," she said, holding her foot out. She had on black ballerina styled shoes allowing for the bandage across the top of her foot, but he couldn't see her toes.

Walter was standing way too close, still in work clothes. She was tempted to take a step closer. If she did, their bodies would be touching. This was the man she should be afraid of. Madeline had warned her he was not one to play with. Still in the backseat, the children hadn't made a sound.

Walter didn't move any closer, it was as if he was waiting

on her permission. Anytime he was near her he needed to push it to the limit. And he liked unnerving her.

Walter's grandfather had been looking out the window, one of his habits. He saw Walter pull up behind the car sitting at the curb. He went to open the front door expecting to see Walter. What he did not expect was to see Walter standing toe to toe with a female. He knew his grandson's body language and he was tempted to turn the hose on him. But he didn't know the girl. The way Walter was standing her face was blocked from his view. He wouldn't embarrass her like that. What was that expression young people used? Get a room. His grandson needed a room. He stepped onto the porch to say something, but the girl beat him to it.

"Walter," Cicely said softly.

He had to lean in to hear her.

"The kids are in the car and I think your grandfather is watching us."

"What is he doing?" Walter asked, not turning around.

Cicely was beginning to find humor in the situation and stifled her laugh. "He's standing on the porch."

"You think this is funny?" he choked out.

She leaned around him, smiled and waved, "Hi."

"Y'all come to see me? Or you gonna stay outside?" Asked Mr. Moore.

Walter moved her aside to open the car door and get the

kids out of their safety seats. He took each child by the hand and the four of them started up the walkway.

Mr. Moore watched the group approach him. Walter was holding the little girls' hands but he wasn't watching his grandson, his eyes were on Cicely. She did not approach shyly. She looked him directly in the eye. This was no girl. Hot damn, Walter had finally found himself a woman. He took Cicely's hand the moment she reached the top step.

She liked him. He reminded her of her Daddy. Not in looks, there was no doubt he and Walter shared the same gene pool, but he looked at her like he would pay attention to what she said. Her Daddy had that gift. He could make you feel like you were the most important person in the world. A good thing when a man lived in a house with five females. But that was almost Walter's household growing up too, wasn't it?

"You're the one that sent the plant." he said rather than ask, pulling her into the house.

"Yes I am."

The living room took up all the space across the front of the house. It had a real wood-burning fireplace. You knew which seat was Mr. Moore's, a worn recliner near the fireplace, crosswise from that was a large flat screen TV. The living room flowed directly into the dining room, which was about half the width of the living room. At the end of the dining room was a doorway, which led to the rest of the house.

He called to his wife as he showed Cicely in, "Mother,

we have company."

Cicely thought it was cute he called her Mother, but she didn't know then everyone, except Walter, called her Mother. The woman she'd met at church came from the direction Cicely thought the kitchen would be drying her hands on a towel.

"You came," she said smiling. "I didn't know if Walter would remember to tell you. Mr. Moore likes to have a face to put with a name and the plant was so pretty." She extended her hand to invite them to sit on one of the two sofas in the room.

"Really, we can't stay," said Cicely trying to stick to her word of not staying long.

"That little one does look tired," Mrs. Moore said looking at Tamequa. "Well at least let me show you where the plant will be living. I love growing things. Bring the girls."

Walter started to follow and his grandfather shook his head no. "They don't need you."

Cicely and the girls followed Mrs. Moore. Immediately beyond the dining room was an odd shaped hall, the center of the house. One door led to a bathroom, on either side of the bathroom was a bedroom. Cicely guessed which one was Walter's grandparents; it looked like they still shared a bed. To her left were two doors, one leading upstairs. Mrs. Moore pointed that one out, "Walter used to sleep up there," she said. The second door was to the basement. Directly in front of them was the kitchen. As they walked through, Cicely could see Mrs. Moore had been in the middle of preparing dinner. Collard greens were soaking in the sink, and a whole chicken was in a baking dish waiting to go into the oven. She led them though the kitchen out the back door.

Walter sat on the edge of the couch waiting for his grandfather to speak. He didn't know how much the old man had seen, but he figured he was in some kind of trouble.

His grandfather took his time getting comfortable in his recliner. He pulled the lever on the side of the chair that would raise his legs and turned the TV on. "She married?" he asked.

The question startled Walter, "No, she's not married."

"Good looking woman not to be married. How'd you met her?"

"Um, her basement flooded." His grandpa was like his uncle. You didn't hit on customers.

"You did a good job on her basement?"

"Yes sir." Walter did not know what his grandfather was up to but it was making him nervous.

"It was nice of her to come by." Another few moments passed before he spoke again. "Those kids like you."

"I like them," said Walter thinking that was a safe answer.

"Much as you like their momma?"

"I…" he didn't know what to say, so he said, "She's not their mother. They're foster kids."

"Well it looks like she treats them as her own. But you

didn't answer the question son."

"It's complicated."

"Walter, I think you know how to handle complicated." And he started flipping channels with the remote.

While Cicely called the enclosed porch at her house a sun porch, this was really a sun porch. The roof had been replaced with glass, and the walls were glass from ceiling to floor. It was like a greenhouse full of plants.

"This is beautiful," said Cicely, turning to take it all in.

"Mr. Moore made this for me as an anniversary present one year." She pointed out the peace lily Cicely had sent. "I found the perfect spot for it. Mr. Moore likes to grow things too," and she gestured to the backyard through the window.

There were rows of greens and tomatoes. All sorts of vegetables. "He'd rather hoe weeds than cut grass," his wife said. "He always made Walter cut the grass."

Cicely smiled at the idea of a knobby-kneed little boy pushing a lawnmower. She'd bet in the beginning it wasn't a power mower either.

"My mother used to have a garden." Cicely said remembering. "She passed away a little over a year ago."

"I'm sorry." Walter's grandmother didn't know what else to say.

"I live in her house now, I said I was going to start one, but didn't get around to it this year."

Mrs. Moore patted her hand. "When you're ready call me. I'll send Mr. Moore around. He won't let this heart attack slow him down. Let me give you some tomatoes."

Tamequa chose that instant to pull on Cicely's top. "Miss CeeCee, I don't feel so good. I wanna go home."

At first Cicely thought the little girl had picked up on her anxiety about coming into the house, but when she looked Tamequa's complexion didn't look good. When she put her hand on her forehead Tamequa threw up all over the floor.

"Poor baby," said Mrs. Moore taking the towel she was still holding in her hand to wipe Tamequa's mouth.

"I'm so sorry," said Cicely not knowing what to do. This wasn't her house, she felt helpless.

"Don't worry about it," said Mrs. Moore touching Tamequa. "She does feel warm."

Shanequa ran to the living room. "Walter, Tamequa got sick all over the floor."

Both men followed her back to the solarium to see Cicely holding a crying Tamequa.

"Walter get some paper towels and the bucket so we can clean this up."

He left to do exactly what his grandmother said without any hesitation.

"I can clean it up," volunteered Cicely, rubbing Tamequa on the back. She would never expect Walter to clean up vomit.

"No," said his grandmother. "You take that baby home and get her into bed."

Walter came back with a bucket filled with soapy hot water and paper towels. Telling his grandmother to leave the mess, he would get it after he saw Cicely to her car.

He waited for Cicely to put Tamequa in the car seat before he spoke, "Call me and let me know how she's doing."

"I will," said Cicely. "And Walter you have wonderful grandparents."

"I'll tell them you said so. My grandpa thinks you're pretty great yourself."

He stood on the curb and watched her drive away before going back into the house to clean up the mess and answer the questions he knew his grandparents had.

Cicely cleaned Tamequa and took her temperature and Shanequa's for good measure before putting her to bed. Tamequa's temperature was 101 degrees, which Cicely didn't think was dangerous for a child, but she called Madeline any way.

Madeline was still at work, but she took Cicely's call. "Just keep her hydrated. It's probably the flu."

"But she doesn't have a runny nose or congestion."

"Cicely, there are all kinds of flu. How's Shanequa?"

"She has a slight fever."

"Then look forward to both of them being sick. Just be happy this has happened before school started."

"Madeline, what am I going to do?"

"Cicely, stop being such a ninny. You have children now. Do what momma did for us. Put them in bed to keep warm, turn the TV on and get them to drink plenty of liquids."

"It's just she threw up all over Walter's grandmothers beautiful sun porch." Too late she realized she'd said Walter's name.

"You and Walter's grandmother are friends now? How'd that happen?"

"They are members of Anita's church, Madeline. Her husband was in the hospital, I sent him flowers. He wanted to meet me." She gave her the abbreviated version, no mention of Walter.

But Madeline was no dummy. "How did you know she was Walter's grandmother?"

"He was with her and introduced us."

"Humph," said Madeline. "Imagine, running into Walter at church."

They talked a while longer catching up. Bernice had gone to her union rep and chances were she would be returning to her teaching job when school started. Of course they would have an aide assigned to her classroom to be on the lookout for any problems. That didn't bother Bernice, anything to keep her in the classroom. Lydia's pregnancy was coming along nicely.

Her due date had now changed to the day after Cicely's birthday. Madeline wanted to know if she threw her daughter a baby shower would Cicely be able to come. Cicely couldn't promise but vowed to look up airfares for the dates Madeline had given her and to inquire if she could take the girls out of state if they were still with her. Now it didn't bother her so much, the idea of her niece becoming a mother, but it created a small ache to think about the girls not being with her any longer.

Finally Madeline asked, "Have you talked to Simone?"

"I keep leaving her voice mails, but she doesn't return my calls. We've never gone this long without speaking to each other."

"Give her time. She talks to Bernice and me. She doesn't sound as angry with you anymore."

"Well I'm glad you think that." Cicely retorted.

"Cicely, did you ever think maybe you shamed her?"

"I have sick kids right now Madeline. I don't want to talk about Simone."

"Okay, okay, I understand. Call me tomorrow and let me know how they are. Love you."

"Love you too," said Cicely and they hung up. She loved Simone too.

By Saturday morning both kids were sick, and in Cicely's bed. By Saturday afternoon she had called their doctor, who told her the same thing Madeline had. She'd see them on Monday if they weren't feeling any better.

Sunday afternoon, her foot was aching from taking each child back and forth to the bathroom. She had cleaned up poop and vomit more times than she wanted to count. Especially the times they couldn't make it to the bathroom in time. She was tired but did not regret one moment of it. She was sitting on the stairs taking a break from the next time one of them called her when she saw Walter coming up the front walk. Evidently he had been to church and still had on his suit minus, the jacket and tie. He was not what she needed right now.

She rushed to the door before he could ring the bell. The girls didn't have a good night and she wanted nothing to wake them.

"You look tired," said Walter taking in her appearance. She had on a pair of saggy sweat pants and a tank top, no bra as usual when she was home, and a scarf tied around her head.

"Yes I am. Not trying to be rude, but why are you here?" She hadn't moved to the side to let him in.

"My grandmother said taking care of a sick child is lots of work. I came to help."

"Well, there are two sick children and you didn't exactly come dressed to help."

He stepped closer and she moved back. He knew she would, so he kept coming until they were standing in the foyer. "It's just a shirt and pants Cicely. When's the last time you had something to eat?"

She had to think about it. Then she said, "I don't know."

He put his hands on her shoulders and turned her around so she was facing the stairs. "Go take a shower, I'll fix you something to eat or you can take a nap. Whatever sounds more appealing?"

"The girls…"

"I'll listen out for them."

"They're in my bedroom." What he offered sounded so good.

"I'll find them. You go." He started toward the kitchen and stopped. "Food or sleep?"

She put a foot on the stair and hesitated.

"You can trust me Cicely. I won't do anything to hurt you or the girls."

"If I can trust you Walter, then I want both," she said before going up the stairs.

Walter entered the kitchen and saw the first thing he needed to do was clean it. Rolling up his sleeves he searched for the dish liquid under the kitchen sink. On the counter were empty soup cans and a bottle of ginger ale. A box of crackers was open on the table. He heard her upstairs and what sounded like a bathtub being filled, not a shower running. Good, he thought he'd seen her favoring her foot, a soak would help.

When he finished the dishes he went upstairs to check on the girls. They were both still asleep so he took the opportunity to look around Cicely's bedroom. Walter didn't know what he'd expected. It wasn't girly. There were pictures on the dresser and what he guessed you would call knick knacks. It was more personalized than his bedroom, but he was a guy. The bedroom was a place he slept and kept clean in case he got lucky. Which, he hadn't in quite some time. But he wasn't looking for lucky anymore. He left the room before he started feeling like a voyeur and stood at the bathroom door and knocked softly.

"Cicely?" When he didn't get an answer he began to wonder if an adult could drown if they fell asleep in the bathtub.

He knocked again a little harder. The door must not have been completely latched because it opened a few inches and he could see her. She was reclined in the old styled tub, her arms propped on the sides to keep her from sliding under. She was sleeping, her head resting on some kind of pillow; he'd seen one like it at his mother's house. Her mouth was slightly open, not in a bad way. If the water had been a bit more shallow he would have been able to see the tips of her breasts. Bubbles were keeping her body hidden from view. But bubbles could not keep Walter's imagination from running wild. Unconsciously he touched the zipper of his pants and his hand rubbed the hardness he felt there. When he realized what he was doing he stepped back from the bathroom door out of her view should she open her eyes. He would have the memory of her in the tub for a long time.

The water in the tub had cooled off considerably and her fingers and toes wrinkled when Cicely opened her eyes. The door was cracked open, something she didn't remember doing, but she smelled something wonderful coming from the kitchen.

She donned underwear and an African print caftan she had bought on a whim. Knew she'd have to change it if the girls started erupting from their body openings again, but Walter had went through the trouble of cooking so she wanted to look nice. After a quick check on Shanequa and Tamequa she went downstairs.

"You look rested," said Walter when she entered the kitchen, where he was setting the table for two.

"I feel much better. Thank you Walter, I needed a break."

He pulled a chair out for her. "The girls had a glass of apple juice and crackers while you were resting. I think their fever has gone down. I got them to eat some ice chips too. And I threw the sheets in the washer that were on the bedroom floor."

"You are almost too good to be true."

"I'm still trainable Cicely. Not old enough to be set in my ways."

"Maybe I'm old enough to be in set mine," she said, looking him directly in the face.

He looked at her with heat in his eyes. While cooking he had turned the radio on and now a slow song was playing. "Dance with me Cicely." He said extending his hand to her.

Against her better judgment she stood and went into his arms.

He held her hand and put an arm around her waist to pull her near. At first they just swayed to the music. Then he took little steps moving her around the kitchen. His arm slipped lower and his hand rested lightly on the top of her buttocks applying pressure to make their bodies closer. He positioned himself so his thigh was resting between hers.

She could feel his arousal against her leg.

They were barely moving now and his breath was hot near her ear. Cicely felt a familiar ache she hadn't felt in a long time and the friction of his leg was making her want more.

The music stopped and they stood there.

Walter stepped away first. "I better go." He didn't wait for her to say anything; he just headed out the front door. But he didn't believe she was set in her ways, taking in two little girls had proven that.

Walter had cooked spaghetti. Doctored some jarred sauce with spices he'd found in the cabinet and added ground beef. He found enough in the fridge to make salad. But Cicely wasn't hungry any longer. Not for food anyway.

CHAPTER 15

Monday morning the girls had gone all night without pooping or vomiting, so Cicely didn't see the necessity of calling the doctor. She could tell they were feeling better, they were getting rambunctious, so back into their own room they went. No more lying in bed watching TV. She gave them each a book and started thoroughly cleaning her room, anything to keep her mind occupied. She had not slept well the night before and when she did, it was to dream about Walter. How his hands felt on her body, the fullness of him pressed against her leg. She could have shifted her body just a little and that hardness would have been just where she wanted to feel it. Thinking about it made her throb even now, a day later. But unless she was open to taking everything Walter was willing to give, Cicely could not open her legs. He deserved more, not a woman beginning to experience perimenopause. Maybe if she denied him what they both wanted he would move on.

She realized she had not moved for a few minutes thinking about Walter, the fresh sheet was still in her hands, when she heard the phone. She sat on the unmade bed to take the call. She recognized the voice of the social worker that had made the home visit.

"Ms. Macklin, I called to tell you the girls' mother is in a half-way house now. She wants to see her girls."

"Is that permissible?" ask Cicely, knowing she didn't want the young woman to come to her home. And didn't she have an ankle bracelet on?

"It's encouraged. The girls haven't seen her in over a month. But she won't be coming to your house. The half-way house she's staying in is family oriented, most of the women have young children. The more the families are involved the better chance these young women have of doing everything they can to regain their children."

"Will any other of Ms. Brown's family be attending?" ask Cicely.

"No, when you got the girls, I thought it was explained to you no family member was willing to take them. Ms. Brown has no family here, only the girls do. And they don't want to be involved with them because it would include their mother. Maybe sometime in the future when she's proven she's turned her life around they'll be interested."

Cicely didn't speak, so the woman continued to talk.

"The half-way house is having a family picnic this Labor Day. If you aren't willing to take the girls we can arrange for a representative to pick them up and bring them back at a pre-set time. That way if you have plans for the holiday this won't disrupt them."

"No, no," said Cicely. "I'll take them. That's not a problem." She reached for a pad and pen and began to write down the information. The half-way house was a thirty-minute drive from where she lived. Not exactly a remote area, but they didn't make it easy for the residents to leave. They had to arrive at a certain time and leave at a certain time. Cicely must show identification for herself and both girls.

Do not bring any gifts. If Cicely had pictures of the girls she could bring those, nothing more. Expect to have her belongings searched, so keep whatever she was bringing to a minimum. When the woman was sure Cicely understood everything they ended their call.

Cicely called the hair salon to make an appointment for the girls. She was going to do that anyway because school started next week and she wanted them to look nice. Maybe she could get some tips on doing their hair herself while there. She couldn't afford to take them to the salon every time they needed their hair braided and maintain her own locks at the same time. After she'd gotten the hang of doing her own hair taking them to the salon wouldn't be an issue. Neither would it be an issue when their mother reclaimed them, came unbidden to her mind. Well at least Walter had left the premises.

She didn't tell them right away they were going to visit their mother. Being children they had no concept of time. Already they were asking her when they could go to school. There were a lot of pictures of the girls on her phone, but she used the camera to take a more so she could get them printed and take to their mother. She scrolled through the pictures on her phone and stopped at the one of Walter trying to jump rope. She should get it to his grandfather, she thought, Mr. Moore would get a kick out of it.

She trimmed the girls' fingernails and buffed them to make them shine, telling them little girls didn't need nail polish to make their hands look pretty. She did give them a mini pedicure painting their toenails a bright red, but she made the mistake of letting them paint her toenails. Now, not only did she have a scar on her foot, but her toes looked like something had gnawed on them. She waited until they went to bed before doing them over herself.

Shanequa asked could they go to church. Cicely was in no hurry to see Walter again but decided to take them anyway. It gave her an excuse to buy them another dress, and it was probably the last opportunity they would have to wear something summery before the weather changed. She had a pair of palazzo pants made of a gauzy animal print fabric; they clung to her hips then flared out. The long sleeved top was sheer but a solid camisole of the same color underneath, made it church appropriate. She lucked out with the girls' and found cotton dresses with an empire waist, one white with a zebra print and the other white with a giraffe print. She joked with them; they could be animals at the zoo. Shanequa and Tamequa insisted on wearing sandals so they could show off their toes.

There was no need for her to worry about encountering Walter at church. He didn't attend. She looked and kept looking. It was hard not to be disappointed. Both his grandparents were there along with his mother, they greeted her and the girls like they were old family friends.

"Are they all better?" his grandmother asked, patting them on the cheek.

'Much better, thank you for asking."

"Did my grandson take good care of you? I told him you would need help." Mrs. Moore asked Cicely.

They all looked at her like she was going to make some profound statement. What was she going to say? Your grandson did a really good job of turning me on, then leaving. Instead she answered, "I got a bit of rest while he listened out for the girls. Thank you for sending him."

Cicely made their good-byes then went to search out her friend.

"You need to join," said Anita. "You attend here most of the time anyway. Did I see you get a group hug from Walter's family?"

"Don't make anything out of it. I sent flowers when Mr. Moore was hospitalized that's all."

"Where's Walter?" Anita asked her.

"How would I know where Walter is?" said Cicely getting in a snit.

"You don't have to get an attitude about it. It just seems everywhere you are Walter shows up."

"Twice, it happened twice."

"And each time he swept you away. Like that TV

commercial."

"You know Anita, sometimes I don't like you very much."

"Come on," said her friend, giving her arm a little squeeze. "I'm just playing with you. Anyone can see he has a crush on you."

"Shush," said Cicely her eyes going to the girls.

"Ooo, forgot about little pitchers," said Anita covering her mouth with her hand. Changing the subject, she asked, "Are you coming by tomorrow? Ben's cooking." Trying to tempt her friend with her husband's cooking skills.

"No, I'm taking the girls to see their mother tomorrow." She hadn't talked to her friend all week, afraid she would blurt out what happened with Walter. This was the first time Shanequa and Tamequa had heard the news too.

"Miss CeeCee you gonna take us to see our momma?" asked Tamequa.

"Yes I am."

"Do we hafta go to jail too?" asked Shanequa, her eyes getting big and round.

"No one is going to jail. Your momma is staying at a house and I'm going to take you there tomorrow."

"You sure we ain't goin' to jail?" she asked taking her sisters hand.

"I'm positive. Tomorrow I'm going to take you to visit

your momma then we come back home. Home.

After visiting their mother, it took Cicely a while to get the girls calmed down enough to go to bed. It had been a long day. She was shocked by the number of children visiting their mothers. The entire visit had taken place outside. The semi-rural setting where the halfway house was located allowed the children to run free and have a stress-free visit with their parent.

As soon as Cicely had them settled she called Bernice to tell her about the visit.

"I really didn't want to like this person," she said to Bernice. "I ended up feeling sorry for her. She had her first child at the same age Walter's mother had him. Then a second one with no help."

Cicely didn't notice Walter's name was creeping more and more into her conversations, but Bernice and Madeline did.

"I wanted to hate her but I couldn't"

Cicely and the girls had arrived at the appointed time. The two-story brick building did not have a welcoming look. It had an institutional feel about it. Like it had always been used to house something unwanted. At some point someone had added a wooden porch along the front to try and soften the appearance, it didn't quite work.

"Cicely, you never hate anyone" chided Bernice.

"She did something stupid that caused her to lose her babies. She's a drug user. This wasn't the first time they took her kids away."

"You said yourself she was young." But Bernice knew what her sister was saying. One day soon this young woman was going to take away the children that Cicely was beginning to love.

"They were so happy to see each other." Cicely hadn't known what to expect at the little family reunion.

The young woman was about Cicely's height, but thin, almost to the point of being gaunt. She had tattoos on both arms, from wrist to shoulder, making Cicely wonder if it was to hide her drug use. Her name was LaShondra and she did not display any hostility toward Cicely, was just sorry a stranger had to care for her children. But grateful Cicely was doing such a fine job. She commented on how nice their hair looked and Shanequa told her mother how Miss CeeCee took them to the hair salon.

Cicely complimented her on how well behaved the girls were.

Tamequa smiled for her mother to show her front teeth were growing in. When Tamequa told her about church and the dancers, LaShondra said no one had bothered to take her children to church before.

"Bernice," said Cicely, "She didn't sound like she didn't have any education, just under educated. That young woman could make something of herself if she left the drugs alone."

"It's hard Cicely, especially for young single mothers with no support system. Walter's mother was blessed. There's nothing to stop you from being part of that support system when she's released."

Cicely didn't acknowledge the mention of Walter's name, but Bernice had given her something to think about later, something that might allow her to stay in the girls' lives. Her sister listened to her go on about how well the visit went, but toward the end LaShondra had started to fidget.

"It probably had something to do with her withdrawal," said Cicely.

She would bring the kids back in two weeks so their mother could see how they were doing in school.

Bernice let the conversation wind down before she spoke again. "Who's going to catch you when you fall Cicely?"

"I don't know what you are talking about Bernice."

"Yes you do. One day someone is going to come and take those girls away from you. Already you love those little girls. I can hear it in your voice Cicely. What are you going to do then?"

"Why do you have to be so bottom line Bernice?"

"Oh Cicely," said Bernice her voice sounding tired. "I'm not trying to be mean. I just know you and how much it will hurt when they take the children. This is the first time you've done this. I don't want you hurt. And it is going to hurt."

"Are you telling me not to love these kids?" Cicely retorted, getting a lump in her throat.

"I'm sorry I upset you."

"No, you're right. I need to keep in mind the situation is only temporary," she sighed. "So, can I ask how you're doing?

"You mean talk about something other than you? I think we can handle that. "

Bernice had seen another specialist who said the only way to have a one hundred percent diagnosis of Alzheimer's was for the person to die and you examine the brain for plaque and lesions. Well Bernice wasn't dead yet, so they could only go by symptoms. And since she'd been wearing the patch, no symptoms were apparent at this time. She and Louis would have to decide if it was worth the risk of not taking the medication for a while to see what happened. There was no history of early onset dementia in the family so Bernice could be an anomaly.

"What are you going to do Burnie?" asked Cicely reverting to the childhood name.

"Well school starts the day after tomorrow, so I guess we wait."

CHAPTER 16

The first day of school Cicely and the girls were excited. The girls had their new backpacks and were dressed in their khaki colored pants and navy polo shirts. Cicely turned from locking the door and saw Walter pull up.

Walter wasn't sure what time to be there. He figured he'd either be too early or too late. They had not seen each other in over a week. The scene in the kitchen had kept replaying in his mind. It had been a rough week for Walter. He'd taken on more work to keep his mind off Cicely. But he didn't forget he had promised Shanequa he would be around for the first day of school. He just didn't know what time to be there.

As it turned out he was just in time.

"Walter, what are you doing here?" asked Cicely. She knew it sounded impolite but she couldn't help it.

"Someone made me promise to walk with them the first day of school." He said looking at Shanequa.

"Don't you have to go to work?"

He was dressed for it. She was dressed for running, he noticed, sports bra under a loose fitting tank top. Black spandex shorts and sneakers and a baseball cap. The cap made her look cute.

"I'm the boss, remember."

"We're walking," said Cicely, headed in the direction of school.

"I can leave my truck here and walk back." Walter said joining them.

Cicely held Tamequa's hand and Shanequa walked a few steps ahead of them. The looked like a family walking together.

They had walked about a block when Shanequa turned around and was walking backwards to look at Walter and Cicely. "Miss CeeCee took us to see our momma yesterday."

He looked at Cicely and she confirmed it. "She is in a halfway house. I took the kids to visit."

Walter wondered how that made her feel? If the mother was in a halfway house she must be getting out soon. Which meant the girls might be gone shortly.

Shanequa continued to walk backwards. "Walter are you Miss CeeCee's boyfriend?"

Cicely knew that question had happened because of what Anita had said about Walter having a crush on her.

He looked at Cicely, but she refused to look at him.

"I don't think Miss CeeCee wants a plumber for a boyfriend." He said it with no inflection in his voice.

"Oh," said Shanequa and turned around starting skipping. She waited patiently at corners for Walter to hold her hand before crossing the street.

They walked the remainder of the way in silence. More

children and parents were joining them as they got closer to the school.

At the gate Cicely stopped and said to Walter, "Will you wait for me? I have to take Tamequa directly to her classroom."

"Sure I'll wait." He didn't know if he wanted to hear what she had to say, but he'd wait.

When Cicely came out of the school Walter was leaning against the fence where she'd left him. More than one woman gave him an appreciative glance as they walked by. He spoke if spoken to but didn't give any one a look that said I'm interested. She knew that look. He stood up straight when she approached.

"What did you have to say to me Cicely?"

"Let's walk," she said heading back the way they'd come. "I never said anything about you being a plumber."

"I know. You just don't want me as a boyfriend."

"True, but your being a plumber has nothing to do with that."

"What does it have to do with Cicely?"

"Look, it's pleasant spending time together. Why can't you leave it at that?" She stopped walking to look at him. They stood in the middle of the sidewalk; parents returning from dropping their kids off had to walk around them. "You can't keep showing up at my house without warning?" Because it unsettled her. It made her remember she was a woman.

"Look, I came today because I promised Shanequa I

would, not just to see you. If you have a problem with me being around the kids while they're still in your care, I'll stop. You explain to them why I don't come see them. I told you in the beginning what I was about Cicely. I laid it all out for you. I made it clear I wanted to get to know you. Maybe I was a little intense so I backed off, but I've given you plenty of opportunity to get to know me." He stepped closer to let someone pass, looked directly in her eyes and lowered his voice. "What are you afraid of Cicely? We both know if this was only about me wanting to fuck you, it would have already happened." It gave him some satisfaction to see her flinch. He remained standing there about three seconds to let it sink in and headed back to his truck.

Cicely stood there with her hands clinched into fist. A heavy set woman walked by, who had obviously heard part of the conversation and said, "Honey if you don't want it, I'll take it off your hands."

She ran for an hour non-stop. The last few blocks she limped home. This was all Walter's fault. It was his fault she'd stabbed herself with a piece of glass. It was his fault she'd ended up running on concrete instead of the softer path in the park like she'd planned.

His fault she wanted to go to bed with him. There, she'd admitted it. But nothing would compel her to take a boy to bed.

'Cept Walter wasn't a boy.

The balance of the week went by without a hitch. No more surprise visits from Walter and Shanequa didn't ask about him.

The second week Cicely volunteered to take all the girls and Jackie could start chauffeuring the girls the third week. She got her routine established during the second week. Walk the girls to school, run for an hour. Go home shower, make beds, but she was training the girls to make their beds as soon as they got up. Tamequa wasn't good at smoothing all the wrinkles out yet, but she was getting there. She'd save other household chores for the weekend.

Two days she actually went into the office, where her boss pretended he didn't know her at first, even though they teleconferenced at least once a week if not more.

She came home one of those days to find the grass cut and the leaves that had fallen thus far, raked and put into bags at the curb. When she went to thank a neighbor, he said a man driving a pick-up truck had done it, not him.

She'd walk to school at dismissal time and go in to fetch the all the girls.

Cicely would have a snack waiting for them, a piece of fruit or peanut butter on a slice of toast. They would sit at the kitchen table to do homework while she started dinner. It was starting to get dark earlier so the girls only had about an hour to play outside before coming in to prepare for the next day.

The beginning of the third week Cicely decided to go to church. She couldn't avoid Walter forever, she liked going to that church and was considering joining. It didn't matter anyway, no one in his family showed up that Sunday. She did as she promised and took Shanequa and Tamequa to see their mother.

LaShondra was confident she would have employment soon and would have her girls back. She had a job interviews scheduled for that week. It took all the Christian, Cicely had in her, not to wish LaShondra bad luck.

This was the week Jackie was responsible for getting the kids to and from school. After seeing the traffic jam around the school she opted to do like Cicely and walk.

That week she had more time on her hands. Once she thought she'd seen Walter drive by and her heart beat a little faster, but the truck never stopped.

When Anita called to see if she wanted to go out Saturday night, she jumped at the chance.

"I won tickets on the radio to this local club. Ben doesn't want to go, told me to ask you. The twins can babysit at your house. Which is the real reason I think he told me to take you. So he can have some friends over to watch the fight on cable. And I'll pick the twins up on the way home. Which I guess makes me the designated driver. Wear something sexy too. I'll have fun watching men hit on you and you turning them down."

"What makes you think I'll turn them down?" asked Cicely mildly offended.

"I'm just sayin'," said Anita.

But her friend was right, she hadn't dated all the while

caring for her mother. And after momma died she hadn't been interested in meeting anyone. That could explain why she reacted so strongly to Walter. After all she wasn't old, just older than Walter. Men still glanced her way when she ran in the park, young and old. So she decided to do as her friend said and put extra care in dressing for their night out.

Walter had had tickets for a while. The plan was to bring Cicely, but that didn't work out, so he sat at the bar alone with a beer. The venue wasn't that large and seating was limited. Walter saw her the minute she walked in. He recognized Anita as Ben's wife as they were led to reserve seating, a small round table. So girls' night out, he thought. He didn't notice what her friend was wearing, but he could certainly tell you what Cicely was and was not wearing. Damn, she had that jiggle going on.

The heels she had on made her almost nose to nose with him. Her black skirt wasn't tight, it had a lot of material, but it was short, hit her about mid-thigh. She had it cinched at the waist with a wide black belt. It looked like a man's white dress shirt she had on, but it was fitted. The cuffs stopped at the middle of her forearms. The collar was turned up in the back and it was only unbuttoned far enough to peak the imagination. She had to have had something on under it, because he couldn't see through it, but she definitely didn't have on a bra.

He considered buying them a drink and saw someone had beat him to it. Walter watched as the waitress put drinks on the table and indicated someone at the bar had purchased them. He craned his neck to see a guy at the opposite end of the bar raise his glass and smile at the women. He wasn't bad looking, had a sprinkling of gray hair in his short haircut, a few wrinkles and the beginnings of a gut.

"Hell no," thought Walter. The man looked to be older than his mother.

The guy was slow, Walter was faster. By the time the man got to the table Walter had snared a chair and was seated between the two women.

"Hi," he said smiling at both women.

Anita spoke and smiled back, Cicely frowned at him. Walter even said hi to the man standing there looking at the threesome, not knowing what to do.

"Grab a chair, have a seat," said Walter. At least he was going to have some say in his competition.

They sat boy, girl, boy, girl. The table was so small it was almost impossible for their knees not to touch under the table.

Anita asked Walter how his grandparents were, and while he answered the stranger took it to mean Cicely was all his. But under the table Walter was making sure his leg kept touching Cicely's.

Cicely was trying her best to ignore what Walter was doing under the table, because for all the world to see, he was ignoring her. He carried on a conversation with Anita, even with the guy whose name was Richard.

The only way she knew Walter was paying any attention

was she'd see the little muscle in his jaw tighten every time Richard tried to look down her shirt. She was getting a little sick of it herself.

The longer Walter sat there the angrier he got. This guy was really trying to make a move on Cicely and she wasn't doing a damn thing to stop him. The show was starting soon, but he couldn't stay and watch what was going on. He abruptly stood ready to walk out, but not before leaning over to whisper in her ear. "He's too old for you."

Cicely put a hand on his arm and said his name. "Walter."

He shrugged her hand away and started toward the door. He didn't know Cicely had followed him until she was outside and heard her call his name. If she wanted to have it out here and now he was more than ready. He stopped walking and waited for her to catch up. He was right about the shoes, they brought them almost eye-to-eye.

"So that's how you roll Walter? Create a little drama, then leave?" she accused him.

He had a hard time looking at her. It was like she was slipping through his fingers. Why couldn't she see he had feelings for her?

"You invited him to sit. Then got angry because I was polite to him?"

"He just wants to get in your pants," he yelled.

"Like you don't!" she yelled back realizing she had

pushed him too far.

Walter opened his mouth to speak. His phone signaled a text message and he angrily snatched it off his belt to look.

"Plumber, always available." Cicely mumbled sarcastically waiting for him to finish.

He looked at her after reading the text. "They just took my grandpa back to the hospital. I have to go."

She caught him by the arm before he walked away. "I hope it's not serious."

He just stared at her before taking off in the direction of his car.

Cicely showed the bouncer her hand stamp and went back to join Anita. Richard had gone, but some other guy was trying to make time with Anita. When he turned to see who was joining them Anita mouthed the word "Help".

"Your husband said he'd be here in about two minutes," said Cicely as she sat.

Dude couldn't get up fast enough. "I'll talk to you later," he said.

"What happen to Richard?" asked Cicely.

"When he saw you take off after Walter I guess he figured he was wasting his time. But I think he heard what Walter said."

"You heard him?" Cicely asked, her eyebrows going up.

"He may have thought he was whispering, but he

wasn't." They both laughed.

"Is he coming back?" Anita asked about Walter.

Cicely shook her head no, "They had to take his grandfather to the hospital again."

They talked about that for a moment, then the lights on stage came on and they enjoyed the live show of jazz played on an electric violin.

Sunday morning, Cicely looked at the clock and rolled back over. She was not going to church she would read the girls a bible story instead. After the club Anita had come in and they'd had a few nightcaps. Her daughters had learner permits and one of them could drive home. And she was not going to walk into the mess left by her husband and his friends sober. They would clean it up tomorrow, together.

She let Shanequa and Tamequa have cold cereal for breakfast promising them they could help cook dinner later. It was about two in the afternoon when Anita called her.

"Have you talked to Walter?"

"No, Anita. I don't think he wants to talk to me right now," replied Cicely.

"Cicely, his grandfather died this morning."

"Oh no." Cicely had been in the kitchen trying to figure out what to cook for dinner. Now she pulled a chair close and sat down. "Oh no," she said again.

"I guess he had a major stoke last night. They took him off life support and he passed shortly after."

Cicely couldn't help it; tears begin to stream down her face. "He was such a nice man. He reminded me of my father. He was the only father Walter knew."

"I thought you would want to know. Are you going to call Walter?"

"Yes. I'll call him later today."

She and Anita promised to talk and Cicely sat there silently crying.

Tamequa came into the kitchen as saw her wet face. "Miss CeeCee why you crying?"

She hugged the girl tightly. "Walter's grandfather died and I'm sad." Cicely wasn't even sure the little girl understood what died meant.

"He gone away and he won't be back? Right?" she asked.

"That's right baby."

"I'm sad too," said Tamequa hugging Cicely back. "Is Walter crying?"

Cicely didn't hesitate. "Yes Walter is crying."

After the girls were in bed Cicely called Walter at the only number she had and got voice mail. "Walter's crew, no one can come to the phone right now. Please leave a message and someone will get back to you shortly."

"Walter this is Cicely. I am so sorry to hear about your grandfather. Please call me at this number." She left the phone number in case it didn't show up on caller id.

The next morning she got the girls ready for school as usual. It was her week to escort the girls to school. Walter had not returned her call the night before, so she promised herself she would try again after her run. She didn't want to call too early. She knew what it was like when a family member died. There were so many arrangements to be made.

The weather was starting to change so she had the girls wear light jackets. Unless the snow was a foot deep they would walk to school, she was not thinking they might be with their mother when the snow fell. Her running clothes had also changed in deference of the weather. Now her spandex pants were ankle length and she wore a lightweight sweatshirt over her sports bra.

When she returned from her run the message light on the phone was blinking. She had missed Walter's call. "Cicely forgot you had to take the girls to school. Here's my personal cell number. Call me. Please."

She called, he didn't pick up, so she identified herself, said it was her cell and he could call at any time.

They didn't speak until late Tuesday night. "Were you asleep?" he asked.

Cicely was in bed dozing, but the TV was still on so she said no. She plumped her pillows and sat up so she wouldn't fall asleep while he talked.

"Thank you for calling. Sorry I didn't get right back to you."

"You were busy Walter. I understand."

"Yeah," he said. "I guess you do."

"It happened to fast Cicely. I wasn't ready for him to go yet."

She could hear in his voice he was trying not to cry. Remembering all the things well-meaning people said to her and her sisters when their mother died, she knew Walter wouldn't want to hear those platitudes either.

"Do you want to talk about him?"

"The only other person to ask me that was my grandmother. And she is hurting just as much as me, probably more. Think she's handling it better than me."

"Walter, if you want to talk about your grandfather, talk about him. I met him and I liked him."

"Did you? Did you really?"

"He seemed like a nice man. Was he a nice man, Walter?"

"He was a great man, but he could be a mean son of a bitch when he needed to be. My bike got stolen. Well I let a kid take it away from me. I was about nine the other kid was about twelve."

Cicely thought she could hear a slur in his speech, but

didn't say anything. If Walter needed a drink right now, who could blame him?

"He took me to get my bike back. He cussed the boy's momma out for letting her son come home with a stolen bike, and he whipped my ass when we got home for letting the kid take it without a fight."

She let him talk for about an hour, telling stories about his grandfather. She'd had to plug her cell in to keep it from dying.

"Cicely, are you falling asleep on me?"

"I think I am Walter. It's after midnight."

"Why didn't you just tell me to shut up?"

"Truthfully Walter, I like the sound of your voice."

"Cee," he said drawing her name out into one long syllable. "That's the first nice thing you've said about me."

"Good night Walter. Get some sleep."

"I can't sleep Cicely."

"Try anyway," she said and hung up before she thought of more nice things to say to him.

CHAPTER 17

The funeral was Friday. Wake at twelve, followed immediately by the homegoing service at one. Cicely figured she could skip the interment and be home in time to pick the girls up from school. Walter hadn't called again; she worried about him.

She did her run and came home to dress. She really didn't want to wear what she had worn to her mother's funeral, all black. Cicely finally decided on a black a-lined dress with a taupe bodice. It had a demure neckline and short sleeves. During the night it had started raining so she would wear her tan trench coat. She stood looking at herself in the mirror, thinking this wasn't the proper underwear to wear to a funeral, black lace panties with a matching bra, but it made her feel good to have them on. She couldn't abide panty hose, so she had on black thigh high stockings. Slipping her feet into a pair of plain black pumps she was ready to leave. She grabbed an umbrella on the way out and thought of Madeline and her rain scarf.

Walter's grandfather had been a popular man; the parking lot at the church was full when she arrived. Cicely parked on the street so she could leave easily after the service. Anita was on usher duty and handed her an obituary and tissue when she entered the church. "You'll need this," her friend said, pressing the tissue in her hand.

She read the obit while she stood in the queue to view the body. The first three rows were filled with family. The Moore family had been very prolific. It seemed Walter's mother was the only one to have a single child and never marry. His grandfather had been one of four brothers, two of whom were still living. He was survived by his wife, three daughters; nine grandchildren and four great-grandchildren. There were two brothers-in-law and their wives, one sister-in-law (widowed) from his wife's side of the family. And many nieces and nephews to mourn his passing. When Cicely reached the casket, she bowed her head and said a little prayer for the family. "Help Walter get through this," was all she said.

She turned to greet Walter's grandmother and mother, the only family members she knew sitting on the first pew. Walter was sitting stoically by his grandmother, on her left, with his mother on her right. It looked like no one had been able to talk him into shaving that morning. His eyes were bloodshot, but she didn't know if it was from drinking or crying. She suspected it was from crying.

His grandmother took her hand and squeezed it. "Thank you for coming. He really took a liking to you. They are having a repast here at the church, but will you come by the house later?"

Cicely looked at Walter, he was watching her, but couldn't seem to make himself speak. He was sitting stock still with his hands on his knees.

"I'll have the girls later, I don't know if I can come."

"Bring the girls," said Mrs. Moore. "I'd like to see them again when they aren't sick and they'll be plenty of children at the house."

"I'll try," said Cicely. She didn't know why she did it, but she reached over and squeezed Walter's hand, like his grandmother had done hers'.

She sat with Anita during the service, and her friend was right. She needed more than the original tissue that had been pressed into her hand.

"Can I bring the kids over after school?" she asked Anita while the mourners were filing out. "I'll feed them before I bring them. Walter's grandmother asked me to stop by the house."

Anita hugged her. "You don't have to feed them, just bring them by."

It was six o'clock when she rang the bell at Walter's grandmother's house. She had plenty of opportunity to change clothes but didn't want to feel out of place. It was still raining which made it seem later than it was. Cicely figured she would stay for an hour and leave. That would be long enough to be respectful. She was glad Lisa answered the door and not some family member she hadn't met yet.

Lisa took her by the hand and led her in. "Mother was asking about you. She thought maybe you wouldn't come."

The house was full. There were children of all ages

either playing or watching TV. The dining room table was laden with food. "Do you want something to eat?" asked Lisa as she pulled her through the dining room.

Cicely shook her head no, not knowing where the young woman was taking her. She caught a glimpse of Walter in the kitchen with a group of men drinking a beer before Lisa propelled her into the room she had guessed was the master bedroom the only other time she had been there.

Walter's grandmother was sitting up in the bed with pillows behind her back. She was surrounded by a group of women, sitting in chairs or on the bed. She still had on the dress she had worn to the funeral, making Cicely glad she hadn't changed. On her stocking feet she had on a pair of worn slippers. "You didn't bring the girls," she said slightly chastising Cicely.

"No, they're with a friend."

"Come sit next to me," and she patted a space next to her on the bed. "This is Cicely, Walter's friend," she said, introducing Cicely to Walter's aunts and great aunt. "If Mr. Moore had lived he would have chased after this one."

Everyone laughed. Cicely was hoping no one was reading too much into the 'this is Walter's friend introduction.' But as she looked at the faces, no one raised an eyebrow or gave a strange look, that she was Walter's friend.

People were coming into the bedroom and paying their respect and leaving. At no time did anyone leave Mother Moore alone a sign of the love they had for her. Eventually Cicely wandered into kitchen and found Lisa washing dishes.

Cicely said to her, "I'll wash, you dry since you know where everything goes," and took over doing the dishes.

Walter walked in at one point saw her and walked out again.

Cicely looked at the kitchen clock on the wall, it was eight thirty, she and Lisa had washed the dishes and put away all the food when Walter's mother came and took her onto the sun porch. It was the only place not filled with people.

"Would you drive Walter home? He's been drinking, but he is not drunk. I wouldn't send you out of here with a drunk, even if it is my own son. He's just dead on his feet. The only time he's been home is to change clothes. I've tried to get him to go home, my mother has tried, but he won't listen to us. Maybe he'll leave with you."

"I'll try," said Cicely.

"Wait here," his mother said and pushed his keys into her hands taking on faith Walter was going to agree.

When she returned, she had Cicely's coat and purse and Walter.

"Walter, Cicely is going to drive you home."

"No Ma, I'm staying here tonight." He looked at Cicely like he dared her to say anything.

"The women are staying with Mother tonight. You can

come back tomorrow."

"Then I'll drive myself home."

"Walter, you're tired. I don't want to have to worry about you. Please let Cicely drive you home."

He looked at the two women and figured this was not going to be an argument he would win. Why Cicely had joined forces with his mother he didn't know. "I'll go say goodnight to Grandma."

While he went to speak with his grandmother, Janice made a plate for him and gave it to Cicely. "See if he will eat something. I haven't seen him eat."

They left the house through the back door, Walter silently followed her to the car, got in fastened his seat belt and let the seat back. She was certain he had fallen asleep.

Cicely didn't know why he was giving her the silent treatment, but she was going to do as his mother asked. When they reached his house, Walter got out and made a great show of looking for his keys. Cicely held them up by the ring and jingled them.

"She thought of everything, didn't she," he said speaking of his mother.

Cicely followed him in, and watched him turn on a single lamp that emitted a dim light and toss his suit coat to the side. His tie had been long gone. He didn't even remember when he'd taken it off. She continued straight through to the kitchen, passing the stairs on her right leading upstairs. No dining room, just what you would probably describe as an eating area and then the small galley styled kitchen. She laid her coat across a chair and placed her purse on the table. She searched the wall for a light switch and could only find the one above the sink. She sat the covered plate on the counter.

"Are you going to eat Walter?"

He didn't answer her. Cicely looked through the cabinets for tea bags but could only find coffee. That was not what he needed if he was expected to sleep.

When she returned to the living room, Walter was seated on the edge of the sofa. His elbows rested on his knees and he held his head in his hands. She stood over him.

"Walter?"

He regarded her for a moment then put his arms around her waist and leaned his cheek against her abdomen.

The only movement Cicely made was to place her hand on the side of his face. She could feel the day old growth of beard.

In a single movement Walter had her straddling his lap. Her knees cradled his hips when he leaned back into the sofa. Her dress had moved up her thighs exposing bare skin where the stockings ended and the hem of her dress started. He pulled her closer so their cores were meeting and slid a hand up her back to her neck and lowered her head so he could kiss her.

Cicely felt her heart skip a beat. She parted her lips to take in a breath and Walter's tongue followed. She could taste the beer he had been drinking earlier and did not find it unpleasant. When he withdrew his tongue, her's went into his mouth not willing to lose the feelings his kiss was creating in her. She wrapped her arms around his neck to bring their bodies closer.

When Cicely put her arms around his neck, Walter's hands slipped under the hem of her dress to rub the bare skin on the sides of her thighs, she felt so warm to him. He'd been cold since his grandfather died. His hands continued up the outside of her thighs to her hips and he pulled her even closer so she could feel the hardness of him. And she rocked against him, which was almost his undoing.

Cicely could not seem to get close enough to him. She broke the kiss and buried her head between his shoulder and neck to catch her breath; she did not breathe this hard when she ran. Her hands worked to unbutton his shirt. Too impatient to wait until the buttons were all undone she placed her hand inside his shirt to feel his skin. Her fingers brushed again his nipple and Walter made a small noise deep in his throat.

Walter's hands went to the zipper on the back of her dress. He pulled the zipper down as far as it would go. Then he pulled her away and made her look at him.

"Cee, I don't want to stop, but if you don't want to do this, I will. I swear to you I will. But you have to tell me now." He was pleading.

In answer, she let the sleeves of the dress slide down her arms and she shrugged out of them letting the dress fall to her waist.

Walter stared at her breasts covered by the flimsy lace material. The vision he had imagined when she was in the bath was real. His fingers fumbled when he reached behind to unfasten her bra. He didn't touch her, just looked. Cicely cupped a breast in one hand and offered it to him. Walter licked the nipple and watched it bead up like a blackberry. With one arm to support her back he latched on and sucked one while he kneaded the other.

His mouth continued the assault on her breasts. Cicely arched her back and Walter held her tight so she didn't fall. That move made her feel his erection straining against her and she groaned.

She made a move as if to stand and remove the remainder of her clothes and Walter wouldn't let her go. He kept one arm around her while he released the buckle on his belt. With one hand he unfastened his pants and freed himself. His hand went between their bodies, he could feel how wet she was and a moan escaped him. He moved the barrier, the scrap of material her panties made between them and slid into her. Cicely rocked once, twice, he could feel the pulse of her orgasm and couldn't control his own.

Cicely didn't remember how they made it to the bedroom. She had a vague memory of them still being joined and Walter going up the stairs with her legs locked tightly around him. Somewhere along the way she lost her shoes.

When they reached the bedroom, Walter turned on the

lights and stood her at the foot of the bed while he removed their clothing.

First he pushed her dress and panties down and knelt for her to step out of them. He slid her stockings down and kissed and nibbled at her inner thighs. Cicely grabbed handfuls of his hair. He stood and removed his shirt, then pants and boxers in a single movement, toed his socks off and stood to let her look.

She ran her hands over his chest and watched his nipples harden like hers, who could have named such a beautiful man Walter. Just above his right hip was an old scar, about the size of her palm. "A burn," he told her, his voice low and husky "from when I was a kid." It didn't take away from the beauty of him. She took a finger and traced the thin dark line of hair she had seen that day and splayed her hand where it became thick. He had not fully recovered but she held his heaviness in her hand.

Walter found the spot just beneath her ear that was so sensitive. Never had a lover found that spot without her directing them to it. He put his mark on her there. Placing his hands on either side of her neck, he slowly moved them down, over her smooth brown shoulders creating sensory memories for both of them

Cicely could feel the calluses on his hands as they moved down her arms to her fingertips. The room was not cold but his slow caresses were causing her to break out in goosebumps.

Reaching her fingertips he entwined one hand with hers. The other he put between her legs and felt the heat and dampness emanating from her.

Cicely couldn't stop the soft mewing sounds escaping her throat as she leaned in to get closer to Walter's body. It had been so long since a man had made love to her, all the sensations he was creating in her were intensified. What happened downstairs was over too quickly.

Walter pulled away slightly to look at her face while he massaged the tight curls at the juncture of her thighs. Seeing her tongue dart out to lick her upper lip, cause his penis to spontaneously bob against her belly. Capturing her mouth with his, he continued the onslaught of her body with his hands. Now he started at her shoulder blades, down to the small of her back, the flare of her hips. To him her body was hard and soft at the same time. His hands encountered the firmness of her muscles from running. But her butt was soft, the flesh yielding to his touch.

Unhurried he dipped his tongue in and out of Cicely's mouth mimicking the move he would make when he entered her.

When Cicely moved her hand between their bodies to fondle him, standing was no longer an option for Walter.

They tumbled onto the bed with Cicely on top.

She was pleased Walter wasn't a hirsute man. A smattering of hair on his chest and slightly more on his belly. Cicely used her hands and mouth to explore his body, stopping at the burn scar. She kissed it before finding herself trapped beneath Walter.

No permission was asked this time before he slid into her,

causing a tremor that would become a full fledge orgasm if he continued to move.

It felt so good to be inside her. It had been a while since he had wanted to make love to a woman the way he was doing with Cicely. Rising up on his arms, he looked at her before moving. Walter wanted to see the look on her face when he brought her to fulfilment.

Cicely wrapped her legs around his hips and pulled him closer. She couldn't wait any longer. She matched him move for move.

He could feel the little tremors starting in her body and he prolonged it. He brought her to pleasure twice before he allowed himself release this time.

Cicely had showered and dressed, now she sat on the bed and watched him sleep. He would be angry when he woke and found her gone, but that couldn't be helped. The girls were with Anita, that wasn't a problem, but waking up with him would be. Her friend had probably figured out where she was and what had happened and was silently cheering. Now she had doubts about having made love with Walter.

It was still dark out when she pulled in to her driveway; the sun wouldn't be up for another hour or so. She checked her phone before getting out of the car and found Anita had texted her at nine-thirty the night before saying the girls were asleep, she could pick them up in the morning. That would give her a chance to get a few hours' sleep

Cicely let her clothes drop to the bedroom floor and put on pajama pants and a tank top. She would never be able to think about that dress in the same way. First she lay on her side with her hands tucked under the pillow, then turned onto her back to stare at the ceiling. Now it washed over her full force what had she done. What had she been thinking? She had let Walter make love to her on the day they had buried his grandfather.

Cicely didn't think when he reached for her. Only felt. He was hurting so bad. She only wanted to… No that was a lie. It wasn't just about comforting him. She wanted to feel his hands on her, feel him inside her. She wanted the sex.

Walter awoke to her scent and his body reacted immediately. He opened his eyes and rolled over to find her gone. A spark of anger flared until he looked at the bedside clock and saw it was ten o'clock the next morning. She couldn't stay she had to get her girls. He just wished she had awakened him before she'd left so they could make love once again. Then it hit him. He hadn't told her he loved her, was in love with her and wanted to be with her.

Her friend lived in a modern brick three bedroom tri-level split home. Before Cicely could ring the bell Anita opened the door took one look at her and said, "You did the do."

"Yes," sighed Cicely. "And it's not going to happen again."

"What do you mean?" asked Anita closing the door behind her.

"It was a mistake."

"It was that bad?" pestered her friend.

Cicely got a dreamy look on her face, she couldn't help it, and her stomach did a little flip. "No, it was that good. Just shouldn't have happened."

"I don't understand," said Anita not letting her friend go any further into the house until she explained.

"You know when someone close to you dies the first thing you do is reach for someone. An affirmation of life. I let his mother manipulate me into driving him home and I was the one he reached for."

Anita looked at her friend sternly. "Bull. You didn't go out and sleep with someone when your mother died."

"Only because I had no one."

"So this was a delayed gratification for you?"

"No. I didn't mean it that way. He needed a release and I was handy."

"So you're saying Walter's a dog and would have slept with any woman his momma got to drive him home?"

"No, I didn't mean it that way either," protested Cicely. Walter was no dog.

"I am so angry with you right now," said Anita shaking her head.

"Because I slept with Walter?"

"No. Because you're trying to reduce what happened between you to just sex. He has feelings for you."

Cicely started to confirm the feelings he had for her was a hard-on. But Walter had definitely made it clear he wanted more than sex. "I'm not going to have a relationship with him."

"Why not?"

"Look at me," said Cicely indicating her body with a sweep of her arm. "I am too old to be doing the walk of shame. I'm a forty-year old woman who never married. I'm caring for another woman's children. I have nothing to offer him." Echoing Simone's words.

"Don't you think he should be the one to decide what you have to offer?"

"He's still young. He doesn't even know what he wants."

"He's not that young Cicely," she said trying to make her friend see reason.

"Young enough it would cause talk when he finally came to his senses and dropped me."

Anita looked at her in surprise. "I'm your best friend. I would never talk about you." Then, "Oh, you mean those nosy biddies at church? The ones that watch Walter's every move. Cicely he didn't even attend church regularly until he knew you would be there."

Cicely didn't speak.

"Those old ladies are jealous because they ain't getting any."

"I let his mother pimp me out. I have two little girls I need to set an example for."

"Cicely, I swear, if you weren't my friend, I'd slap the black off you. You worry about him being too young. You worry about what those church ladies are saying. You feel you got to be this paragon of virtue to raise kids. Don't make excuses why you went to bed with him. Simple fact you want him. God created us as sexual beings. Go with the flow." Anita stalked from the room to tell the girls Miss CeeCee was there to pick them up.

Cicely looked at her friend's retreating back. Anita hadn't talked to her that bluntly since they were teenagers. Regardless, she wasn't prepared to accept what Walter was offering. It would be hard enough to face him in daylight knowing him as intimately as she did now.

Walter made it to his grandmother's house in time to eat. The women had prepared a brunch and for the first time in a week he felt like eating. He had showered and shaved a fact his mother took pleasure in pointing out.

"You slept," said his grandma walking past his seat and giving him a kiss on the top of his head. They were alone in the kitchen.

"Yes ma'am," he said his mouth full of food. He wanted to give Cicely a chance to get home before he called. He wasn't going to tell her he loved her over the phone, but he wanted to speak to her. He wanted to hear her voice.

"I am going to miss your grandfather so much," she said taking the seat opposite his.

Walter stopped eating and looked at her. He had been hurting so bad himself he had forgotten how much his mother and grandmother must hurt. "I'm sorry I haven't taken time for you."

"Walter, I didn't say that to make you feel guilty. We all have to deal with it in our own way, but I thought I was losing you this week too grandson. Your body was here but you weren't."

The past week had passed in a fog for him. His grandpa had been his rock. He had built a shell around himself to contain the hurt and the only time it had cracked was the night he had talked to Cicely. When their phone called ended he cried. At his grandpa's house, upstairs in his old bedroom, Walter laid across the bed and cried like a baby. Downstairs his mother and grandmother could hear his grief and shed tears for him and the man they had all lost. At the funeral his eyes had were red because he had been unable to shed any more tears. His heart ached. Walter pushed his plate away.

"Don't," said his grandmother covering his hand with

hers. "You were in a good mood when you came in, now I've ruined it."

"No, grandma you haven't. It's going to take time like you said."

CHAPTER 18

She did everything she could to avoid Walter. After collecting the girls she kept them out all day. Going to the movies, out to eat, anything, so no one would be home if he stopped by. Sunday instead of church she took them by the address she'd gotten from Madeline where Simone was supposed to be staying but no one answered the door. All his calls she let got to voice mail.

Walter stayed away as long as he could. He assumed she was upset because he hadn't been to see her after their night together. The guests that had come from out-of-town to the funeral were still around and he felt obligated to spend time with them when it was Cicely he really wanted to be with. He had driven past her house so many times the past three days someone might get the impression he was stalking her. The only reason he didn't stop was because her car was always gone.

He was waiting for her Tuesday morning when she returned from her run. He never thought she was avoiding him on purpose.

It was Jackie's turn to escort the girls to school so Cicely got her run in early before going to the office. She saw his pick-up before she saw him sitting on the top step of the porch. The back of his truck was filled with supplies; she hoped that meant he wouldn't stay long. The neighbors probably wondered why the plumber was at her house so much.

As she got closer she saw he had shaved and didn't look

as haggard as the last time she saw him, asleep naked in his bed.

"Walter," she said, "Why are you here?" She stayed on the walkway not trusting herself to get any closer.

Walter had stood and was smiling as he walked toward her. "You shouldn't have to ask that Cee."

Without meaning to, Cicely took a step back.

Walter stopped his approach, frowned and waited.

"Walter," Cicely began. "What happened the other night was a mistake."

"We made love the other night Cicely." He didn't move any closer.

"We had sex. It was a mistake."

"Are you saying I forced you do something you didn't want to do?" he asked becoming angry.

She could see the muscle working in his jaw. "You didn't force me."

"Well, at least you admit that much."

"It never should have happened. It wasn't appropriate under the circumstances."

"Circumstances? It was obvious I wanted you and I thought I was pretty good at judging if a woman wanted me or not. Was I wrong?"

"You weren't wrong. The timing was wrong."

"I'd say the timing was damn near perfect." He grinned,

the anger falling away.

"I'm trying to be serious here."

"And I'm trying to stop you from saying something stupid. I love you Cicely. And I'm pretty sure you feel something for me."

Cicely opened her mouth to speak.

"No denials, no nothing. You can't make me go away so easily. I'm not some kid that tells a girl I love her, just to get her into bed. Did I enjoy the sex? Hell yes, I loved the sex, but that's not all I want from you. I think you are beautiful. I love your hair and when you paint your toes red. I love that your breasts jiggle when you don't wear a bra. I love you took two little girls into your home and heart even though it's going to hurt you like hell when they go. I also love that when we made love you didn't hold anything back. So don't say one word about how what happened was a mistake or inappropriate. I know my grandpa died and if his death is what brought us together then I accept that. I'll be here Cicely when you realize you need me just as much as I need you and not just because you want me in your bed."

And while he had her speechless, Walter took advantage, because until he figured out how to make Cicely accept what was happening between them, this was going to have to hold him for a while. Closing the distance between them he kissed her and didn't care who was watching. Turning turned their bodies so her back was facing the house and no one from the street could see what he was doing with his hands, he grabbed her by the buttocks and pulled her close and up so Cicely knew exactly how much he wanted her at that moment. When she opened her mouth to protest he dove right in with his tongue.

After the initial shock, but not before she felt his erection, not before his tongue played havoc with her senses Cicely got her hands on his chest and pushed him away.

Her first instinct was to knee him in the groin, but Walter anticipated that and blocked her knee. So she slapped him as hard as she could manage.

Walter staggered back, okay, she hit very hard for a girl. He backed up down the walkway his hand to his face and watched her stomp up the stairs.

"Cicely," he called out. "I love you don't hit like a girl."

She didn't get a chance to process what had happened, the house phone was ringing incessantly. She didn't even try to disguise the anger in her voice when she answered it.

"Hello," she snapped

"Ms. Macklin?" questioned the person on the other end.

"Yes"

"This is Mrs. White, Shanequa and Tamequa Brown's caseworker. There is no good way to say this. The girl's mother, LaShondra Brown died of a drug overdose Friday night."

Cicely just sat on the floor. Friday night while she and Walter had been making love the girl's mother OD'd.

"She didn't return from a job interview on Thursday," continued the woman.

"But she had an ankle bracelet on," protested Cicely.

"They are not foolproof Ms. Macklin for a person that wants it off. The police don't believe the overdose was intentional."

What difference did that make? Cicely thought. Dead was dead. "You said she died Friday. Today is Tuesday."

"The police found the body sometime Saturday. It takes time for things to get through the red tape. I was informed yesterday. I'm telling you today."

Cicely didn't respond.

"Would you like me to send someone over to help you tell the girls their mother died?"

"No, I'll tell them." But she didn't know how she would do it. "What about funeral arrangements?"

"No family has come forward to claim the body. We are checking into that though. They were told. I will keep you informed."

"What happens if no one steps forward?"

"They hold the remains for a set amount of time before disposing of them. Either burial or cremation. You could claim them since you have guardianship of her children, but that would make you financially responsible for the disposition of the remains."

Cicely knew she couldn't afford that expense. Why did everything have to come down to money?

"Can the children claim the body?"

"I'm afraid not, they're minors."

How do you explain to children their mother had died, but there would be no funeral or memorial to mark her passing?

"How long will they wait for someone to claim the body?"

"They may wait as long as ten days. But this isn't a matter of no one knew who she was. This is a matter of the family doesn't want to be responsible."

"What happens to Shanequa and Tamequa now?" Cicely didn't want to ask the question, but she had too.

"For now they stay with you. But that can change. When you got the girls you were told no one wanted them. That was probably because they would have to deal with the mother. These people are related to the children, not their mother. The mother isn't in the picture anymore."

"Can't I just keep them?"

"The children are not property. Possession is not nine tenths of the law. The court will look at family first."

Why would the court give children to people who didn't even have the decency to bury their mother?

"Do you have any more questions Ms. Macklin?"

"No, I'll call you if I do."

"Are you sure you don't want us to send a grief counselor to help with the girls?"

"No, I can handle it," said Cicely, hanging up. What could a stranger possibly do? But she had no idea either.

She couldn't be still. If she hadn't already gone for a run, she would have done that. Work was out of the question now; she wouldn't be able to concentrate. Madeline and Bernice were the first to come to mind to call for advice, but they were at work and this was not a conversation that could take place in five minutes. They could explain how they'd told their children their grandfather had died. But these children were different. They had spent months at a time in the care of someone other than their mother. And what to tell them about how she had died? They would want to know, at least Shanequa would.

She wouldn't tell them it was a drug overdose. Maybe when they got older. That stopped her. There was no guarantee she would have them when they were older and able to understand.

After pacing through the house for about a half hour and praying to God for help, Cicely took a shower. Thinking of death she thought about Walter and his grandpa. He was wrong; she wasn't in love with him. She had just isolated herself too much from male companionship while caring for her momma. That would have to change. Even if the girls stayed, that would have to change. She was guilty of letting Walter waltz in and out when he pleased. Time to put an end to that.

At lunchtime she still hadn't figured out what to say, so

when the phone rang she answered it without looking at caller ID.

"Cicely, don't hang up." It was Walter. He had taken a lot of ribbing at work about being late. And his face was still tingling from her slap. "In the paper they said they'd identified a body found over the weekend as LaShondra Brown. Wasn't that Shanequa and Tamequa's mother?"

"It was."

Cicely told him everything she knew except her uncertainty about the girls. After the promise to herself, she was letting him back in.

"I can give you the money to have her cremated Cicely. That way when they become of age they can decide."

"Walter, I wouldn't ask you to do that."

"Then I can loan it to you."

"No Walter. I think I just have to let that go. The family has to be held accountable some way."

"Do you want me to come over when you tell the girls?"

"Isn't this a little close to home for you?"

"Maybe that's why I can be of help."

There were two little girls and she only had one pair of arms. They knew Walter and liked him. They knew his grandfather had died. This was the last time she would have him here, but she agreed. He promised to be there when the girls got home from school.

Walter didn't ring the doorbell not trusting himself to be alone with her. He sat on the step waiting for the girls to come home. They pulled away from Jackie as soon as they saw him and came running calling his name.

"Walter, we missed you."

He picked Tamequa up like he always did and she patted his bruised face. "Walter what happened?"

Cicely chose that moment to open the door and waited to see what he would say.

"It's just a love tap." He could still smile at Cicely, even under the circumstances.

"Then I don't want no love tap," said Shanequa walking past everyone into the house.

The girls did what they always did when getting home from school. They headed straight to the kitchen for their snacks. After which they would do their homework while Cicely started dinner. Walter looked at Cicely, where did she want to tell them?

She decided on the living room. She turned on lights so the room wouldn't be so dim in the fall afternoon. Walter could tell the room wasn't used much, everything seemed to have a place. He knew she had a TV in the bedroom and could picture her and the girls cuddled in bed watching television. Tonight would be one of the nights the little girls shared her bed.

"Are you bout to tell us our momma is coming to get us

Ms. CeeCee?" asked Shanequa. The little girl was very attuned to things out of the ordinary.

"No," said Cicely sitting down. She and Walter had the girls sit between them on the sofa. "Walter I don't know if I can do this."

He took Tamequa's small hand in his large one. "Ms. CeeCee told you my grandfather died."

Both girls nodded yes. "He was old," said the youngest. "I saw him before I got sick."

"Yes you did," said Walter. He had been at the hospital with his grandfather when he died. He wanted to believe his grandpa knew he was there. These girls did not have the luxury of being at their mother's bedside. There would be no funeral for them to go to. Did they even understand the concept of heaven? Cicely took them to church, but he didn't know their history before that. He looked at her and saw her eyes were becoming wet. He had to hurry this up.

"Your momma can't come get you," said Walter. "She died. She went away like my grandpa did."

The girls looked at Cicely for confirmation and she could only nod.

"She just left us?" asked Shanequa.

"Baby, she couldn't take you with her," answered Cicely.

Shanequa stood and looked at them. "She is always leaving us," she screamed. "I hate her, I hate her."

Walter stood and picked her up. She felt so tiny and frail in his arms. Her arms went around his neck and he cooed in her ear. "No you don't. You don't hate your momma. You hate she went away. She didn't want to leave you. She died Shanequa. That does not mean she didn't love you."

Cicely put Tamequa on her lap. Her thumb was back in her mouth. She had not seen her sister act this way before and it scared her. Their momma had left them before, how was this different? Her momma wasn't old like Walter's grandpa. Maybe she could come back. "Are you gonna be our momma now Miss CeeCee?" asked Tamequa.

Walter looked at her. She hadn't said one word to him about what would happen to the girls.

"I don't know," is all she said.

He knew she desperately wanted to be their momma, without her saying a word.

Food was comfort. They all went into the kitchen while Cicely prepared the girls' favorite meal, spaghetti and hot dogs. It kept her busy cutting the hot dogs into little circles while Walter continued to comfort the girls.

The only ones who ate were Walter and Tamequa. Shanequa pushed the food around her plate and Cicely had lost her appetite.

All through the meal Shanequa was whispering to Walter. Did he think her momma was with his grandpa? Was that in heaven? How would her momma and his grandpa know each other? He would nod and patiently try to answer her questions.

Tamequa was only four, but Cicely knew that she would probably on occasion ask when her mother was coming back or could she go visit.

Cicely watched Walter. He kept his focus on Shanequa, giving her his undivided attention. Tamequa usually monopolized Walter whenever he was around, but she seemed to sense her sister needed him more right now. She was glad she agreed to let him come over.

The only jewelry she'd ever seen him wear was a watch on his right wrist. Now she noticed he wore a gold chain around his neck with a plain gold cross. She guessed correctly it was his grandpa's. She'd have to check if anything had been left for LaShondra's daughters.

Walter stayed until she put the girls to bed; she walked him to the door, promising the girls she'd be right back. They girls were in her bed and she'd have to remember the pad to put under Shanequa when she went back up in case the bedwetting started again.

They stood at the outside door in the small entryway. Cicely raised her hand as if to touch the bruise on his face and let it drop. "I'm sorry I hit you."

Walter slid his hand to the back of her neck and pulled her in and kissed her forehead. "No you're not," he said. "But I ain't mad at cha. I'll be by after I finish up work tomorrow."

Walter's presence had made the task of telling the girls

their mother had died bearable. It seemed natural to talk to him about what to do about the girls and school. He was the one that suggested she talk to their teachers and get a recommendation.

It was hard to keep thinking of him as a boy.

She watched him walk to his truck with the swagger that was uniquely his. Reminiscent of how he used his hips in bed. Yes, if she let herself she could fall in love with Walter.

Shanequa and Tamequa had fallen asleep when she went back upstairs, so she used that opportunity to call Bernice and Madeline. Neither sister was surprised to hear Walter was instrumental in breaking the news to the girls. They had talked among themselves about Cicely's growing attraction to Walter. Madeline thought it was a good thing. Bernice wasn't sure.

"Cicely what happens to you if they take the girls?" asked Bernice.

"I'll deal with it. I knew going in it would be short term, I just thought it would be their mother they would be going back to."

It was still early by adult standards, so Walter stopped by his grandmother's. Her widowed sister had decided to stay for a while after the funeral and both women were still up.

"What happened to your face?" Was the first thing his grandmother asked.

"Cicely hit me," he said truthfully. "But I deserved it grandma."

"You didn't hit no woman, did you Walter?"

"No ma'am," he said following her into the house.

"There is no right or wrong way to tell someone Walter," his grandma was telling him, after he explained how they'd told the girls about their mother.

"I offered to pay for a cremation," Walter said. He was sitting at the dining room table eating a piece of cake. His grandmother and his great aunt had enough food to last a week from dishes people had brought by the house.

"You can't take care of everybody Walter," said his grandmother.

"I'm only trying to take care of one person and right now she comes with a package."

"So, did she take your money?" asked his great aunt.

"No, she ain't like that Aunt Willie."

"What other use she got for you?"

Walter looked at his grandmother for help. He didn't want to disrespect her sister.

"I mean, she's older than you," continued his aunt. "Probably better educated. You dropped out of college to be a plumber like your uncle."

His grandmother was not going to come to his rescue. She looked at him like, if you want that woman, then you have to act like it.

If it had been one of his mother's contemporaries he

would have said they complemented each other in bed. But he wouldn't bring up sex in front of his grandmother. Not even to shut her sister up.

"How old do you think she is Aunt Willie?" he asked.

"She look like one of them cougars to me," she said, her false teeth clicking.

Walter laughed. If Cicely was a cougar, then why was he the one doing the chasing?

CHAPTER 19

Cicely spent the better part of the next day tracking down La Sondra's belongings, or if she had any. She discovered the half-way house had some things and would hold them for her. She left a message with the caseworker to give her phone number if anyone wanted to talk to the girls She kept expecting someone to call and inquire about the girls' well-being, but that didn't happen. But Cicely had never heard Shanequa or Tamequa say anything about cousins or aunts and uncles.

How could someone become so isolated from their family? She and Simone still weren't speaking to each other, but she knew Bernice and Madeline were speaking to her. She had cousins she wasn't close too, but had an address book handy with everyone's phone number and address.

After speaking with the school counselor, which both girls teachers recommended, Cicely would send them back to school on Friday. That way they wouldn't fall too far behind, but have the weekend off. With no funeral there would be no real closure for the girls.

True to his word, Walter was there before the girls went to bed. He explained to Cicely he couldn't come back before the weekend because of the work he'd missed since his grandpa's death. But when he heard she was going to the half-way house he insisted on driving her. They would go Friday while the girls were in school. Neither of them mentioned 'that night' which was fine with Cicely.

It was a bright green tote. It held all of LaShondra Brown's belongings. Cicely had to show identification identifying her as the girls' guardian to take possession of the tote. The drive home was quiet. Both of them thinking how sad it was a person's life could be reduced to the contents of a plastic tote.

Cicely expected Walter to leave, but he carried the tote into the dining room for her and put it on the floor. "What do you expect to find?" he asked.

"Some clue as to who they are."

The bulk of the tote was filled with clothes. Cicely would give those away. But packed in the bottom was a small photo album. She sat crossed legged on the floor and started thumbing through it. Walter sat on the floor with her, his arm draped over his knee.

The album had baby pictures of both girls. Luckily someone had written dates and names on the back, or Cicely would not have been able to tell which baby was which. There was a picture of a lone female, when Cicely turned it over, it only said Momma RIP. It must have been LaShondra's mother. There were other pictures, but no names were written on them.

"You should get copies of their mother's death certificate." Walter told her.

"I can do that?"

"Just go downtown and pay for it. The girls might need it one day. What about their father?"

"I was told there was no father in the picture."

"Do you have a copy of their birth certificates?"

"I do," said Cicely. "But no father is listed. Didn't you ever want to know who your father is?"

"I know who my father is Cicely. I just don't have the need to meet him face to face. I know where he lives, where his parents live. My mother has all the information if I want it. But I don't want it. They didn't care enough to see how I turned out."

"But I want to give Shanequa and Tamequa the same choice you had. If I find a relative I don't plan on shoving the girls down their throat. I just want them to know there is family out there."

"And what happens when they find out no one wanted them?"

"I want them Walter," she said.

"I know," he said pulling her into his embrace resting his chin on the top of her head.

"Is that what happened to you?" She could smell his scent and didn't resist as he held her loosely in his arms.

"Cicely I was never made to feel unwanted."

"Aren't you even curious if you have brothers and sister out there somewhere?"

"The only time I was curious is when I thought I might have sex for the first time. Didn't want that to happen with a sister."

She started to feel warm at his mention of sex and pulled away from him. "I want to be able to say I did everything I could for them."

"Even though it could come back and bite you on the ass?"

She took a deep breath and audibly let it escape. "Yes"

Now she'd given him another reason for loving her. He untangled himself from the floor and stood. "Try getting their original birth certificate from downtown. It might have a father listed. Even if he didn't sign it." He took her hand and pulled her up. "I have to get back to work. There's talk of firing the boss," he said with a smile.

Walter held her hand as they walked to the door and gave her a brotherly kiss on the cheek. Unable to resist he pulled her close for a hug and whispered in her ear, "It'll be all right." She needed the physical contact.

Cicely stood there a minute or more. She didn't know how much longer she could hold out against Walter or why she should. Her excuses for not taking him as a lover were flimsy. Where he was concerned she was becoming a horny middle-aged woman. Why couldn't she just lie with him and be done with it? Because only three days before he'd told her he loved her.

She took the tote upstairs to her bedroom before looking through it one last time to see if she had missed anything. In the bottom of the tote was a pair of gold hoop earrings. She put those to the side. Once more she flipped through the album. She would show this to the girls. They'd probably seen it before. And maybe knew some names. This time she did find something. The return address from the corner of an envelope was tucked behind one of the pictures. It did not have a name, just the street address and city. Walter was right. This could end up backfiring on her. But if she didn't do something she'd never forgive herself.

Walter didn't call until Saturday night, asking could he pick them up for church. Cicely doubted the wisdom of them arriving together, but agreed. He was her friend and a good friend to the girls. Nothing was going to happen between them again, let the church ladies talk.

They walked into church like a family. Cicely had talked to Anita about the circumstances and Anita talked to the minister. He made a special point of mentioning the girls by name and asking people to pray for them during this time of their lost. Shanequa cried and Tamequa held her hand.

Anita couldn't contain herself and pulled Cicely to the side after service while Walter took the girls to speak with his family. "Well are you a couple now?"

"No. He's just helping with the girls. I told you I was going to try and track down some family."

"I don't know what to say about you. Anyone can tell he's not just hanging around for the girls. He brought you to church. He didn't arrive late and sit next to you. You walked in together. I don't know why you are in denial. I like seeing you with Walter."

Walter walked up to hear the last of the conversation and said, "I like seeing her with me too."

Anita put a hand on his arm. "I'm on your side."

"Thanks," said Walter. "I need all the help I can get." He turned to Cicely. "My cousin Diane is having small birthday party for her oldest. Basically cake and ice cream since it's so soon after grandpa's passing. She wants you to bring the girls." He didn't say he had made the suggestion to his cousin the girls be invited.

Cicely looked at Walter and Anita. It was like they were in a conspiracy against her. The girls looked at her expectantly and she wondered how many birthday parties they'd been invited to. "We'll come, but I'll drive. You don't have to come pick us up."

"Sure," said Walter smiling. "But do I still get to take you out for breakfast?"

"Please Miss CeeCee," said Shanequa.

No way was Cicely going deny the girls a chance to go to breakfast with Walter or a birthday party. But she was not going to feed into the impression they were a couple by letting him bring them to the party.

His cousin lived in a development that was being built

when she'd first left the city. Neat identically styled ranch homes with attached garages. Hardly any trees on the block, in a city known for its tree lined streets.

She didn't know what to expect when she got there. On the way she had stopped and bought card, slipping a few dollars in it. Money was always a good idea for a gift when you didn't know the person. They had changed clothes and the three of them had on jeans, hers a little snug. Guaranteed to make him look at her behind, something she hadn't consciously thought about when she put them on.

Walter had told her to be there by five and exactly at five o'clock she rang the doorbell.

Walter answered the door surrounded by little kids. "These are my cousins," he said. "Actually, my cousins' children." He knelt to introduce Shanequa and Tamequa to the four children following him. After shedding their coats and tossing them to Walter they followed them to another part of the house.

She recognized some faces from the funeral and greeted everyone. Walter took her coat and led her to the kitchen to introduce her to his cousin Diane, who was busy putting candles on a cake.

Diane took the card she offered, "You didn't have to bring anything. I just wanted to do a little something for Lilly even though we just buried granddad."

"I understand," said Cicely but not understanding why

she was there. It was obvious everyone there was family. None of Walter's aunts and uncles was there. Nor his mother or grandmother, only his cousins and their children.

Walter was trying very hard to integrate her into his family.

CHAPTER 20

Monday morning Cicely took the kids to school and skipped her run so she could check out the girls' birth certificates and get a copy of the death certificate. Shanequa's birth certificate wasn't there. She hadn't been born in Buffalo. But Tamequa's was. Walter was right. A father was listed, but he hadn't signed the birth certificate. She sat down and composed a letter to persons unknown at the address she had found in the photo album. It was the same city Shanequa had been born in.

She had shown the pictures to the girls, but the only ones they recognized were the pictures of themselves. They didn't remember a Daddy. Shanequa did know her mother's last boyfriend but only his first name. That was no help and Cicely didn't want to keep questioning them.

She included all the pertinent information. Gave the caseworker's name and phone number, along with her own. She started by asking whomever received the letter if they weren't the correct person and knew the whereabouts of that person would they please contact them to relay the information. Cicely knew she was doing the right thing, but it still worried her. The person didn't even live close. If they had she would have driven there and confronted them. The same way she wished she could confront the family here that had abandoned Shanequa and Tamequa to strangers.

At the birthday party she learned Walter had been working long hours to get caught up and she really wasn't expecting to see him anytime soon, so she was surprised when he showed up Wednesday night at dinnertime.

"You didn't call first," she said letting him in.

"I won't stay long. I just stopped by to see how Shanequa and Tamequa were doing." He still had on his work clothes and boots.

"Come eat," she said. "We were just sitting down."

Before sitting down, he meticulously washed has hands at the sink.

"Hope you like mac and cheese," Cicely said to him placing another plate on the table.

"Show me a black man that don't," he replied reaching for a piece of the chicken she had cooked to go with the mac and cheese and broccoli.

"I helped with the macaroni and cheese," said Shanequa.

"It tastes good," he told her after taking the first bite. He asked them both how school was going and received news they weren't the only kids who's momma had died.

Cicely sent them all in the living room to watch TV while she cleaned the kitchen. It didn't take her long, but when she walked in the girls were sitting on the floor and Walter had taken his boots off and fallen asleep on the couch, curled in the fetal position with his hands tucked between his knees. He had turned his back to the TV. She left him there and took the girls upstairs and got their school clothes ready for the next day. She had an appointment for all three of them at the hair salon the coming Saturday so she tied their hair up in a scarf while giving them a bath. Now she had Shanequa read the bedtime story before putting them to bed.

She went downstairs to wake Walter and send him home. She shook him gently.

He was dreaming about Cicely. It was one of those dreams you knew was a dream but still felt real. He could feel the pressure of her touch on his shoulder and covered her hand with his own. "Come back to bed," he told her. In his world they had just finished make love and he wanted her again.

"Walter," she called his name and shook him harder.

That woke him, but Walter didn't immediately open his eyes. He turned onto his back and stretched, thrusting his hips upward.

It was a nice sight, thought Cicely.

He sat on the edge of the sofa and put his boots on without tying them. "You sending me home Cicely?" He asked.

"Yes Walter," she said. Seeing him sit on the couch brought back memories.

He stood and stretched again. That done he pulled her close and nuzzled that spot on her neck. The mark he had made there before had faded. He let his hands roam down her back and cup her round bottom, the dream fresh in his mind. "The girls still in your bed Cee?" he asked.

She put her hands on his chest and stepped back out of his embrace. "It's not going to happen Walter."

He dropped his hands to his sides. "Okay Cee. I'll play by your rules. But I had to try. Wouldn't be a man if I didn't at least try." He said apologetically. As much as he wanted her, Walter wouldn't pressure her back into bed.

When he left Cicely pressed her forehead to the cool glass of the front door, wishing he had tried harder. Then remembered when they had made love he'd asked her if she wanted him to stop he would. Like now, he would do as she asked, and play by her rules. If Cicely wanted Walter to make love to her again, she was going to have to give him an unequivocal yes.

CHAPTER 21

Two weeks had passed since Cicely had mailed the letter with no word back. During that time she'd called the morgue every other day to see if anyone had claimed LaShondra's remains to find no one had stepped forward. It got so the coroner knew it was her.

Walter had taken them to church and breakfast the two previous Sundays but had made no other move to get intimate with her. He'd invited her and the girls to watch him play basketball at the Y one Saturday and they went. She enjoyed watching him play, but was uncomfortable with the looks he kept giving her. His young friends notice too and teased him about it. But she didn't know, this was the only time he had invited a woman to a game. Their girlfriends and wives came to watch all the time and Walter never brought anyone. They were giving him a hard time because his friends knew he was serious about this one.

She increased her days in the office to three, mostly so she would have other adults to talk to.

There had been a parent teachers meeting at school. Tamequa would be five in January and her pre-K teacher wanted to move her to a kindergarten class, saying the current class wasn't challenging enough for her. Cicely agreed not knowing if the girls would still be with her or not. Shanequa's teacher said she was doing fine, but had a tendency to stare into space sometimes. Both women agreed those were probably the times she thought about her momma.

Madeline and Bernice each called her separately. She didn't tell them what she'd done as far as sending the letter. Madeline was thinking about an early retirement to help care for her first grandbaby. Cicely knew that wouldn't last long. Madeline loved her job.

Bernice was doing better than expected. Louis had removed all processed food from their diet and was slowly removing meat. As a result they had both lost ten pounds with no real exercise involved but walking. Their daughter was doing well in her freshman year of school and was on course to make the dean's list her first semester.

And par for the course Simone was talking to them but not to Cicely.

Cicely had not given up on her though. She still called Simone and left messages.

She missed her baby sister. She needed someone to talk with about Walter. Anita wouldn't listen to her any more. She was staunchly on Walter's side and didn't understand why Cicely wouldn't just have an affair with him for as long as it lasted. She couldn't get Anita to understand she was afraid Walter would break her heart no matter how much he said he loved her now.

Walter was done waiting on Cicely to make a move. His plan was to get her away from the girls and seduce her. He wouldn't give her a chance to say no. Tuesday he called her and made a real date with her on Friday. He would pick her up at her door and take her somewhere nice and feed her. And before the night was done he would have made love to her. Made her believe how much he loved her. He wanted to wake up every morning with her next to him. Walter wanted her to yell at him for putting his feet on the coffee table, scream at him in the middle of the night for leaving the toilet seat up. He wanted to have fights and mad make-up sex.

It was dark when he got home from work Thursday evening. She was sitting on his steps. He hadn't seen Perri in almost four years.

She stood when he approached. She had a backpack and a duffle bag next to her. Perri was almost as tall as he was. Her build was slender and she wore her naturally curly hair close cut. Her complexion was light and some would mistake her for Puerto Rican until they heard her speak. She was definitely a black girl. Her eyes were dark, fringed with dark lashes, her lips full. She was a few years younger than Walter and at times their relationship could have been called volatile.

He walked right past her without speaking and unlocked the door. Perri followed him in and dropped her belongings on the floor.

Walter moved around the room turning on lights.

"I need a place to stay for a couple of days Walter."

"Maybe my mother will let you stay with her." He answered.

"All the women in your family hate me. You know that."

"Whose fault is that Perri?"

"Walter I promise only a couple of days. I can sleep in the second bedroom."

"Don't have a second bedroom anymore. I use it as an office now. No bed in there."

"Well I guess sharing your bed is out of the question."

"I'm seeing someone Perri."

"Did she need saving too? You always liked a damsel in distress."

"Perri, why you trying to make me angry if you need a place to stay so bad?"

"You're right." She said as she took off her jacket and tossed it on the couch. "I was always good at pushing your buttons." She had on jeans that fit her like a second skin. A large oversized sweater to hide her chest. Perri was always self-conscious about her small breasts.

"How's your grandfather?" Another thing she was good at, changing the subject.

"He died a few weeks ago."

"I'm sorry to hear that." And she was. She genuinely liked Walter's grandfather. "He liked me."

"He liked all pretty girls."

"I just got back into town Walter…"

Walter's cell phone rang. He looked at caller ID and saw it was his mother. He held up his hand to stop Perri from talking.

"Hello."

"Walter, was that Perri I saw going into your place?"

He turned his back on Perri and walked into the kitchen. "Yes it was."

"Why is she here?"

He rubbed his hand over his face. "She needs a place to stay for a couple of days Ma."

"Give me one good reason why you should let her stay with you?"

"We used to mean something to each other. I never hated her."

"What has that got to do with letting her stay with you? What about Cicely?"

"Ma, Cicely has nothing to do with this. This is part of my past. It has nothing to do with how I feel about Cicely."

"Are you going to tell Cicely about her?"

"Yes I am. I don't want to hide anything from her."

"Make sure you do Walter. I don't like getting in your personal business, but…"

"Then stay out of it Ma." He couldn't deal with his

mother and Perri at the same time. He knew she was right about Perri. She'd created havoc in his family. She flirted with every male that noticed her. His cousins, his cousins' husbands, boyfriends, his uncles, his friends, it didn't matter. Thinking back on it, if he had really cared about her the flirting would have bothered him more than it did. They'd fought about it, but only because the women in his family expected him to put a stop to it. They didn't understand it was part of her personality, her insecurities.

"Well did momma say I could stay?" she said to him when he came back into the room.

"Perri, don't do that. If I had listened to my mother we wouldn't have lasted as long as we did. How long do you need to stay?"

"I'll be gone Saturday."

"You can sleep on the couch." He went upstairs and came back carrying a pillow and bed linens.

"What happened to us Walter?" she asked taking the items from him.

"I think we grew up." He didn't want to make small talk with her. She didn't even come close to what he wanted in his life now. He wouldn't turn her away because that wasn't in him. But he didn't want her sticking around either. "If you're hungry check the kitchen, you know where everything is. I'm going to bed. I have an early day. Saturday Perri. Outta here by Saturday."

"Can't we at least sit down and catch up a bit? You said you were seeing someone."

"Perri, you have no rights here. I'm letting you stay because we used to be close. Take what I'm giving you and leave it at that." And he left her standing there.

Walter sat on the bed and took his shoes off. He looked at the clock on the nightstand, Cicely would be getting the girls ready for bed. Tomorrow would be soon enough to tell her about Perri. He rehearsed in his head what he would say. Perri was an ex. She needed a place to stay. She'd be gone by Saturday.

"Damn," he thought, that interfered with his plans for Cicely. Naw, Perri had to leave tomorrow. He'd put her up in a hotel, because he would not take Cee to a hotel. He wanted her in his bed. He'd call her later before she went to sleep. Walter didn't even get a chance to remove his clothes before he was dead to the world.

Walter woke up in a good mood. He showered. Then shaved so he wouldn't have to when he came home later. Dressed then went downstairs to make coffee. Perri was rolled up in the covers on the couch.

He saw the kitchen and winched. Perri had cooked, but had not cleaned up after herself. He didn't even try to be quiet as he fixed coffee.

Perri came wandering into the kitchen stretching, wearing only her panties and a tight fitting camisole.

"You're pregnant," Walter said, seeing her small round

belly.

"If you had taken the time to speak to me last night I would have told you."

"Baby daddy?" he asked.

"No longer in the picture. I was kinda hoping you might want that role."

He looked at her, "Go put some clothes on."

"Guess that's a no," she said walking away. "There was a time when you couldn't get enough of this Walter."

"Be ready to leave when I get home today," he called out to her.

Perri turned back to him. "You said I could stay until Saturday."

He shrugged. "Things change."

"Is it because I came back pregnant?"

"Perri, if you're happy you're pregnant, I'm happy for you. This has nothing to do with that. I told you, I'm in a relationship." At least he hoped after tonight he would be. "I'll spring for a room tonight."

She had put her loose sweater on and was struggling into her jeans. "Walter if you weren't in a relationship would you take on that role?" She was curious.

He had filled his go cup and was ready to leave. "No, I wouldn't."

"Why, because it's not yours?"

"No, because it's yours." He felt cruel saying it, but it was true. He had outgrown Perri.

Perri sat on the sofa and cried when he left. She'd been doing that a lot since becoming pregnant. She did have some place to go Saturday, but this was not the Walter she knew. That one would have been happy to see her. They would have fallen into bed and had sex most of the night. Loving him had nothing to do with it. She didn't love Walter any more than she loved her baby's daddy.

Cicely wanted Walter to make love to her again. There would be no rules. That he wanted more than that, well they would cross that bridge when they came to it. She knew his plan to take her to dinner was a ruse and she planned for it accordingly. Condoms in her purse and a speech prepared to tell him no more unprotected sex until they were both tested. The twins were coming over to spend the night. She had ordered pizza and all they had to do was heat it when they were ready to eat. She had bathed and smoothed lotion on her body from head to toe. The scent wasn't heavy and you could only smell it if you got very close. She intended for Walter to get very close. On the bed was a black leather skirt she had bought months ago and never worn. As much as she hated panty hose she loved the look of textured tights and a black pair lay on the bed next to the skirt. The weather was now cold enough to wear them.

She didn't feel ashamed of wearing a skirt that hit her at mid-thigh at forty. By the bed was a short black boot with a chunky heel that accentuated the shape of her calves. Her toenails were red, because Walter said he loved them.

Cicely had bought new underwear. She didn't need it. It wasn't like Walter had seen her collection of underwear. She wanted something new for him. She now wore sheer red panties and matching bra. When he got her undressed down to her undies her nipples would show through the sheer fabric. She had a cream-colored cowl neck knit sweater made from cashmere and silk that showed a little cleavage. The fabric was thin and if you looked closely you would be able to see her red bra.

She put on very little make-up, because she didn't want to leave a mess on Walter's pillowcases.

Her outerwear was a long black full-length trench coat. She'd briefly considered wearing nothing under it but the red undergarments, then decided against it. Who knew what could go wrong. And it had been done so many times on TV. Let Walter work a little.

Walter did not even look at Perri when he came in. He did notice her bags neatly stacked and that was enough for him. "I won't be long." He said, taking the stairs two at a time.

"Fine," she answered.

Perri had cleaned the kitchen, but was still a little peeved. Walter didn't want her any longer. Pregnancy hormones were messing with her emotions or she wouldn't have cared.

Soon she'd have to get some pants with elastic in the waist, her jeans were getting too small to leave unzipped. She still had on the camisole she had on that morning when Walter left. Perri looked down at her breasts. She'd have to be a lot more pregnant before they got any bigger.

Walter was scowling as he dressed. He'd forgotten to change the sheets on the bed and it was too late now. There was only enough time to take Perri to a hotel before picking Cicely up. He'd figure something out.

He dressed in charcoal grey slacks, black shoes and socks. The V-neck t-shirt wouldn't show in the open neck of the royal blue dress shirt he wore. The black sports jacket he planned on wearing was downstairs in the small closet. At the last minute he remembered to put lotion on his hands before putting his watch on. He didn't hear the doorbell.

Perri was about to slip her sweater on when the doorbell rang and ended up just pulling her top down over her little baby bump and unzipped jeans.

Cicely pulled up to Walter's duplex just as dark was taking hold. She hoped her surprise would work as planned. The lights were on and his car was still there so she'd gotten there before he'd left. She walked up the stairs and rang the bell, her heart beating rapidly in her chest.

Perri was not expecting a woman to be standing on the other side of the door.

"Is Walter here?" Cicely didn't know what else to say.

Perri stepped aside, let Cicely enter and closed the door behind her. This was the woman Walter was in a relationship with? "He'll be down in a minute. I'm Perri," she said sticking her hand out.

Cicely looked down at her hand and saw the baby bump. Her coming to his home was a mistake. The young woman looked to be about four or five months along. The number of months Cicely had known Walter. When he told her he had no baby momma drama in his life. This was the type of person she imagined him to be with. Young, thin, tall and model like. Her mind's eye saw them fitting together perfectly. Would he have said anything if she hadn't shown up at his door? She had the urge to pull her coat closed. Cicely felt like a cougar on the prowl.

Perri had to fight the impulse to look at her own breasts. This woman's boobs were made for Walter's hands. Her curves made Perri's look like a broomstick. This woman was beautiful. Jealousy rose in her like the morning sickness she'd experienced at the beginning of her pregnancy.

Cicely reluctantly took the offered hand and gave her name.

Perri was really self-conscious now. This Cicely was dressed to show off her every asset. She retrieved her sweater and slipped it over her head, giving Cicely a better view of her bulging stomach. Cicely clamped her lips together.

As was his habit, Walter was walking down the stairs buttoning his shirt. Both women's eyes turned to him, before looking at each other suspiciously.

Perri was the first to speak. "This isn't what it looks like."

Cicely looked at Walter, then back at Perri. "I think it is," she said and started toward the door.

Walter pointed at Perri and said, "Don't open your mouth." To Cicely he said, "I was going to tell you." Which didn't sound any better.

Cicely threw open the door and bolted to her car.

"What did you say to her," he demanded of Perri.

"I didn't say anything Walter. She just got here." But knew saying nothing was just as bad.

Walter took off after Cicely. She had already gotten in her car and started the engine. He stood in front of the car with his hands on the hood.

"Don't leave Cicely. I can explain everything. It is not what you think."

"Move Walter," she shouted. "Move or I will run you down."

He stayed where he was. "Damn it, roll the window down. Let me talk to you." He didn't know whom he was angrier with; Perri, for coming to him, himself for letting her stay, or Cicely for believing he would do something like that.

"That is not my baby Cicely."

He'd seen how Cicely was dressed and knew she had come ready to let him make love to her. He was not going to let what they had started end like this.

Cicely let the window down and said again. "Move Walter." She'd heard what he'd said about the baby not being his, but the woman was at his house. She was letting everything hang out in front of him with a familiarity that Cicely hadn't developed with Walter yet. How could she know this baby wasn't a product of an act done months ago? Cicely didn't want to wait around and find out. She didn't want to lay with him and think of him comparing her body to this Perri's body. Walter was thirty-one years old, he certainly wasn't celibate before she came along and wouldn't be after she was gone. How did she even know he hadn't shared something with this woman while waiting for her to make up her mind? It had been a month. He was young. She said again, "Move Walter."

He slapped the flat of his hand against the car hood. "Cicely, you have to let me explain. I have not lied to you about anything. I love you." He enunciated the last three words.

She was not going to stay here and be humiliated. Cicely put the car in neutral and gunned the engine. The car moved just enough to make Walter move out of the way, she put it in drive and pulled away screeching rubber.

Walter stood in the middle of the street and watched the taillights of the car get dimmer as she drove away. He turned and saw Perri standing in the doorway. His angry stride took him back into the house. He grabbed her bags and threw them onto the sidewalk. "Get out." He said, his voice was low and deadly.

Perri had never seen him this angry. "I'm sorry Walter," she looked close to tears.

He didn't care. "I said get the hell out of my house."

"I don't have any place to go." She was pleading.

"I'm sorry. Isn't that what you always say Perri? I'm sorry. Well sorry ain't gonna cut it this time. I want you gone. You've disrupted my life for the last time."

He got his car keys and put a jacket on and waited for her to do the same. Walter left her standing on the sidewalk in front of his house while he went after Cicely.

Cicely would not go home. Walter would come looking for her there, and she knew he would come looking. Anita's was her first thought. But by having the twins spend the night at her house, she had promised Anita and Ben a romantic night alone. She wanted a drink. There had to be a bar somewhere she could go and have a drink alone without looking like a prostitute.

Walter parked in front of the house and waited. Her car wasn't there so he would wait for her. One way or another she would listen to him. The lights were still on, so the girls and their babysitters were still up. He wouldn't cause a scene in front of them but he had to talk to Cicely. He called her cell. She hadn't thought to block his number yet, so he left a message.

Cicely ended up at a bar downtown. She remembered hearing it advertised on the popular black radio station. A place a person could network with other professionals. It was happy hour for the white-collar crowd. She was able to get a seat at the bar and order something to eat, but when the food arrived she didn't have an appetite. Vodka rocks, was her drink of choice but being alone she settled on a white wine. Vodka on an empty stomach wouldn't sit well or driving. Finally she nibbled on the French fries that had come with her meal.

The crowd was a mixed group of professional looking people, different age groups and ethnicities. She saw a lot of business cards being passed back and forth. Luckily there was a television above the bar she could pretend interest in because she was there for an hour before anyone spoke to her. She thought the guy was trying to slip between her and the person sitting next to her to order a drink, but he had a business card in his hand.

"You look like you could use a lawyer," he said.

She looked at him. He was average height, nice hair and teeth and he was white.

The only thing she could think of was Walter accusing her of only going out with white men. She took the card any way.

"Do you specialize?" she asked with a smile.

He pointed at the card. "Mark Jones, Tax law."

"What a coincidence,' she said. "I'm a financial advisor."

Walter refused to leave. He eventually fell asleep in his car. And was still asleep when Cicely pulled into her driveway.

She and Mark had talked for hours over a few drinks he paid for. When she made it clear nothing was going to happen sexually they'd actually talked some good business. She might be able to send some business his way and vice versa.

She went in the house got a piece of paper and wrote a note on it in crayon. One he was sure to see when he woke up. She put it on the windshield, driver's side. He would have to get out of the car to remove it.

"YOU BETTER HAVE NOT GIVEN ME A DISEASE."

Saturday morning Janice let herself into Walter's place with her key. She'd heard and seen everything that had went on the night before and knew she would find him brooding and angry. Feeling sorry for her, she had even let Perri spend the night on her couch.

He stood in the kitchen, with the same clothes he'd had on last night. He was sipping on a cup of coffee and just looked at her. His eyes appeared more brown than green, a reflection of how he was feeling. "Don't say anything Janice," he said to her.

"May I have a cup of coffee? I ran out."

He indicated for her to help herself. But he knew his mother. She never ran out of anything.

As she fixed her cup she took a good look at him while pretending not to. He was in his stocking feet and it was obvious he had slept in his clothes. Janice wished she could hug him. The last time they had hugged was when her father died, his grandpa. Before that she couldn't remember when. They had a good relationship, but he didn't come to his mother when his heart was hurting. She didn't know if he went to anybody. Except the night they buried his grandfather. He'd let Cicely in.

Janice knew about it. She'd come home for a few things before spending the night with her mother and sisters and saw Cicely's car was still in front of the house. She didn't feel guilty manipulating Cicely into bringing him home. Walter let very few things get under his skin and Cicely was one of them. She felt she understood Cicely. Not that she'd ever been in a situation like the one her son was in with Cicely. But with the age difference Cicely had to feel she wasn't right for Walter. If her son wanted that woman he was going to have to fight for her.

"What are you going to do about it?" she asked. It wasn't necessary for her to ask about Perri. She knew that baby wasn't his. After his father's abandonment of them he would never do that to a child and its' mother. Janice also knew that if Cicely wasn't in the picture Walter would have sheltered Perri and her unborn child for as long as it took.

"Why did you never marry?" he asked her point blank, ignoring her question.

"Do you think knowing the answer to that is going to give you some insight into why Cicely has never married?" she threw a question back at him.

She saw the muscle in his jaw work and knew she had hit on part of his reason for asking her. "No one ever asked me," she said.

His eyes widen slightly. That was not the answer he was expecting to hear.

"What if someone asked you now?"

She wasn't seeing anyone special right now but didn't feel she was too old to still happen upon the right person. "I'm still young enough to be open to that possibility Walter. Now answer my question. What are you going to do?"

"I honestly don't know. I screwed up Ma." He said shaking his head.

Janice tried to dig deep and think of something her father would say to him. Something profound.

"I don't understand her. "

"Well gee Walter. Men have been saying that since Adam and Eve." She said trying to elicit a smile from him. It didn't work.

"She won't listen to the truth."

"Walter, try to look at this from her point of view. I know that's hard for you, because you are a man. She's older than you."

"Ma, that ain't even an issue," he protested.

"I know that. Let me finish. You're young and good-looking. Basically you could have any woman you want. And that's not just your mother speaking. You want her. I know it, your grandfather knew it. Hell the whole family knows it."

He did smile at that.

"Cicely is at what I like to call the in-between age. Young and old men are still attracted to her. Both want to take her to bed."

Walter opened his mouth to argue he wanted Cicely more than in his bed, but his mother held up her hand to stop him.

"I know you want more than that Walter. She's very attractive. I'd think you were stupid if you didn't want her that way too. The thing is, she doesn't understand you want the whole package."

"I've tried to explain that to her."

"She's insecure."

"Insecure?" His voice went up an octave. "You've seen her. She's the most confident woman I know. Well, next to you."

"She doesn't believe a young stud muffin like you wants her for more than a short term roll in the hay."

"When did you start talking like that?"

"Whatever the situation calls for," she said waving away his remark. "She thinks you will leave her when something younger comes along."

"Like Perri?"

"Like Perri."

"There is no competition between her and Perri. Ma I've seen Cicely with nothing…."

"TMI, Walter."

"I didn't mean with no clothes," but he paused and got a dreamy look on his face before continuing. "With no make-up. None of that stuff you women do to make yourselves look good and she looks damn good to me. So what do I do to show her I'm in it for the long haul?"

"Keep at it. That's what your grandpa would do when Mother got particularly upset with him. "

"Cicely is not going to speak to me any time soon," he said running his hand through his hair. The note she'd left on his car let him know exactly how she felt about him right now. He'd been careless their night together but when Cicely didn't deny him all he could think of was being inside her. How could he explain he was reduced to only what he could feel, physically and emotionally? No words existed to describe the pure joy he'd felt when they made love.

She didn't have to worry about catching anything.

"But that doesn't stop you from speaking to her." Janice looked at her son. She set down the cup of coffee she hadn't touched and headed toward the door to leave. "Walter you need a haircut."

Walter came after her. He stopped her at the door and put his arms around her. "I love you Ma," he said.

Janice didn't even come to her son's chin, she hugged him back. "Love you too Walter."

CHAPTER 22

Cicely deleted all messages on her cell phone without listening to them. If someone besides Walter had called they would have to call back. She told Anita about the surprise she'd found at Walter's house. Not that the woman was pregnant only she was young and pretty and clearly she and Walter shared some kind of past. Anita tried to tell her she may have been reading too much into the whole thing, but she wasn't listening. Cicely felt that maybe she had been a distraction for Walter until he mended things with this woman.

"Walter doesn't seem to be that type," Anita objected.

"How would we know?" said Cicely. "It's been a long time since we've been in that dating pool. Young people do a lot of bed hopping now."

"I don't think he falls into that age group." She was going to have to question her husband more closely about Walter.

"Either way, he and I are not going to be a couple."

"Did he give an explanation why she was there?"

Cicely admitted she didn't give him a chance.

"It could have been innocent," said Anita, she liked Walter.

If her friend knew the whole story she wouldn't say that.

But she wasn't going to tell her. It was still too raw.

It was a nice fall day and she and the girls made a game out of raking the leaves. Shanequa and Tamequa did more jumping into the piles she created than raking. At four she didn't really expect Tamequa to be much help, so she let them play. She had a lot of yard and had appreciated it when Walter had come by and done that chore for her. In the end she would hire someone to do the job for now it was outside time for the girls.

When the postal truck pulled up Cicely didn't much pay attention. It wasn't until the mailperson began walking toward the porch did she stop her.

"May I help you," she called out from the side yard.

It was a registered letter from the city she had sent her letter. Cicely held the large manila envelope in her hand and felt sick to her stomach. It was thick. She placed it on the dining room table and went to the bathroom upstairs to throw up. She didn't want the girls to hear her vomiting into the toilet.

She came back down and told herself she would open it after she washed Shanequa's hair. Then it was I'll open it after dinner. At bed time the envelope was still sitting on the dining room table.

Sunday morning she got the girls up to go to church. Walter's presence was not going to keep her from church. Cicely had some serious praying to do. She had initiated contact with these people and would have to pay the consequences.

They left for church through the front door so she wouldn't have to see the envelope sitting on the table.

Walter was late for church. He saw her sitting in the same pew she always sat and he felt no compulsion not to join them. Tamequa immediately climbed over Cicely to sit on his lap. He saw her shoulders stiffen, but to him that meant he had some kind of effect on her even if it was anger.

Cicely refused to acknowledge him, but she was aware of him. No suit this week, black jeans and a black V-neck sweater. Shanequa was sitting between them and he put his hand, palm up on the little girl's knee, inviting Cicely to take hold of it.

Shanequa looked at the adults on either side of her. She didn't know why Miss CeeCee was being to mean to Walter. If Miss CeeCee wouldn't hold his hand she would. Shanequa placed her small hand in Walter's. In gratitude he gave her hand a gentle squeeze.

Walter left church right after the sermon, not waiting for the benediction. He said something to the girls before leaving. Cicely strained to hear what he said but couldn't. She still took them to breakfast because they'd come to expect that treat after church.

It should not have surprised her to find the yard cleared of leaves, the grass cut and the trash bags lined up at the curb when they returned home. On the porch he'd left a huge pumpkin for Shanequa and Tamequa.

Sunday afternoon she called Jackie to ask if she could

send the girls over for a while. She had procrastinated about opening the envelope for long enough. Cicely couldn't help but think how much easier it would have been if Walter had been there.

Finally she made herself a cup of tea, Madeline's cure for everything, and sat at the dining room table to open the envelope. She opened it and dumped the contents onto the table. There were a number of photographs and a hand written letter. Cicely chose to look at the pictures first.

The first one was of LaShondra holding a toddler and, a woman standing with them. A post-it stuck to the picture said "Baby Shanequa and LaShondra's mother shortly before she died. Cicely looked closely at the photograph. You could see the aura of illness around the older woman even though she smiled. There was one of the woman identified as LaShondra's mother with another female closer to her age. This one was marked sisters. The person that had sent the envelope had taken the time to include photos of LaShondra growing up, pictures of Shanequa and Tamequa's great grandparents. Only one baby picture of Tamequa was in the group and a note on the back requesting it be returned, as it was the only one they had.

Cicely reached for the letter. The handwriting was firm and legible. A few spots contained words that had been scratched out, as if the writer was in a hurry and didn't want to start over.

"Dear Ms. Macklin

Thank you so much for informing us of my niece's passing. Words cannot express how grateful we are to you for contacting us and caring for her daughters.

Forgive me for taking so long getting back to you. We had moved but the new owners tracked us down.

I did contact the morgue and unfortunately my niece's remains had been cremated. I will claim them though. Perhaps sprinkle them over her mother's (my sister's) grave.

I know you have questions about how LaShondra ended up there with two small children. I will try to answer some in this letter, but I think the bulk of it should wait until we see each other in person."

Cicely stopped reading. The woman planned on coming? She scanned the rest of the letter until near the end.

It said, *"We will arrive Friday. Would like to meet the girls then and if everything goes well, leave Sunday so they may be enrolled in school on Monday."*

She couldn't hold back the sob.

First thing Monday morning she called the caseworker Mrs. White. Cicely had to call numerous times and leave messages before the woman called her back.

"How could you let this happen," she demanded of the caseworker.

"Ms. Macklin I have to remind you, you instigated this.

You contacted them, they contacted us," she was losing her patience with Cicely.

"But they want to take the girls."

"They are blood relatives. That's always preferable to foster care."

Cicely wanted to wail into the phone. It was taking all her control to keep her voice neutral. "You know nothing about these people."

"Ms. Macklin, it's not like we're going to dump the girls on them."

"No, you're going to let them come to my house and take them."

"We can arrange for the transfer to take place somewhere besides your home."

Cicely willed herself to be calm. "No, no. Here will be fine." She had to see the people she was relinquishing her girls to.

"When this family member received your letter she immediately contacted child services to get the facts. I'm sorry she wrote to you before we were able to tell you. This isn't a situation of foster care. This is family taking on the responsibility of other family members. Of course the agency in their state will monitor the children to make sure things are fine."

During her discussion with Walter, Cicely had pointed out the importance of a family connection. She still believed that, but this was turning into a nightmare for her. She stopped short of calling her lawyer.

After school on Monday Cicely began preparing the girls for what was about to happen. She showed them the pictures of the aunt and cousins. Explained the aunt had been looking for them and would be there in a few days. They took it better than she did. But they had been through this before.

When she was able to, Cicely made herself read the rest of the letter.

LaShondra's mother had died when Shanequa was about three. Her father had died years before. After her mother's death LaShondra was of legal age so she took off with her boyfriend, Shanequa's father. The only other time she'd heard from LaShondra was when Tamequa was born. She'd sent a card with money, which is how Cicely had gotten the old address. LaShondra had kept it. Everything else was speculation. Any relatives located where Cicely was could have only been the girls' father's relatives. Well Cicely knew a little bit more than that. The girls had different fathers, so somewhere along the way LaShondra and Shanequa's father had broken up.

Either way she and Pauletta Sims would speak in person.

Cicely wanted to make memories the last week she would share with the girls. Together they made cookies for the girls to take to school for Halloween. While they slept she put together little scrapbooks for them to take. She took pictures of Jackie's daughters to include in the scrapbook, being sure to include names, dates, and addresses. That brought Walter to mind. Regardless of what was happening between them he had the right to say good-bye.

She didn't have to call him. He showed up, beggar's night, the night before Halloween. He wanted to see what they had done with the pumpkin, so he said.

The pumpkin sat on the front porch, so she didn't have to let him inside. Still it felt as if he was invading her space.

She'd been barefoot when she first answered the door and knew Walter noticed her feet. When she sent the girls outside after putting them in jackets she slipped her feet into her worn house slippers before stepping onto the porch, taking a hoodie for herself at the last second.

When she stepped out the first thing Walter did was look down. He smiled to himself, thinking, she remembered he loved her toes and was trying to hide them. He looked at her closely in the dim porch light. How could she think Perri was any competition for her?

Cicely watched him squat to examine the jack-o-lantern with the girls. He always did that, got down to their level. That's one of the reasons she loved…. Cicely quickly turned her back to the group.

When had that happened? When did she slip into loving Walter?

She didn't know he was standing behind her until he said her name.

"Cee, what's wrong?"

Her eyes were filled with tears she didn't want him or the

girls to see. She took a step toward the darker shadows of the porch and turned around. "The girls will be leaving Sunday. An aunt and uncle are coming to get them. I was going to call you in case you wanted to say good-bye."

"Are you alright with that?"

"It is what it is Walter. The state pays me to take in kids."

"Cicely I know you didn't do it for the money. This is me you're talking to. Don't try to pretend to be something you aren't. I know it's going to hurt you when they leave, but I know how strong you feel about family ties. You are only doing what you think will be better for them in the long run. Give them some roots."

Cicely had folded her arms across her chest and now gave her face a swipe to wipe away a tear that had fallen.

He didn't come any closer, but ran his hand down the side of her arm. How it must have hurt her to see Perri at his house. "Cee I'm sorry. We need to talk."

"You don't have to explain anything to me."

"Yes I do Cee. I love you."

"Can we not talk about this now?"

"Sure, okay," he said. He would have her undivided attention after the girls left.

"I'll be here for you Cee. Can I come by Saturday to meet the people?" The first time he had asked permission to come by.

She nodded. "We'll see you then."

The girls were allowed to wear their Halloween costumes to school and Cicely allowed them to pick what they wanted to be. Since television had been limited in the household they went with storybook characters. They wanted to be princesses, but African princesses. Cicely took the African print caftan she'd worn when dancing with Walter and cut it up to make them headdresses and sarong style dresses over their school uniforms, making sure she took pictures. She walked them to class and told their teachers Friday would be their last day. Cicely wanted transcripts of their school records to send with them so there would be no delay. She was hoping Tamequa would be admitted to kindergarten in her new school.

She went out and bought a legal file folder to put all the girls' records in and luggage. Cicely didn't want them to leave her house with backpacks like they'd come.

She and Jackie took all the children trick or treating for a short while and she explained the circumstances to her neighbor. Jackie said she figured it was something, but didn't want to pry.

Cicely mustered the courage to call Madeline and tell her what had happened. She sat crossed legged on the bed while they talked. For once Madeline didn't say, "I told you so."

"Are you going to be alright?"

"I don't think I can do this again," admitted Cicely.

"Yes you will," said Madeline. "Those girls are better off having known you. I wish I had met them. You did a good job. I know it wasn't easy, but it was your first time. You know like sex. Didn't turn out like you thought it would, but you kept at it anyway."

For the first time in days Cicely smiled about something other than what the girls had done.

"Do you speak to your daughter like that?" laughed Cicely.

"Yes I do," said Madeline. "Don't want her to make the mistakes I did."

"You didn't tell her about...." Cicely remembered the conversation she and Madeline had the beginning of the summer.

"No," said Madeline. "Momma got to have some secrets."

Cicely hadn't mentioned him so Madeline brought it up. "How's Walter?"

"He's going to come by and say good-bye to the girls Saturday. They like Walter."

"Wasn't asking about the girls and Walter, Cicely. I was asking about you and Walter."

"There is no me and Walter."

"You may not have realized it baby girl, but lately every time we speak Walter's name comes up in the conversation."

"Oh."

"Oh, that's all you got to say 'oh'?"

"Let's just say you were wrong about Walter. He would have been very amenable to scratching my itch and moving on. He's found fresher lawns to mow."

"You mean younger?"

"Younger, thinner, pregnant." Cicely didn't know why she let that slip out.

"Pregnant? The bastard," said Madeline.

"He is you know."

"Is what?"

"His mother had him when she was seventeen."

"Cicely, that's not very nice." But she knew. Bernice had told her.

"I know, I know," and she had never thought it before. Walter was being so kind to her and the girls. Talking to Madeline just brought back all the hurt she'd felt that night at his house on top of losing the girls. "He said it wasn't his."

Bells went off in Madeline's head. "And Walter's the type that would deny a child of his?"

"No, "said Cicely defending him, "but that doesn't mean he didn't sleep with her."

"Well did he?"

"I don't know," admitted Cicely. "I didn't ask."

"So you're upset with Walter because he may or may not

have slept with someone other than you."

"You make it sound silly."

"So he had to say something to you. What did he say?"

"He said I love you."

Cicely hadn't meant to say that. She hadn't told Madeline she'd been to bed with Walter. She certainly didn't mean to blurt out he'd said he loved her.

Finally Madeline said, "And what did you do?"

"I slapped him."

Madeline laughed. She laughed so hard she was snorting. "Wait a minute, let me get this straight. You catch Walter with another woman. He tells you he loves you and you slap him?"

"That's not the exact order of events," said Cicely tautly.

"I'm listening."

Cicely got up from the bed and started pacing. She tried not to dwell on what Walter had said. She'd only reacted to him manhandling her in public.

"He takes the girls and me out to breakfast after church. I come home and he's cleaned the yard. When Shanequa and Tamequa were sick, he came by and cleaned the kitchen and cooked. He invited all three of us to a cousin's birthday party."

"Cicely," Madeline said stopping her. "He's courting you."

"If he's courting me, why was that bitch at his house?" she had begun to shout and had to lower her voice so she wouldn't wake the girls.

"You're jealous," stated Madeline. This was probably a new emotion for Cicely. "It didn't have to be a young woman; any woman would have pissed you off."

"You're the one that said he was too young for me," countered Cicely.

"No, I did not. What I said was he was nothing to play with. But I was trying to stop you from hurting him, not the other way around."

"Walter don't need nobody protecting him. He does just fine," retorted Cicely. She was getting angry, angry enough to cry.

"Cicely have you fallen in love with Walter?

How could Madeline know that? She had just come to that realization herself.

"Are you crying Cicely?" asked Madeline hearing her sniffling.

"No, I'm coming down with a cold."

"Do you need me to come? I can come for the weekend."

"I don't need you to come Madeline."

She knew Cicely was lying about crying. "You need to take time and talk with Walter. Get this whole thing straightened out."

"No, I need Walter to leave me alone. I can't deal with him and losing the girls at the same time."

"Cicely, he's probably trying to help. He knows how you feel about those girls."

"I can't think when he's around Madeline."

"Then tell him. Not that you can't think. Tell him you need a little space, some time. If he loves you, he'll understand, as long as you don't make him feel you're completely shutting him out of your life."

Cicely stopped pacing and sat on the bed again.

"What about that woman?"

"Cicely you want to punish him for something you don't know he did."

She did want to punish him. "He won't be over until Saturday. He wants to meet the people taking the girls."

"Well ask him about it then. And then tell him you need a space."

"I will"

"Promise me Cicely," demanded Madeline.

"I promise."

Madeline told her she would tell Bernice about the girls so Cicely wouldn't have to repeat the heartbreaking news twice.

CHAPTER 23

Cicely didn't sleep the night before the Sims's were due to arrive. No amount of make-up was going to cover the bags under her eyes.

The Sims' hadn't given an ETA, she suspected it was to catch her off guard. Cicely wanted them there before Shanequa and Tamequa got home from school so she could get a first impression. The caseworker said she would be there at five. Paperwork had to be signed. Cicely could only hope they would be there by then.

She made sure the house was spotless, but no way was she going to give them a tour. She would introduce them to the girls in the living room, then excuse the girls to their room. That was the plan anyway. She'd been unable to eat breakfast with the girls for fear it would come back up.

Without meaning to she had dressed in all black, black jeans and a black pullover sweater, like she was in mourning. Then she remembered how Walter had looked dressed in all black last Sunday at church. Her life was becoming full of reminders of him. She was thinking about changing when the doorbell rang.

Looking at her watch, Cicely saw it was one o'clock. She should have asked Anita if she could come. Someone to have her back.

Standing at the door was a perfectly put together Simone.

"Not today," thought Cicely, "Please God, not today."

She let her in without speaking.

It was cold outside, Simone had on knee high dark green suede boots with a flat heel. Rust colored tights and a straight wool skirt the same green as her boots, a cream-colored silk blouse that tied at the neck and a green suede jacket. Over this she wore a black wool cape. She tossed the cape over the newel post at the foot of the stairs.

"You look like shit," she said to Cicely.

"What do you want Simone?" She was too down to muster the energy to fight.

Simone took Cicely by her hand and began to pull her up the stairs. "Is this the picture you want those girls to remember you by? All dressed in black like a funeral?"

"How do you know…" began Cicely.

Simone stopped walking up the stairs long enough to turn around and look at Cicely. "Just because I am not speaking to you doesn't mean I don't know what's going on with you."

"Madeline."

"Don't forget Bernice," said Simone pulling her along.

"They made you come."

"No one makes me do anything. You're my sister and I love you. I stayed away to make you suffer. You've suffered long enough so here I am," smiled Simone.

Cicely refused to budge from the stair where she was standing. "I am so sorry Simone. I never thought about how you would feel with Olivia gone."

"Apology accepted, but you were right. It took me a while to accept that. I wasn't the person Olivia needed to be with then. Had to get myself straight and I'm working on that. I'm sorry I've ignored you for so long. Now come on, can't have you meeting these people dressed like this."

Simone put her in a pair of black leggings and a light grey cable knit pullover that hit her at mid-thigh and made her wear a pair of black ballerina flats with black socks. She still looked somber, but not as severe as before. With a little make-up Cicely didn't look as drawn. She liked Cicely's sister locks not a look for her but Cicely could handle it.

Cicely protested when she saw herself in the full-length mirror. "I look too, I don't know, hip," unable to think of a better word.

"Cicely that's you. My trendy older sister. I was so glad you didn't wear make-up. I was so jealous of you. I hated when I'd bring boys home. You would walk through the room and they'd forget about me. They would not believe you were four years older than me."

"Guess I got a lot to apologize for."

"Cicely you do not apologize for how you look. All us Macklin sisters look good. That's a blessing."

They talked about Shanequa and Tamequa, well Cicely

did. Simone didn't mention she'd seen them with Walter that summer.

She waited for Cicely to mention Walter but she never did. Simone figured there'd be time to talk about Walter after the girls were gone.

Simone got to meet the girls after school. She was sorry she had wasted the summer being angry with Cicely. She liked children and these girls would have helped with her missing Olivia. Now she and her daughter talked with each other, not at each other. She and Evan even talked. It would not have happened if Cicely hadn't sent Olivia to her father.

At exactly five the doorbell rang. Cicely looked out expecting to see only the caseworker, but there were three people. Evidently the Sims had met with Mrs. White before coming to her house. Simone was with the girls upstairs waiting to be summoned.

Cicely put a smile on her face like she was pleased to see these people.

Mrs. White introduced the couple. Cicely held out her hand to greet Pauletta Sims and her husband Bernard. The woman appeared to be only a few years older than Cicely. She was brown skinned and had her permed hair pulled back into a bun fastened at the nape of her neck. Pauletta wore glasses and shook Cicely's hand vigorously thanking her again for reuniting her with her nieces. She and Cicely were about the same height. Pauletta was a few pounds heavier. How Cicely imagined she would have looked if she had been blessed with children.

Already the woman had prominent laugh lines, which Cicely hoped indicated a generous spirit.

Her husband Bernard was about Walter's height, but a few pounds heavier, also unlike Walter's sometimes wild afro, his hair was close cut. To Cicely he looked mean, but when he smiled she saw what Pauletta must have seen in him. He squeezed her hand gently and patted their clasped hands with his free hand and also said thank you.

Cicely showed them into the brightly lit living room.

"The girls are upstairs with my sister. I thought we could talk for a while before you meet them."

Pauletta did most of the talking. They had three children, ages seventeen, fifteen and twelve, all boys, but room for more. She was looking forward to having girls in their new home. She'd brought more pictures and Cicely could see the resemblance to Shanequa and Tamequa.

Pauletta went on about how the holidays were hard because LaShondra was missing. Besides Pauletta and LaShondra's mother there were three brothers. She and her sister were middle children, two brothers older and one younger. Shanequa and Tamequa had lots of cousins waiting for them back home.

Cicely told them Shanequa sometimes wet the bed and Tamequa sucked her thumb when upset. Both girls were excellent students and liked school. Generally they were well behaved.

LaShondra had been a good mother other than that neither the caseworker nor Cicely could give them much information about her life. And Pauletta became emotional when told about the drugs. She could only shake her head and comment, "A life wasted because of drugs."

They had picked up her ashes earlier that afternoon.

Pauletta had been a stay at home mom until her youngest started school. Now she planned on cutting back her hours at work until the girls became acclimated to their new surroundings. She was a beautician.

Bernard was a foreman at a manufacturing plant and would also welcome the girls into their male dominated household. They attended church on a regular basis and were happy Cicely had introduced the girls to that practice. They did plan on adopting the girls formally.

The caseworker had Cicely sign papers saying her time fostering the girls was done. Cicely turned over all the papers she had neatly organized and went upstairs to get the girls.

Simone looked at her sister and asked, "Well?"

"They're nice. A nice couple."

Each woman took a child's hand and walked them downstairs.

Pauletta and Bernard were waiting at the bottom of the stairs for them.

Pauletta had to stop herself from grabbing them up in her arms. These were her sister's grandbabies.

They only stayed a half hour longer not wanting to overwhelm the girls. Pauletta had shown them pictures of their cousins and included Cicely when showing them their new bedroom.

"Will you spend the night?" Cicely asked Simone as they washed the dinner dishes. The four of them had sat down to eat as soon as the Sims's left.

"I was just waiting for you to ask me," said Simone. "I have a bag in my car."

Cicely was glad Simone had come see about her. They shared Cicely's bed, talking until they fell asleep. Something that hadn't happened since they were little girls. Simone confirmed the vibes she got from the Sims were good too. They were due back at eleven the next morning to get better acquainted with the girls. Simone was sure she heard Cicely crying during the night.

At breakfast all Shanequa and Tamequa could talk about was they had an auntie and an uncle. As sad as it made Cicely feel, she was happy for them.

When the Sims arrived the first thing the girls wanted to do was show their auntie and uncle where they slept. Cicely led the way. She and Pauletta could help the girls pack. Bernard seemed out of place in the little girls' room, but he bravely listened to their chatter as the women packed.

Simone answered the door when Walter came.

"Hi Walter," she said. He looked as good as she

remembered.

"Simone," was all he said. He stepped into the foyer looking for Cicely. "How is she?"

No, how are you? No, are they here? First question was how is she? So Madeline was right.

"She's fine Walter. They're upstairs packing. The people are nice."

He took the time and really looked at her. Simone was different. Didn't have the edginess to her like when he'd first met her. "How you doing Simone?"

"I'm doing okay Walter."

He kept looking upstairs.

"You can go up if you want," she told him. "I'll take your coat"

Walter gave her his black leather jacket. "I'll wait." He stuck his hands in his pockets and stood there.

When he started to pace Simone said to him, "Go on up. I don't know how long they're going to be. It's already been about an hour."

Walter wondered why she was there. Was it for moral support, or to keep him from getting too close to Cicely? He didn't know the details, but knew Simone and Cicely had been estranged for several months. Either way he was resentful of her presence. This sister had come on to him when they first met. He wasn't interested then, he wasn't interested now.

Simone hadn't done anything to make Walter look at her with distrust. She was about to give him some attitude when he blurted out,

"I love Cicely."

She walked past him smiling to herself. "I'll just go tell them you're here."

When Shanequa and Tamequa found out Walter was there they called his name and came running. They coaxed him up the stairs, Tamequa by pulling on his hand, Shanequa pushing him from behind.

"We got cousins," Tamequa told him.

"Just like you do," interjected Shanequa, recalling meeting Walter's cousins at the birthday party. "We got a Auntie and Uncle too. And Miss CeeCee's sister said we could call her Auntie Simone."

"Auntie Pauletta said Miss CeeCee can come visit. You have to come too Walter," said one of the girls.

He didn't know which one. They had reached the bedroom and Cicely was sitting on the floor folding clothes and placing them in the suitcase. He searched her face for a sign of how she was doing. His heart flipped at the pain he saw there and it was nothing he could do to make it go away.

"Hi," he said to her, basically ignoring everyone else in the room.

Simone stood to the side and watched. There was definitely something happening between these two. Madeline said no, but Simone would bet all her hair pieces these two had, had sex.

Madeline had said, "Go see about your sister. You've stayed away from her too long and she needs you. And don't allow her to let Walter walk out of her life. Do you hear me Simone?"

"Yes Madeline," she'd said, not knowing how Madeline expected her to accomplish that task. Hell, she had screwed up her own marriage.

Cicely spoke and was about to introduce the Sims when Bernard rose from the rocking chair to reach out to Walter. He was obviously relieved there was more testosterone in the house.

"Walter is our friend," said Tamequa.

"But not Miss CeeCee's boyfriend," added Shanequa shaking her head.

All the adults looked at each other before releasing a nervous laugh.

Cicely looked like she wanted to disappear. Walter looked like he wanted to shout, "Yes I am." And Cicely was trying not to look at him.

"I'll explain later," Cicely said to Pauletta quietly. She didn't want them to think Walter had been spending the night while the girls were living with her.

Shanequa went on talking unaware of the embarrassment she'd caused the adults. "This is my Auntie Pauletta and Uncle Bernard. Walter is a plumber."

"Tell you what," said Simone. "Why don't the men go downstairs? Has to be some kind of sports on TV. Us girls will stay up here."

The minute they walked into the living room Walter picked up the remote. He may not be Miss CeeCee's boyfriend, but damn it, he was the alpha male in this house.

They sat on opposite ends of the couch trying to size each other up.

The men sat there for about an hour watching college football. They talked about nothing important. Neither got particularly excited about the game, both preferring pro-football. Each expressing disappointment in their home teams.

Tamequa entered the room and went directly to Walter. She stood at his knees until he noticed her. She started to talk and Bernard watched Walter lean forward and gently pull her thumb out of her mouth.

"What did you say," he didn't yell at her, just quietly asked what she had said.

"Auntie Simone said we gonna get hungry in a little while and you should go get us something to eat. And you should take Uncle Bernard with you." She was slow getting Bernard's name out.

"Is that all she said?" asked Walter.

"No, she said Miss CeeCee would probably like some ribs." She stumbled over the word probably.

Walter looked at Bernard, he knew where they wanted

ribs from.

Bernard stood and asked, "Is this what it's like to live around a bunch of females?"

"Pretty much," said Walter remembering his grandfather's stories.

"Think they'll get upset if we pick up a six pack?"

For the first time Walter smiled at the stranger taking Cicely's kids. "We'll find out."

Despite the circumstances while the men were gone the women began to bond. Cicely sent Shanequa and Tamequa on an errand to get something downstairs and explained the background behind Shanequa's "Walter statement". It gave Pauletta some insight to her niece's need to have a man take care of her.

"Probably because her father died at an early age," supplied Pauletta. "My sister never remarried." After a few moments of silence she spoke again. "Walter made quite an impression on them, does he have kids?"

Simone waited for Cicely to answer. She didn't know Walter all that well and was interested in the answer herself.

"No, no kids. Lots of cousins all ages."

"How old is he?" asked Pauletta.

"Thirty-one."

"Wow," said Pauletta. "That's unusual. Most men his age have at least one baby momma in the background. I worry about my sons."

Cicely wasn't going to reveal Walter's parental pedigree to anyone else so she changed the subject. The girls were lucky they had someone that knew how to take care of their hair. It had been a trial for her.

By the time they returned everyone was hungry. Simone took a beer, Bernard had one and Walter drank two. Pauletta and Cicely declined, but didn't object to the men indulging.

The women spread the food out on the dining room table. Cicely set out plates and paper napkins and let everyone help themselves. Walter had brought enough to feed ten people and wouldn't let Bernard pay for anything except the beer and soft drinks.

Simone, Pauletta and Bernard all noticed how the girls went to Walter and Cicely for everything, fill a cup, clean their hands. Walter ended up letting Tamequa sit on his knee at the table.

Simone had seen all this before at IHop, so it didn't surprise her. What did surprise her was Cicely. While they were cleaning up Cicely said she thought they should take the girls that night.

"Are you sure?" asked Pauletta.

"It won't be any easier in the morning," said Cicely.

"I see how much you and Walter care for them, and honestly if we lived in the same area I would consider leaving them with you." They lived four hours away in Ohio. "But they are my sister's grandbabies."

Which was a moot point, thought Cicely. Because if Pauletta and her husband had been nearby, Cicely would have never met the children.

"I think tonight would be best," Cicely said. She was tired and couldn't hold up the pretense that everything would be fine much longer.

Discovering the Sims's didn't have safety seats for girls, Walter got Cicely's keys and removed them from her car to the Sims's, telling them not to worry about returning them. He helped Bernard carry the luggage out. They would spend the night at the motel and leave first thing in the morning. Cicely promised to send anything that had been left behind. The only thing left to do was say good-bye.

They all stood at the curb with the exception of Simone. She stayed on the porch.

Walter didn't kneel. He picked each girl up individually, hugged them tightly and told them how much he would miss them. In return each girl squeezed him around the neck as tight as they could and kissed him on the cheek. Tamequa put her hands on his cheeks to make him look at her. "Don't worry, Walter," she said. "I'll be your girlfriend when I grow up."

Both girls cried when it was time to say good-bye to Cicely. They wanted to be with family, but felt loyal to Cicely.

"I will come see you," Cicely said.

"Do you promise Miss CeeCee?" asked Shanequa. "Do

you promise?" It was cold and dark and snot was beginning to run from the girls' noses.

Pauletta fumbled in her purse for tissue. She needed one herself.

"She promises," Walter said for her.

Cicely looked at Walter and nodded in acquiescence. If she spoke her tears would flow.

Walter made sure the girls were fastened in the seats correctly then stood on the sidewalk with Cicely. His hand sought her cold fingers and held them tightly.

They both watched until the car was no longer visible.

Cicely pulled her fingers from Walter's hand. "Good night," she said and walked with Simone into the house and closed the door.

Walter stood there not sure what to do. She'd left him standing there alone. All day she'd said less than ten words directly to him. He got in his truck and rested his forehead on the steering wheel. He reached into his jacket pocket for his keys and realized he still had Cicely's. Walter got out of the truck, walked up the front walk, he was about to knock on the outer door when he decided to use her key.

Cicely was seated at the bottom of the staircase. Her face was buried in her hands on her lap. Walter couldn't hear her crying but he could see her shoulders shaking. Simone sat on the stair above her, rubbing her back with the flat of her hand trying to comfort her.

Only Simone looked up when he entered the house, though Cicely had to have felt the draft when he opened the door.

Simone stood and walked upstairs to Cicely's bedroom, closing the door when Walter approached the crying Cicely.

She knew he was standing there, but Cicely refused to acknowledge him.

Walter took her by the forearms and made her stand. Standing on the last step she was nose to nose with Walter. Cicely threw her arms around his neck like Shanequa and Tamequa had and buried her face in his neck. Walter just slipped his arms around her body and held her.

Walter just let her cry; he didn't know what else to do. When she didn't stop he began to worry. "Cee, you have to stop. You're going to make yourself sick."

After a moment she raised her head and looked at him. "I need to blow my nose." Her eyes were red and her eyelashes were in wet clumps.

He tried to step away to get her a tissue or something and she held on tight, not letting him move away from her.

In the end Walter pulled his shirt out of the waistband of his pants, unbuttoned it and gave her his shirttail to blow her nose.

He had on a white V-neck t-shirt. Cicely could see the gold chain and cross he'd inherited from his grandfather. A few hairs were showing in the deepest part of the V and Cicely rubbed at them with her fingers. She wanted to forget about Shanequa and Tamequa. Cicely could look directly into Walter's eyes. The color seemed to shift between green and brown. She couldn't read what he was thinking. Cicely kissed him.

Walter put his hands lightly on her waist and kissed her back.

Cicely broke the kiss and whispered in his ear. "There are no children in my bed."

Walter dropped his hand from her waist. Cicely pushed his jacket and shirt off his shoulders and down his arms, like she'd done her dress the first time they'd made love, letting them fall to the floor.

She ran her hand down his chest past the waistband of his pants and searched for what she wanted. She made a sound and took a sharp intake of breath when he began to grow hard and thicken under the touch of her hand. Cicely put her arms around his neck and pulled up, wrapping her legs around his waist. There was no doubt he would hold her there.

Walter walked up the stairs with Cicely wrapped around him. He stopped on the landing and pinned her against the wall. He began to gyrate his hips against her applying more and more pressure.

"Bed," Cicely gasped.

Walter carried her up the remaining stairs and turned toward her bedroom.

"Simone's in there," she whispered.

But he continued in that direction. Cicely didn't care, they would tell Simone to get out.

He knocked on the closed door and Simone called out to come in.

He put his hand on the doorknob and said to Cicely, "I said to you once, I would stop if you asked me to. You didn't ask me Cicely, but I'm saying stop."

She was so shocked her legs fell from around him. Her toes were barely touching the floor because he still held her.

Walter put his arm under her knees, carried her to the bed and dumped her unceremoniously next to Simone.

He made it down the stairs and when he picked up his jacket and shirt from the floor he looked at the wet stain on his jeans. Well, that hadn't happened to him since he was about seventeen. At least now he washed his own clothes.

He was in his truck, before he realized he still had her keys. There was no way he was going back into that house now. Cicely would be seething, but at least she wasn't crying anymore.

Simone pursed her lips together so she wouldn't say anything. She knew anything she said now would be wrong.

Cicely pounded on the mattress with her fist before sprawling face up on the bed.

Simone wanted to laugh. She knew how Walter got her sister's mind off the girls, but he had not followed through. If she didn't get out of there Cicely was going to find a way to blame this whole thing on her. Simone scrambled off the bed and left the room. It would be even better if she left the house. But if Cicely did have a meltdown, someone had to be there. Somehow though, Simone thought Walter had nipped that in the bud.

Cicely stared at the ceiling, thinking how shallow she was. She would have had mindless sex with Walter in order not to think about Shanequa and Tamequa. And he wouldn't let her. It's a wonder he didn't tell her to "grow up". Life brought pain.

Cicely turned over onto her stomach and grabbed a pillow. Until the girls and Walter, she wasn't feeling anything. She had shut down since the death of her mother. The ache was still there, but now love was crowding the space.

She fell asleep, when she woke in the middle of the night Simone was in the bed with her. Cicely got up, put on her pajamas and went back to bed.

The next morning the sisters did not mention what had happened the day before. Cicely was now a little bit ashamed of what she had done with Walter and had trouble looking her baby sister in the eye.

They didn't really speak until dinnertime.

"Momma would beat our behinds if she knew what we were doing right now," said Simone.

They were sitting on Cicely's bed eating Chinese food. Momma never approved of eating in the bedroom. The TV was on and they had spread a table cloth over the bed to catch any fallen food. Both were in their jammies even though it was barely dark outside and had a collection of their favorite food sitting in containers on the bed.

"You're right about that," said Cicely using chopsticks to pick up a steamed dumpling, one of her favorites.

"They retired momma's preacher," said Simone, also using chopsticks to scoop up some rice noodles.

"Seriously," said Cicely with disbelief. "How do you know that?"

"Been going to her church," said Simone, her mouth full of food.

"Get out," said Cicely jiggling the bed and having to catch a container before it spilled over.

"I've been doing that a lot lately. Sunday service, Wednesday night bible study, the whole nine yards."

Cicely waited for her to say more.

"They have a younger minister, more contemporary. Think they are trying to grow their young people membership."

Cicely didn't want to hear about the church, she wanted to know what else Simone had been up to.

"I quit my job Cicely. I'm going back home to Evan and Olivia."

Cicely paid no attention to the food on the bed and reached over to hug her. "I'm so happy for you. What bought that on?"

"Some deep soul searching and counseling. You all made me look at my self- destructive behavior. Evan and I have some work to do, but I think we can make it. He's already downsized so between us we should have a comfortable life."

"You could always move back here. I got plenty of room."

"Cicely, you tell Walter what he wants to hear and you won't have all these empty rooms. Walter would steal kids for you."

"Walter deserves to have kids of his own."

"Cicely, you're only forty...."

"Forty-one, have a birthday next month."

"Okay, forty-one, those eggs are still poppin'."

"Simone, I think I've started perimenopause. I couldn't tell you the last time I had a regular period.' Cicely didn't want to talk about it.

"Then you need to see a doctor, because that is not normal. Tell me one thing," said Simone pointing her chopsticks at Cicely. "How is he in bed?"

"The best," said Cicely without thinking then putting her hand over her mouth at what Simone had got her to admit.

"I knew it," said Simone giving the bed a bounce. "Madeline said she didn't believe you had done the nasty with Walter, but looking at him I knew she was wrong. You wouldn't be able to hold him off long if he made up his mind. Tell me about it."

"I'm not going to do that," Cicely clearly embarrassed.

"Why not? We used to when we were younger. Remember lying in bed saying so and so didn't know what to do with his equipment. And I told you it took Evan more than a minute to get the hang of it."

"Okay," said Cicely ready to throw her a tidbit. "Walter ain't need no minute."

"Ooooo," said Simone. "Then why you keep blocking him?"

Cicely had spent a lot of time thinking about that during the night. She could no longer say his youth. Walter's actions the night before proved he had more maturity than she'd given him credit for. "I'd have to surrender Simone. And I don't know if I can surrender."

"We're more alike than I thought. We both want control of the situation. Face it Cicely, you are not going to be able to control Walter. Just because you're older than him doesn't mean you know everything. Look at Madeline. She doesn't know everything. She didn't know you were sleeping with Walter."

"One time, well one night."

"Oooo, twice in one night," commented Simone.

"Actually three times," confessed Cicely.

"Now you braggin'," said Simone. "You better surrender big sister."

Walter didn't expect to see her at church Sunday, when he accompanied his grandmother. He saw her friend Anita and for a change he was the one giving the update. Shanequa and Tamequa were on their way home with family.

"So you and Cicely settle that misunderstanding about the woman at your house?" asked Anita.

Walter rubbed the back of his neck. "You know about that huh?"

Anita looked at him and waited.

"Short version?"

"Any version," said Anita. As much as she liked Walter he had hurt her friend.

"Ex. Haven't seen her in four years. She's pregnant and needed a place to stay for a couple of days. I was going to tell Cicely, but she showed up before I had a chance."

Pregnant? Cicely hadn't told her that part, no wonder she had been so determined not to talk to Walter again.

"We straight?" Walter asked her.

Anita gave him a thumbs up.

CHAPTER 24

Monday morning Cicely couldn't find her keys. She searched an hour before remembering Walter letting himself into the house. She had to use her emergency set of keys to go to work which meant she had to talk to him and possibly see him. She was still mortified by her behavior, though Simone tried to reassure her Walter would understand.

"Face it," Simone said. "He loves you and you love him."

Re-connecting with her sister felt good. Cicely always thought it was her responsibility to watch out for her baby sister. Now Simone was watching out for her.

Simone had returned to her place that morning to start packing for her return home. Cicely volunteered to help, but Simone said she had it, for Cicely to go to work and not think about Walter or the girls. Her plan was to leave Wednesday morning and take her time driving home. She and Olivia would share a room until she and Evan felt it was going to work out. Simone was confident it would.

Sunday night after she and Simone cleaned all the Chinese food off the bed they called Madeline and Bernice to assure them Cicely was going to be just fine. Simone would call them later and tell the older sisters exactly why Cicely would be fine. The Sims's called to let her know they had made it home safely.

Madeline was right. Cicely would take in more kids, she just needed time to recoup in between.

Wednesday started out like any other cold rainy November day. She and Simone had an early dinner together the night before because Simone was leaving in the morning. Now, Simone felt guilty leaving Cicely alone and nothing had been resolved with Walter yet. Cicely had not given up hope Simone and Evan might consider moving to Buffalo. It didn't have everything to offer Chicago did, but the cost of living was much cheaper. She would have liked to have one of her sisters near.

As much as she wanted to, Cicely didn't call the girls. She and Pauletta had agreed to give them some time to get settled before she talked to them. That way the separation from Cicely wouldn't be so fresh.

After working in the office three straight days she came home tired. With no children there was no reason for her not to work nine-to-five, but it wasn't something she was used to. The only up-side was she was too tired to dwell on Walter. She still hadn't talked to him and missed him.

Wanting to feel warm and toasty she decided a bowl of soup and a grill cheese sandwich would be dinner. And nothing would be more comfortable than a pair of sweat pants and sweat shirt with her ratty bedroom slippers. Simone had called her at lunchtime to say she was on the road, expected to be home in a few hours, and would call her back then.

The phone rang just as she was about to take the first spoon of her soup. So sure it was Simone she didn't look at the caller id.

"Cicely?" It was Evan.

"Evan," she was glad to hear from her brother-in-law. "Simone told me you were…"

"Simone is dead Cicely." He said flatly.

"No, Evan, I talked to her. She's just taking her time coming back to you and Olivia."

"They think her vehicle started to hydroplane in the rain and she crashed into a bridge abutment. She was almost home." He was starting to cry.

"That's wrong Evan. Simone was a very good driver. It must be some kind of mistake." Cicely was starting to shake. "She was coming home to you and Olivia." She repeated.

"I had to identify the body Cicely." He was openly weeping on the phone now.

She dropped the phone and hugged her self. She could still hear him talking as if through a tunnel. "I've talked to Madeline and Bernice. You were the last one I called. I have to go home and tell Olivia. I have to tell my baby her mother is dead."

Cicely hit the end button on the phone. She put on the jacket she had worn to work and picked up her keys and walked out of the house. She passed her car in the driveway and kept walking. She didn't know where she was headed until she showed up on Walter's doorstep.

Walter had been trying to figure out his next move with Cicely. He'd finished up his latest job and had come home taken a shower and wanted to relax. When the doorbell rang he thought it was his mother wanting to talk about their newest project.

Cicely stood before him, cold wet and shivering.

"My sister is dead Walter. Simone is dead." She said without feeling.

Walter gathered her in his arms.

"Make love to me."

He removed her wet coat and tossed it to the side.

Once they were in the bedroom he removed the rest of her wet clothing and used the damp towel lying on the floor from his shower, to dry her off, rather than leave her alone the few seconds it would take to get a dry one.

Walter pulled the covers back so Cicely could slip between them. Quickly he removed his clothing and laid next to her.

Since uttering her declaration he make love to her, Cicely had not said another word.

Walter looked at her face. She lay perfectly still. He saw tears trickling from behind her closed eyes and he pulled her into his embrace.

Finally he felt her body relax and she fell asleep. Slowly

he eased out of bed trying not to disturb her. Putting his clothes back on Walter watched her sleep. Much like she'd watched him the first time they'd made love. Every once in a while her body would shudder and she would whimper in her sleep.

Though it had felt like hours, only an hour had passed since Cicely arrived, it was only eight o'clock. Walter had heard his cell ringing continuously while he held her and it was ringing now as he came downstairs.

"Walter," said Anita. "Is Cicely with you?"

"Yeah, she is."

"Is she alright?" She and her husband had gone by the house to look for Cicely when Madeline had called and said she wasn't answering her phone. Walter's was the only place she could think of where Cicely would go.

"She's taking it very hard. I think she's in shock."

"Have her call her sisters."

"I will," said Walter before hanging up. He wouldn't disturb her now. Then he heard her phone ringing in her jacket pocket.

"Hello," he answered seeing it was her sister Madeline.

"Cicely," the woman cried in response. "You aren't Cicely. How did you get my sister's phone? Who are you?"

"It's Walter, Madeline. Walter the plumber. Cicely is with me."

"Let me speak to her," she sobbed. "Walter I have to

speak to her."

"She's sleeping Madeline. I don't want to wake her." He was speaking softly and glanced up the stairs to see if Cicely had stirred.

Madeline was crying uncontrollably on the phone and the next voice Walter heard was male.

"Hello, I'm Preston, Madeline's husband. Is Cicely alright?"

"She's asleep. I really don't want to wake her. She's at my house."

"You know what happened?" asked Preston.

"Only Simone died. I just saw her a few days ago."

"There was a car accident. She was on the interstate."

"Oh God," said Walter as he sat on the sofa, he rubbed hand over his face.

"We've been trying to call Cicely."

"I got her," said Walter. "I'll take care of her. She'll be okay with me."

"Walter I imagine we'll be talking a lot the next few days."

"Take my number." And Walter gave both his cell numbers.

"I'll call Bernice and tell her we found Cicely," said Preston. "If you would call her friend Anita and tell her Cicely is with you."

"I just spoke to her," replied Walter.

"Good, good."

"Is there anything else I can do?"

"Evan, that's Simone's husband, is going to call back tomorrow. I'll talk to you then. Thanks for seeing to Cicely," said Preston, then hung up to take care his wife.

Now he was back upstairs watching Cicely sleep. Walter saw her shudder again and climbed back into bed with her. She was cold even under the covers. He undressed while under the covers and pressed his body to hers to share his body heat.

Walter put his arms around her to pull her even closer. He pressed his lips to her neck. "Poor Cee," he whispered.

It was after eight the next morning when Walter woke up again. Cicely was still by his side, her back to his front. She no longer felt cold to his touch.

"Cee," he gently shook her shoulder.

"I just want to sleep Walter. I won't bother you. Just let me sleep."

"You have to call your sisters. You have to let them know you're alright."

"I'm with you. I'm alright. Simone knows I'm with you."

Walter felt the hairs on his neck rise. "Cicely, everyone knows you are with me. Please call your sisters. They are worried about you."

"Just let me sleep Walter. I'll call them later."

"Cicely, I'm going to get dressed. When I'm done you are going to call your sisters."

She didn't even look at him when he got up naked. Walter grabbed everything he needed and left her alone.

An hour passed before he went to check on her. She was shivering again and crying. He found an extra blanket to throw over her and went downstairs to make a call.

"Ma," he said. "Can you come over? I'm worried about Cicely. She's here. Her sister died in a car accident yesterday."

"Poor girl. First the kids, now this. Give me a few minutes. I'll be right there."

"Can you bring a night gown or something? She showed up last night soaked to the bone. I think she walked here."

Walter opened the door a crack so his mother didn't have to use her key. When she came in she thrust a paper bag into his hands. "Make a cup of hot tea, put plenty of sugar in it and some lemon." In her arms she had a bundle of clothes. She left him to do what she'd said and went directly upstairs.

Janice couldn't even see the top of Cicely's head when she walked into the bedroom.

"Go away Walter." Cicely's voice was muffled by all of the covers.

"It's not Walter," said Janice sitting on the edge of the bed near Cicely's head.

Cicely peeked at her and started to bawl.

"Let's get some clothes on you before you make yourself sick." Janice helped her slip a flannel nightgown over her head. Over that she put a hoodie with a zipper. She searched Walters's dresser drawers until she found a clean pair of sweat socks and slipped them on Cicely's ice cold feet. Then she wrapped her arms around the younger woman and let her cry. Janice was sure Walter had done everything right. But he could only postpone what Cicely was going to have to go through. When he appeared in the doorway with the cup of tea, she took it and shooed him away.

When Cicely finished her crying jag, Janice went to the bathroom and brought back toilet paper for her to blow her nose. "I told my son, everyone needs to keep a box of tissues. The only time he listened is when he has a cold."

Cicely managed a small smile for her.

"Now drink some tea." Janice placed the cup in her hands making sure she gripped it with both hands to feel the warmth of the cup.

Cicely had only taken a few sips when she tried getting out of the bed. "I think I'm going to throw up."

Janice moved out of her way and followed her to the bathroom. While Cicely leaned over the toilet, Janice pressed a cold rag to her neck.

"Is everything okay?" Walter called up the stairs hearing the rapid footsteps and Cicely's retching.

"Nothing out of the ordinary Walter," said his mother. "Go back to doing whatever it was you were doing."

Walter looked at his hands. He wasn't doing anything. He didn't know what to do.

"I'm sorry," said Cicely as Janice wiped her face and mouth with the cool face cloth.

"Honey you have nothing to be sorry for. You just lost your sister." Janice led her back to the bed.

Tears began to fall from Cicely eyes again, this time without the body racking sobs of before.

"Have you talked to your sisters?"

Cicely hung her head. "No."

"Walter," Janice called. "Bring Cicely her phone so she can talk to her sisters."

"Do you want me to leave?" Janice asked when Walter put the phone in Cicely's hand.

Cicely shook her head no. Walter left without being told. He couldn't stand to see her cry. It didn't feel strange to him, he called his mother to help care for a naked woman he had in his bed. The woman he wanted to make his wife.

"Cicely are you alright?" Is the first thing Madeline said. "We were so afraid when we couldn't find you."

"I'll be okay. I'm at Walter's."

Janice held her hand as she talked.

"How are Evan and Olivia?" Cicely asked.

"We haven't talked to him yet. Bernice is here. Cicely this was not supposed to happen. She was going home." Fresh tears started for Madeline.

"She told me. I told her, she; Evan and Olivia should come live with me."

"You know she wasn't angry with you anymore?" asked Madeline.

"I know."

"You aren't going to be alone are you Cicely?"

Cicely squeezed Janice's hand. "No I have someone with me. Call me as soon as you know something"

"I will. And Cicely call me if you need me or Bernice. I love you"

"I will. I love you too." She ended the call.

Janice threw the covers back so Cicely could slip between them. "You go to sleep. You'll sleep better now that you've talked to your sister."

Walter met his mother at the bottom of the stairs. "Is she okay?"

Janice looked at her son. He wasn't like his father. She had her father to thank for that. "Let her sleep. Then take her home. When you take her home, stay with her. I don't want to see you back here." But she knew without saying it, Walter wouldn't be back. It would take dynamite to move him from

Cicely's side.

While she slept Walter packed a bag and put it in his truck. No need to let Cicely see what he was planning. He threw her wet clothes in the dryer, looking at the scruffy slippers, he put them in the dryer too. He didn't know how she'd made it to his house essentially barefoot. It was after the fact but he became angry with her for walking to his house. Anything could have happened to her. The idea scared him shitless.

Walter was still angry when he took the dry clothes to her.

She was awake and sitting on the side of the bed.

"Why didn't you call me? You know I would have come to you."

Cicely looked at him standing there. He was angry; she could see it coming off him in waves.

"Something could have happened to you. You could have ended up in one of those boarded up houses and nobody'd find your body until spring. Dammit Cicely, that was a stupid thing to do." He held her dry clothes out to her.

Seriously, she thought. She had just lost her sister and he was upset about something that didn't happen. Cicely didn't even remember making a conscious decision to come to Walter. All she knew is she felt completeness when he put his arms around her and now he was angry. She couldn't help it, her eyes filled with tears. She was sad and angry. Her sister had died, she'd come to Walter for comfort.

Walter hadn't meant to make her cry. He wanted her to understand just how much she meant to him. How as he going to explain to his mother he'd made Cicely cry again?

Cicely stood, took her clothes from Walter and went into the bathroom to change. She didn't care they had shared a bed together. Many times during the night she had awakened and felt his body heat and heard the soft words he was murmuring to her. Cicely was not going to give him the satisfaction of seeing her naked.

Walter didn't move. He preferred the Cicely that took swings at him when she was upset with him. Not the silently crying one.

She did not talk to him at all during the ride home. She did look at him strangely when he followed her into the house, but didn't object. The bowl of soup and grilled cheese were still sitting on the kitchen table. It would be a very long time before Cicely could eat that meal without thinking about Simone. But looking at it she was now ravenous. She hadn't eaten since noon yesterday. Cicely looked at Walter, if he had breakfast at his house he certainly had not offered her any.

Since it had been raining Walter went to the basement to make sure everything was still dry. He stayed down there as long as he could without it becoming obvious he was avoiding Cicely. When he came back up she was standing in the kitchen eating a peanut butter sandwich. He knew that because he could smell it. Cicely also had a glass of cold milk. Walter couldn't help it, his stomach growled.

She looked at him and retrieved the jar of peanut butter from the cabinet and made a second sandwich, put it on a saucer and thrust it at his belly.

Walter looked at the sandwich and said, "I didn't ask you to fix that for me."

She moved away and made like she was going to toss the sandwich in the garbage. Walter stopped her and held the saucer above his head. "Why you have to be so ornery?"

"In case you forgot, my sister died yesterday."

"Is that the only time you're willing to have sex with me Cicely? When someone dies?" He regretted the words the second they came out of his mouth.

"You never refuse," she yelled. Her fists were tightly balled at her sides and she was trying very hard not to cry. "Oh, I forgot, yes you did. The night they took the girls from me you refused. And last night. You refused last night. What happened to the Walter that said he would be there for me? The one that said if I need him, he would always be there."

He dropped the saucer, it shattered on the floor and he wrapped his arms around her.

She had her face buried in his chest and pounded on his arms with her fists.

"I'm sorry," he crooned. His chin rested on the top of her head. "I'm sorry Cee, I never meant to hurt you. I love you so much."

"They're gone Walter. Simone is gone. The girls are

gone."

His phone was clipped to his belt and began to ring. With one arm still around Cicely he answered the phone.

"Hello"

"Walter, this is Preston."

He told Cicely who it was and she pulled away to get a paper towel to clean her face.

"I don't have any information," Preston said. "Evan can't make any decisions. Madeline and I are flying out tomorrow to help him. Bernice and her husband Louis are coming to be with Cicely."

Walter told Cicely Bernice was coming. And she nodded.

"Are you at Cicely's house?" Preston asked.

"Yes we are. Have them call me and I'll pick them up at the airport."

"Will do," said Preston hanging up.

Walter clipped the phone back on his belt. Cicely tried to walk past him and he stopped her by grabbing her arm. "I'm new at this Cee. Don't hold that against me."

"I have to make some phone calls Walter. I can't leave everything to Madeline and Bernice. Other people have to be notified."

He nodded and released her arm. He found the broom and swept up the mess he'd made wishing he could clean up the mess he'd made with Cicely that easy.

Anita was there as soon as she finished work. She brought food. If she was surprised Walter was there, she didn't show it. She and Cicely ensconced themselves in Cicely's bedroom leaving Walter alone. He ate and cleaned up after himself. He took a plate up to Cicely, because he hadn't seen her eat anything since the peanut butter sandwich she hadn't finished and asked Anita to make sure she ate something.

While they were in the bedroom he went out to his truck and got his bag and stuffed it in the downstairs closet. He figured there would be another argument when Cicely found out he was intending to stay. Walter checked the voice mail on his business phone and transferred them to his uncle. He didn't know how long Cicely would need him. When he couldn't find anything else to do he settled in front of the TV.

"I'm so sorry," Anita was telling her best friend as they sat on the bed. "Simone could be alright when she wanted to." If anyone else had said that Cicely would have jumped to Simone's defense.

"She went back to momma's church." Cicely told her.

"Did they kick her out after that stunt Madeline pulled?"

Cicely related what Simone had told her.

"So, she was going to church?"

"And going back to Evan." Tears started falling again.

Anita passed her a bottle of water and urged her to eat. "You're going to get dehydrated and sick if you keep this up."

"I can't stop."

"Yes you can," said Anita in her no-nonsense voice. "Stop dwelling on it. You made up, dwell on that. Everyone doesn't get that opportunity. You're making yourself sick and worrying Walter to death."

"Easier said, than done."

"I never said it would be easy. In all the years I've know you, you've never done things the easy way. But you do get things done. So I know you can do this."

"I feel like I've lost so much."

"And you have. We should not have to deal with a sibling dying at our age. That shouldn't happen until we're back in diapers."

Cicely could help it, she smiled at the image that statement created.

She hugged her friend. "What would I do without you?"

Anita returned the hug. "You'd be downstairs jumping Walter's bones. Some of that affirmation stuff you were talking about."

Cicely dropped her arms. "I was wrong about that."

"So, you gonna admit I was right and he has feelings for you?" asked Anita

"No." It wasn't that simple and Cicely was still trying to digest the fact Walter hadn't left.

Anita shook her head. She loved her friend dearly, but

Cicely's need to be right all the time puzzled her.

"I'll be back tomorrow," she said promising to bring more food.

Cicely walked her friend to the front door and cast a glance at Walter in the living room. In what she believed was typical male fashion, he was sprawled on the couch asleep with one hand covering his lap. She wondered why men did that. She entered the room and removed the remote from his other hand and turned the TV off. She would leave him right where he was.

Cicely went upstairs to get ready for bed. She'd have to get Bernice's old bedroom ready tomorrow.

An hour and a half and she still hadn't fallen asleep. There were no little bodies in the bedroom next to hers anymore. And even though Simone had only been there a few days, she missed her sister's warm body next to her, because it would never happen again. She went downstairs.

She lifted his hand and let it fall back into his lap, startling him.

Walter opened his eyes and looked at her. The TV was off and she had turned on every light in the room so he had to shield his eyes with his hand. Cicely had on pink flannel pajamas with ugly black cats. On her head was a bonnet thing. If he wasn't mistaken she still had on his socks. He waited for her to tell him to get out. There would be an argument, because he wasn't going anywhere.

"Are you spending the night?" she asked

"Yes," he said hesitantly not sure of what to expect.

Cicely dumped the blanket and pillow she was holding on his head and turned to leave the room.

Walter moved fast and took her by the hand.

"I love you Cee. And I'm going to keep saying it until you believe me. I want a relationship with you. You take care of everybody; I want to be the one that takes care of Cee. I don't want you to feel that I am not here for you. This is a hard time for you and it was my job to understand that better. I failed I'm sorry."

"Walter," she began. She wanted to say he didn't fail her.

"You don't have to say anything. Just listen. I'll be by your side through all of this, even if you fight me. You wouldn't fight me if you didn't feel something. I'm not going to let you push me away. When we met I told you all about me. I said we could be friends if that's all you wanted. But I can't just be your friend. I want to be your friend, I want to be your lover. I may say things in the heat of the moment, like I did earlier and I'm sorry. You got a temper. I got one too. I've never been in this position before. Never felt about someone the way I feel about you. I shouldn't have said that about you crawling in my bed. Cee, I'll take you crawling in my bed any day. I love you." He gave her hand a squeeze and let her go.

It was a long time before either of them fell asleep.

The next morning she wanted to run. All the recent

upheavals had caused her to renege on her routine. This morning she wanted to run, gloomy skies or not. There was no rain to deter her and the cold weather wouldn't bother her. Anita was right. She and her sister had made up. She would dwell on that.

Walter was in the kitchen having coffee when she came down dressed to run. She knew he had checked on her during the night because she'd heard him creep up the stairs and stop in her doorway, before turning and going back down stairs.

He looked at her over the rim of his cup. Thinking of the past few days he asked, "You up to that?"

She began doing stretches to warm up before running. "Yes, I need this. I have to get back on track."

At least she was talking to him. "Anything you want me to do before your sister gets here? If not I have some errands to run."

"Do your errands Walter. They can call me if they can't reach you."

It seemed they had a truce. She hadn't kicked him out. Pushing the envelope Walter kissed her on the forehead. He was surprised she let him.

Cicely didn't have to think while she ran, basically put one foot in front of the other. She didn't have to think about Shanequa and Tamequa, though she was sure they would be fine. She didn't think about Simone or Walter.

Physically she was feeling good. She had a good pace going, so she was totally unprepared when the nausea struck.

Cicely stepped off the path and stood in the grass dry heaving. There was nothing to throw up but the juice she drank before leaving the house.

No one paid attention. They just assumed she was another runner trying to push herself.

Cicely dropped to the cold damp grass and sat crossed legged trying to breathe through her nose to fight the feeling. A woman pushing a toddler in a running stroller stopped and leaned over her.

"Are you alright?" the concerned woman asked.

Cicely nodded yes, she wasn't quite ready to trust herself to speak.

"Are you pregnant?" asked the woman. "I was the same way with this one," she said indicating the child in the stroller. "First trimester I had to give up running. Not this one though," she said patting her burgeoning stomach.

"Here have some water. No, on second thought that might make you sick again. She rummaged in her bag and pulled out animal crackers. "Have some of these. I always carry them with me for my son."

Cicely took the cookie and gingerly bit into it.

"You shouldn't keep sitting on the cold ground. Are you sure you're alright?" The woman asked again when Cicely unsteadily got to her feet. "I would drive you home, but I walked here."

"I'm not pregnant," Cicely finally managed to say.

The expectant woman began to apologize profusely. "It's not like you're fat or anything. I guess I see a woman throwing up in public and assume she's pregnant like me. Please forgive me."

"Thank you for the cookies," said Cicely as she tried to distance herself from the stranger.

She walked home slowly. She was not pregnant. Granted she had not thought to ask Walter to use a condom until after the fact, and that was to prevent getting an STD. It never occurred to her she might get pregnant. Women her age needed help getting pregnant. Evidently Walter was the only help she needed. Except she wasn't pregnant.

She wasn't pregnant. Her sister had just died. This was not a convenient time to be pregnant. What had Simone said to her? Let Walter give you babies. Cicely let out a sob and then glanced around to make sure no one was looking.

She was weepy because her sister was dead. She was weepy and throwing up because she no longer had Shanequa and Tamequa, not because she was having Walter's baby.

Oh God, Walter. Walter never said he wanted babies. He said he wanted her. If Walter wanted babies he would have had them by now. Pauletta had said as much.

She wasn't pregnant. She was emotionally overwrought because of everything that was happening. So she'd let some crazy pregnant woman get inside her head.

The closer she got to home the faster she walked. Okay,

when was her last period? After the girls started school, when she'd had no intentions of having sex with Walter. Her menses were starting to become further and further apart. Just because she did not have one last month did not mean she was pregnant.

When she got home she would go buy one of those home pregnancy test. No need to panic until she was sure. It wouldn't be the first time she missed because she was stressed.

Cicely turned the corner to her street and saw her car was gone, but Walter's truck was still there. Bernice must have called and he'd taken her car to the airport. Why hadn't she taken her keys back from him? She *didn't* have keys to his house or vehicle.

She didn't know how long he'd been gone. Checking her cell, he nor Bernice had called her. There was no way she could make it to a store and back on foot before he returned with Bernice and Louis. She would have to come up with an excuse to leave the house, like Bernice would let her leave the house alone.

Cicely put her hand to her mouth to check her breath and caught a faint whiff of vomit. First order of business, get cleaned up.

CHAPTER 25

Bernice recognized Walter at the airport from when he'd worked at the house. Despite what Madeline said, she wasn't sure this was the man for her sister. Personally she thought he was too young. She was cordial when she introduced Walter to Louis, but was shocked to see he was driving Cicely's car.

"Why didn't Cicely come?" asked Bernice as they loaded the luggage in the trunk.

"We didn't know you were coming this early, so she went for a run."

We, thought Bernice. When had they become a couple?

They rode to the house in silence.

Cicely had brushed her teeth, taken a shower and now was behind the closed door of her bedroom studying her nude body in the mirror. The scale hadn't shown any weight gain. She cupped her breasts, they were no bigger. Did your breasts get bigger in six weeks? She looked closer in the mirror. Were her nipples always that dark? She should have checked the internet for pregnancy symptoms before coming upstairs. Why were the only symptoms people talked about were missed periods and nausea?

Cicely placed her hands on her bare belly where Walter's baby would be growing, if she was indeed pregnant. She'd be forty-one years old. This situation was not unheard of.

She turned from the mirror to pick up her cell. She texted Anita.

"Bring pregnancy test when you come."

Immediately she got a text back.

"??????!!!!!"

At the same time her cell rang someone knocked at the bedroom door. She hadn't heard anyone come in the house.

She grabbed the discarded towel to cover herself before Bernice entered without waiting for permission.

"Cicely, I thought you had gotten over that walking around naked," said Bernice stepping into the room and closing the door.

"I was about to get dressed Bernice." Her phone was ringing incessantly. She knew if she didn't answer Anita would not give up. "I have to get this," she said, wrapping the towel about her.

"I can't talk now, Bernice is here," she said before Anita could get a word in.

"Are you?" is all Anita said.

"Don't know," said Cicely. "I'll see you later," and ended the call.

The sisters faced each other. Bernice looked good with her weight lost. Cicely thought they looked like each other more than ever.

Bernice was slightly embarrassed to see her sister standing there with just a towel wrapped around her, but needing to touch her overrode that feeling. She gathered Cicely into a hug.

Again it hit Cicely their baby sister was dead.

Louis hadn't formed an opinion about Walter yet. They shook hands at the airport and that was about it. The boy had a firm handshake. At fifty-two he could have been Walter's father. The only thing he knew about Walter was he had his own business. That was enough to earn the young man some respect, but Louis didn't have time to worry about Cicely. He was too busy praying this tragedy wouldn't cause Bernice to begin having symptoms. There had been none since the doctor had placed her on medication.

Walter let Louis lead the way upstairs as the carried the bags, because he wasn't sure which room they were sleeping. Cicely's door was closed. So she and Bernice must have been talking. He felt Bernice's coolness toward him, but her husband was a little harder to read.

The men ended up in the kitchen waiting for the women. Louis asked Walter had he known Simone and the truth was he had met her but really hadn't gotten a chance to know her. They'd become acquainted the same time he'd met Bernice, when the basement flooded. Walter didn't feel comfortable talking to Louis about how hard Cicely had taken it when she gave the girls up, so he decided to leave.

He called up to Cicely to tell her he was leaving. She

told him to wait and came downstairs to see him out.

"I'll be back later. You aren't going to get rid of me this easy. Just want to get some things done and give you some time alone with your sister and brother-in-law."

"Walter," she started.

Cicely wasn't sure what she wanted to say. It wouldn't be fair to tell him she might be pregnant and it turned out to be a false alarm. And she didn't want him to feel obligated.

"You don't have to sleep on the couch tonight." She ended up saying.

He smiled at her. Cicely had just invited him to her bed.

Bernice spied on the couple from the top of the stairs. She still wasn't sure what to make of Walter. "Do you think it's okay he stays here?" she asked when the door closed behind him. "I mean, Cicely, he has a key to the house and everything. What if he'd been the one to walk in on you instead of me?"

"News flash Bernice, he's seen me naked."

"You don't have to flaunt him in front of family."

"Bernice what do you have against Walter? He doesn't hide me from his family." And Cicely realized that was true. He'd never tried to keep her hidden. His mother held her hand while she was throwing up in the toilet. How many ways was she going to make Walter show her he loved her?

"I could be that boy's momma," said Bernice coming down the stairs.

"But you're not. And he is not a boy. He's a grown ass man," said Cicely heading toward the kitchen, because now that the nausea had passed she was hungry.

She left Bernice standing on the stairs with her mouth open.

Madeline called later to say she and Preston were with Evan. She had given it a lot of thought and wanted to bring Simone home. If Evan would agree, Simone would come home.

Bernice was upstairs and Louis was watching TV in the living room when Anita arrived. Cicely dragged her into the kitchen.

"Did you bring it?" she asked

Anita held up the drug store bag apart from the bags of food she had brought. "Tell me he used a condom and it broke." She said in a hushed voice, unable to prevent taking a poke at her friend.

"Not funny," said Cicely taking the bag. "I'm going to the downstairs bathroom, I don't know when Bernice will come down, but to keep her from asking about me, I'll leave it in there, under the sink. After the time limit you can go read it for me. If I keep running back to the bathroom she'll know something's up. And I don't know when Walter will be back."

"And if it's positive, how you gonna keep that off your face? You're either going to be grinning like an idiot, or crying like a fool."

"Please Anita I could use a little compassion today."

"Go," said Anita. "I'll start unpacking the groceries."

Cicely sat on the toilet and read the instructions. She peed on the stick and placed it in the vanity cabinet. She would get rid of the evidence later. Five minutes it said. She stopped in the living room to invite Louis into the kitchen to see what Anita had brought to cook, holding up her hand to let her friend know how long to wait. And started talking to Louis to see which ingredients they could use.

Anita was about to check when Bernice called Cicely's name.

She followed Cicely to the foyer where Bernice was holding the test stick.

"Are you pregnant Cicely?" She demanded.

How was she to know her sister would come downstairs to use the bathroom when there was a perfectly good toilet right across the hall from her room?

"You have to tell me Bernice," said Cicely indicating what Bernice was holding in her hand.

Bernice thrust it at her, almost dropping it before Cicely had a chance to take it. She and Anita both looked. Plus three weeks it said.

Anita was happy for her friend, even if Cicely wasn't

sure how she felt about it yet.

"How could you let that happen?" questioned Bernice.

"I imagine the same way it happened to you."

Anita hid her smile behind her hand.

"And does your young boyfriend know?" asked Bernice with her arms folded across her chest.

"No," said Cicely shaking the stick at her. "And don't you dare tell him. Don't you tell anyone. My priorities right now are Simone, and Evan and Olivia." She couldn't help it, she began to cry and took off for the privacy of her bedroom.

Bernice brushed pass Anita to go into the kitchen with her husband. It was always Cicely and Simone that caused the chaos in the Macklin household. How would she explain to her teenaged daughter her forty-year-old aunt was unmarried and pregnant? It had been bad enough telling Jeanine the reason Evan and Simone had broken up. Some people called her old fashioned, she didn't care. That's how she was raised and she wanted to instill the same values in her daughter. That she'd put her daughter on birth control at sixteen didn't factor into anything.

Anita tapped on the door before letting herself in. "Happy tears or sad tears?" she asked.

"Both," said Cicely staying prone on the bed.

"How far along?"

"About six weeks," sniffed Cicely.

She knew the only time Cicely and Walter had made love. "He caught that the first time, huh?"

"The only time. How could I have been so stupid?"

"You weren't stupid," said Anita. "You were ready. He loves you. And don't deny you love him."

"This isn't a good time," said Cicely, rolling over to sit upright.

"If it wasn't a good time God would not have let it happen. He sent you a man now He's sending you a baby."

"What do I say? Oh by the way Walter, you knocked me up."

"Well you gonna have to tell him soon. At six weeks it won't be long before you have a little baby bump. And with him being around twenty-four seven he's gonna notice something."

"I could send him away until I'm ready to tell him," she said knowing that wasn't a viable solution.

"Cicely I think you've tried that. It ain't working."

"I don't want him to be around just because he got me pregnant." Cicely finally admitted.

"I don't know why you doubt how that man feels about you. All you're doing is tormenting yourself and him."

"I have to at least wait until everything with Simone is concluded."

Anita agreed on that point but said, "You got to get yourself to a doctor. Now wash your face and come downstairs.

Don't let Bernice make you hide in this room. I think I heard the doorbell. It might be Walter and he'll know something else is going on if you stay up here."

"Walter has a key," said Cicely casually, rising from the bed to do as her friend suggested.

Anita looked at her with a raised eyebrow. Walter was moving things right along and she approved. She would stay this evening to offer moral support against Bernice, but after that Cicely was on her own.

It wasn't Walter at the door, but a few cousins. Hearing the news they had come to offer their condolences. No one seemed to notice that Bernice was pre-occupied and barely speaking to Cicely.

Walter arrived shortly afterwards and no one took offense that he was there. They accepted him as Cicely's friend and left it at that.

He waited until everyone had gone to bed before retrieving his bag and going upstairs. The only light in the room was from the TV. Walter stripped to his underwear and slid into bed. Cicely had on those god-awful pajamas but snuggled up to his body heat the minute he got settled.

Walter had lived with Perri for a little while and he took the pajamas to mean don't touch me. 'It's that time of month.' That was okay. He wasn't going anywhere. He turned off the TV and went to sleep.

He woke up in the middle of the night to find Cicely tucked neatly under his arm and her bent knee trapping his thigh. Her hand rested on his chest, he covered it with his own. She had a soft snore so he knew she was asleep. "I hope when all this is over you will marry me Cicely Macklin," he said into the darkness.

Madeline and Preston arrived Sunday afternoon with Evan and Olivia in tow. Evan had agreed to everything Madeline suggested. While they did have friends where they lived, where Simone had grown up was a centralized location for family and friends still in the area. Madeline had talked to the funeral director that handled their mother's homegoing and he would take care of everything. The new minister at Momma's church remembered Simone and would do the funeral service that coming Wednesday. Afterwards she would be cremated.

Madeline wasn't surprised Walter picked them up at the airport. Preston, Madeline's husband gave him a much warmer greeting than Louis. He said he was glad to be able to put a face to the person he had spoken to on the phone. Olivia gave Walter a hug and Evan looked shell shocked.

The first one Cicely hugged was Olivia then Evan. His expression was the one Walter had when his grandfather had died. The house was full now. All the remaining sisters were back home. Six months ago none of them would have thought to be back at the house under these circumstances.

The first chance she got, Madeline pulled Cicely to the

side. "How far along are you?"

Cicely quickly glanced around to make sure no one else had heard. "How do you know?"

"All somebody has to do is take a good look at you. And I dreamt about fish. Remember Momma said when you dream about fish somebody is pregnant. Lydia is already expecting so it had to be you."

"I haven't told Walter yet."

"Why not?"

"I just found out. First about Simone's death and a day later finding out I was pregnant. I'm on sensory overload Madeline."

"He's a good man Cicely."

Cicely looked over to see him talking to Evan. "Yeah," she said. "I know"

"Bernice knows," she informed Madeline. "And is not pleased."

"Are you pleased, baby girl?" Madeline asked her.

Cicely smiled. "I am."

"I'll keep your secret." Madeline said before hugging her.

Bernice couldn't wait to get her older sister alone so she could spill the beans. "Cicely is pregnant."

"I know. I know she wants to keep it quiet right now too

Bernice. We need to respect that." They were in Madeline's bedroom talking as Madeline unpacked her and Preston's clothes.

"He is sleeping in the bed with her. Right next to the bedroom Olivia will be sleeping in. Doesn't that mean anything to you?"

"I'm sure Olivia knows men and women live together without the sanctity of marriage. Can't you let Cicely have a little happiness in her life? When did you become such a prude?" Then Madeline looked concerned. "Your condition hasn't worsened has it? The stress of Simone dying hasn't brought on more symptoms?"

"Nothing has changed with me. I just don't want to see her hurt. She's forty years old and he is...."

"In love with her," finished Madeline. "No one knows how long anything is going to last. Evan and Simone were proof of that. You and I have been blessed. Let Cicely have her little piece. You were never spiteful Bernice. Don't ruin it for her."

"She's too old to have her first baby. I don't want to lose another sister." Tears were leaking from her eyes.

"No she is not. I see older mothers all the time. Besides it's done. Be happy for her and think happy thoughts. I don't want to hear anything negative from you. Just like you refuse to submit to your diagnosis, refuse to believe anything bad will happen to Cicely. When they make the announcement congratulate them."

"You know the older you get, the more you sound like Momma," said Bernice.

"I take that as a compliment," said Madeline giving Bernice a hug. She figured they'd all be giving out a lot of hugs in the coming days.

Monday before the funeral service Walter found Cicely sitting alone on the unheated sun porch, snow was predicted in the forecast. He gathered her in his arms to share his body heat. "Why you sitting out here by yourself Cee?"

People had been coming and going all evening as the news spread about Simone's death. All her nieces and nephews were due in the next evening. "Too many people."

Walter knew what she meant. He was having trouble not thinking about his grandpa's death. "Want to go to my house tonight Cicely?"

"I'm not sure I should leave Madeline and Bernice to do everything."

"Go pack a bag," he said. "I'll tell Madeline we're leaving."

She was in the kitchen. Someone always seemed to be in the kitchen cooking something. He didn't mince words, didn't make any excuses. "I'm taking Cicely to my house tonight. We'll be back tomorrow."

"Take her," said Madeline. "She's not getting any rest here. I wish all of us had a place to escape to for a little while."

"Thanks Madeline."

"Take care of my baby sister Walter. That's all I ask."

While Walter drove to his house Cicely fell asleep in his truck. It didn't occur to him to wake her; he just picked her up and carried her into the house. His mother had left a lamp burning in the living room. He was contemplating taking her directly to the bedroom when she spoke.

"I'm awake Walter," she said softly.

He removed his arm from under her knees and let her slide down along his body. Cicely put her arms around his neck and pulled him down to kiss her. She'd missed this.

Walter couldn't feel her through the bulk of their coats and shrugged his jacket off and unbuttoned her coat without breaking the kiss. His hands went under her sweater to feel the bare skin of her back. He didn't feel a bra and groaned in pleasure and sought to cup a breast with his hand.

Cicely couldn't help it, she flinched. It hurt when he touched her. That's why she didn't have a bra on. They hurt and there was no opportunity for her to go out and buy new ones. No one had told her, her breasts would become so sensitive so soon.

Walter pulled away. "I'm sorry. I didn't mean to hurt you."

"My breasts are tender." She didn't have to tell him why did she? She wasn't ready to tell him.

"I can wait Cee. We don't have to do anything. I can wait until you feel better."

Cicely frowned at him. What was he talking about? Wait until she felt better? "What are you talking about Walter?"

Walter hunched his shoulders. This was making him uncomfortable. "You know. Some women's breasts hurt that time of month." He had the good graces to look embarrassed talking to her about other women's breasts.

Cicely wanted to laugh at him. He was as far away from the truth as you could possibly get. "What if I don't want to wait?" She said closing the space between them. With nimble fingers she unbuckled his belt and pulled it from the belt loops. Then unbuttoned his jeans and pulled the zipper down. The entire time he had spent in her bed Walter had not touched her. Now she knew why.

Cicely removed her coat and took off her shoes, leaving her socks on. She made a production out of getting out of her pants. She stood before Walter in her sweater, panties and socks.

Walter wondered how she managed to look so sexy to him. Her dreads were hanging in her face and her panties were plain white bikinis hugging her hips. His socks, the ones she'd never given back, were on her feet. Why would her having on his socks make him want her more? Because she'd made them hers. Just like she was making him hers.

He kicked off his boots and pushed his jeans and underwear down together and stepped out of them. Walter would never get tired of carrying her up the stairs when he knew what waited at the top.

They didn't return until the next afternoon. Madeline studied them closely. Cicely looked well rested. Good, the pregnancy wasn't taking a toll on her. Her first doctor's visit wasn't until Friday and Madeline wasn't leaving until she'd accompanied Cicely to that appointment.

Walter looked like the cat that ate the canary.

Despite everything that was going on around them, Madeline was happy for her sister. Her own pregnant daughter would be arriving that evening. Entering her eighth month, Madeline had tried to discourage Lydia from coming, but her doctor had given her the okay to fly. Jeanine, Bernice's daughter wouldn't be in until morning right before the funeral. She was flying in and out because of school obligations.

But the only people staying in the family home that night would be the sisters and the men that loved them along with Evan and Olivia. The children of Madeline and Bernice would stay at a hotel. Lydia and her husband would join them later after she had a visit with her mother and aunts.

Walter wanted to take Cicely back to his place, but knew this was necessary for her.

The women congregated in Cicely's bedroom. Madeline moved the old rocking chair into the room so her daughter could sit in it. Cicely sat on the floor leaning against the bed. Madeline and Bernice were on the bed with Olivia stretched out between them.

Downstairs the men sat in semi-darkness watching TV. Preston was in a quiet conversation with his son-in-law and Louis. Walter sat in a chair away from them and Evan sat alone on the ottoman holding a beer he had hardly touched.

Walter looked around, these were the people Cicely loved. If things worked out for him and Cicely, he would have to learn to love them too.

He and Preston were on friendly terms, but for some reason Louis remained cool toward him. Walter suspected it had something to do with Bernice. He didn't know why she had something against him. Preston's son-in-law had not been there long enough for him to make a connection. Evan didn't have much to say to anyone.

If circumstances where normal, like a family reunion, Walter, the son-in-law and Evan would have hung out.

Walter tried to put himself in Evan's place. He couldn't. Having found Cicely he couldn't imagine life without her. Even if things did not work out for them, he would know she was still out in the world somewhere. Evan did not have that comfort. Walter's grandparents had been together for over fifty years. Watching Evan he did not know how his grandmother coped day to day. But Evan did have Olivia.

He remembered when his grandpa died. Cicely had let him go on for hours, talking about his grandpa. From what he'd seen, no one had offered Evan that opportunity.

He began to have a pain in his chest imagining the pain

Evan was going through. Walter abruptly stood and sought Cicely.

The sisters frowned at his interruption, but he couldn't help it. Walter pulled Cicely into the darkened bedroom Shanequa and Tamequa once shared.

He held her tightly in his embrace.

"Cee, I love you," he murmured into her hair. "I love you so much."

Cicely didn't know what brought on his frantic declaration.

"Marry me Cee?" he asked. "I know this is not the right time. The circumstances are not the best, but I couldn't wait. What if something happened before you know I want to marry you? Marry me Cee? Let me give you babies, foster kids, whatever you want."

"Walter what did you say?" she asked trying to see his face in the darkness.

He sat her on one of the twin beds and knelt on the floor, laying his head in her lap.

"Marry me Cee?"

"Everything, I mean tell me everything you said again."

He was on his knees and took each of her hands in his. Walter could feel her trembling and hear the tears in her voice.

He said it again. "Marry me Cee," he drew her name out into one long syllable that made a chill go down her spine, like the first time he call her that endearment. "Let me put babies in you. We can get foster kids. However you want to do it. Let me be the one to share it with you. I love you."

Cicely couldn't stop the tears. She had never said the words to Walter. She had fought him at every turn. And he kept coming back.

She put her hands on the side of his face like Tamequa had when she said he could be her boyfriend when she grew up.

"I have to tell you something first."

"I know you love me Cee," he said. He didn't have to hear the words now. He could wait until she was ready to say them. He took her hands and kissed the palms of each one.

She was scared. Despite what he said, she was afraid. Then she felt a strong nudge at her shoulder. Someone or something prodding her on.

"I'm pregnant Walter," came tumbling out

He peered at her in the darkness. "You having my baby Cee?"

He felt her nod more than saw it. After all his upbringing Cicely was the only woman he'd slept with without using a condom.

"You have to say yes now,' he said hugging her. "Or Janice will come over here with a shotgun and make you marry me"

She hugged him back. "Yes." Followed by, "I love you

Walter."

When Walter left Cicely he felt settled. They were going to get married and she was having his baby. The baby part did not feel real to him yet. Until he met Cicely he'd hadn't given a lot thought to getting married. He enjoyed children but thought fatherhood would not be in his future.

Cicely was having his baby.

It was hard going back downstairs to join the men. He and Cicely agreed to keep it to themselves until after the funeral, but Walter had all this joy inside him. He sobered when he saw Evan still sitting alone.

He tapped Evan on the shoulder and with his head indicated the man should follow him. They stopped in the kitchen and Walter poured them both a glass of the Hennessey Preston had purchased earlier, and continued to the sun porch. It was dark and cold out there, but it suited the purpose of what Walter was hoping to accomplish. Since Cicely had taken the rocking chair inside the only seating available was the old sofa and the ratty recliner. Walter chose to sit next to Evan on the sofa.

"Tell me about her," he said to Evan. Walter touched his glass to Evan's as if making a toast.

It took a few sips of his drink before Evan's tongue was loose enough for him to begin talking. He didn't know Walter and with the combination of alcohol it made it easier to talk. Once he started talking Walter took the drink from him. It would do no good for him to get his future brother-in-law wasted the night before the funeral.

Evan initially talked about what a bitch Simone could be, the anger that she was dead and had left him alone, before the love started coming through. He had no doubt when she returned home they would make it. They had a beautiful daughter together. His heart hurt, he told Walter. He had physical pain.

Walter knew what he was talking about.

They all stared at Cicely when she returned to the bedroom.

"Well what did he want?" asked Bernice

"He's going to stay at his place tonight. We have enough people to get ready tomorrow and he doesn't want to be in the way."

"That was considerate of him," said Madeline in a kindly fashion, trying to make up for the biting tone of Bernice.

"He's taking Evan with him," added Cicely.

"But what about Olivia? His daughter needs him," shot back Bernice.

They all knew Evan has been useless when it came to Olivia.

"Olivia can sleep with Cicely tonight," said Madeline. "Evan needs some time to himself." She understood completely.

They heard Evan in the next room gathering his things to stay with Walter. Walter would sleep on the couch and let Evan have his bed. Evan would be alone without having to worrying about his daughter hearing him cry. He and Walter would be back before the limo arrived to take them to the church.

The funeral was short and dignified exactly like Simone would have wanted. The talk Evan had with Walter and the time alone was cathartic for him and he was there for Olivia. Something he had been unable to do before.

After the service the immediate family only stayed long enough to say thank you to everyone. They encouraged everyone to stay and partake of the repast the congregation had thoughtfully provided, so the family would not have to entertain people at Cicely's home. Simone's remains would be cremated and shipped to Evan. He could have a memorial service in their hometown if he found the strength to go through it all again.

It was no surprise to Cicely that Walter's mother and grandmother came to the house. They had attended the homegoing.

Bernice tried to act indignant the women hadn't done as requested, but Madeline greeted them warmly. She wanted to meet the women who were influential in Walter's life. They didn't act like guests, both pitched in to get food on the table, because no matter if you tell people you want to be alone, they show up anyway. Even at her advanced age his grandmother made sure dishes didn't stay dirty long.

"We like Cicely," Walter's grandmother said to Madeline. "She was a great help when Mr. Moore died."

"I like Walter," was Madeline's response.

"She was really good with those children," continued the older woman, noticing Madeline only spoke for herself when it came to liking Walter. "We hope we are going to continue seeing her."

Madeline gave an enigmatic smile. "I'm sure you will."

Walter was never far from Cicely's side after the funeral. Whenever they were within touching distance of each other one of them always reached out. It might only be a brush of their fingertips or a rub on the back, but the concern was always there. Madeline hadn't said anything, but Walter had done for Evan what none of them had been able to do, so wrapped up in their own grief. Her sister had a good man.

"Do you mind not staying here tonight?" Cicely asked him. They were sitting on her bed. "Bernice and Louis are leaving tomorrow morning and I want to tell them about us before they leave."

"You don't want me to be here when you tell them Cee?" he asked, hurt at her request.

"Bernice knows I'm pregnant."

"So she should be happy we are getting married," he insisted. "But Cee I don't want anyone to think we're only getting married because you're pregnant."

"Walter, people are going to think that no matter what.

Just let me do this. I want them to know how much I love you. Why I love you."

He took her hand and brought it to his lips. "Why do you love me Cicely?"

She thought of the litany of things he had told her, but could only say, "You are God's gift to me. You never turn down a gift from God. And..." she took his hand and placed it low on her belly, "You gave me this Walter."

Walter wanted to make love to her, but feeling secure in their love he would go. He was going to miss having her next to him in bed, even if it was only for a night, the way she intertwined herself around him, her soft snore. Whatever her reasons, he would do as Cicely asked.

Walter was going to let himself out, but heard someone in the kitchen. Seeing it was Bernice he stood in the doorway between the dining room and kitchen. She was there alone making sure the kitchen was spotless. He couldn't tell if she was actively ignoring him or didn't see him, so he cleared his throat. Bernice jumped so he gave her the benefit of the doubt.

"Can we talk?" he asked trying to keep his voice neutral.

Bernice sat at the table and waited for Walter to take a seat.

"I love Cicely," he said. "I thought you would be okay with that. When we first met you and I were okay."

"That was before you starting sleeping with my sister and moving in on her."

"Moving in on her," he said incredulously. "The only thing I want from Cicely is for her to love me."

"Why Cicely, Walter?" Bernice asked.

He looked at her. Did she have such a low opinion of her sister? Couldn't she see everything Cicely had to offer as a person? Then it hit him. Cicely wasn't lacking. It was him. He wasn't good enough for her. Walter looked as his hands. Yeah he had a dirty job. Sometimes he literally shoveled shit, but he never came home with dirty hands. Cicely never chided him about his hands. Bernice thought Cicely had chosen beneath herself.

"You think Cicely is slumming," he finally said. "You wished she had kept her ghetto trash out of sight until all this was over.

Bernice didn't respond.

"But now the whole family knows Cicely is sleeping with a plumber. And pretty soon they gonna know this plumber," he said tapping his chest, "Got her pregnant."

He was becoming angry and was having a hard time keeping his voice low. Walter didn't want to bring the whole household into this conversation.

He stood and had to catch the chair before it hit the floor. Walter pointed his finger at her in controlled fury. "You know what Bernice? If I thought for one minute, for one freaking minute, I could not make Cicely happy I wouldn't be here. I'll tell you like I told Cicely. I'm not going anywhere. We're getting married," he said forgetting his promise to Cicely. "And until that day comes when she can absolutely convince me she no longer loves me I'll be here."

He didn't wait for Bernice to say anything before he left.

Madeline had been walking up from the basement when she heard Walter's voice. Not wanting to interrupt their conversation she stood on the top stair with the door ajar, doing what any big sister would do, she eavesdropped. Hearing the same words Preston had said to her.

When Walter left she came from her hiding place.

"Well?" she asked Bernice, startling her yet again.

"I heard what I wanted to hear," she mused. "He said he loved her."

"Momma and Daddy would have just asked him," laughed Madeline.

Cicely was waiting for Bernice in the kitchen the next morning leaving Olivia sleeping. Her niece has elected to sleep with her even though her dad was there. Evan and Olivia would be leaving on a later flight. She was too nervous to sit and leaned against the counter waiting.

Cicely didn't want any animosity between herself and Bernice. They were sisters and would not always get along, but her marrying Walter was non-negotiable.

"Walter asked me to marry him." Cicely said instead of

good morning when Bernice entered the kitchen. "I said yes."

"Is that so?" replied Bernice not giving away Walter had spoken to her the night before.

"You know what Bernice? I just want you to be happy for us. Bernice I want what you and Louis have. I see how he takes care of you. Why can't you see how Walter takes care of me? If it had not been for Walter, I don't know what would have happened to me the night Simone died. If it doesn't work, at least I'll have memories. You're the one told me that when I decided to take in foster kids."

"Well say something Bernice," said Madeline. She had entered behind Bernice.

Bernice walked to her baby sister and put her arms around her. "You have my blessings."

Madeline joined in the hug fest and said, "Mine too."

EPILOUGE

They got married the Saturday after Thanksgiving at her mother's church. Following tradition, she would join Walter's, the one her best friend Anita also attended. Left to Walter they would have gotten married at city hall with no delay.

Anita helped her pick out a dress. It was tea length, like her Momma's, with a scooped neckline and tight bodice, that in a few weeks she would never have been able to wear. It had princess darts that were fitted at the bosom and flared out to swirl gently around her calves. The sleeves were fitted and elbow length. She chose it in ivory satin covered in ivory lace. On her feet, even though it was cold and damp outside she wore ivory peep-toed pumps with ankle straps so Walter could see her red toenails.

Walter surprised her by paying the airfare for Madeline, Bernice and their husbands to come back for the wedding. Otherwise they would not have been able to come. Cicely made note to tell him any future large financial expenditures must be discussed as a couple.

Cicely shocked Walter by kicking him out of her bed until after the wedding. Her reasoning, they'd never had sex in her bed and it would make their wedding night that more special if they waited. Walter didn't understand, but his mother did, so she kept him on a short leash the two weeks before the nuptials.

His grandmother and mother didn't blink an eye when he informed them Cicely would be having his baby in about seven months.

They had a small reception at his grandmother's home. No need for anything big when they would be combining two established households. His new in-laws agreed to stay with his grandmother so Walter and Cicely could be alone on their wedding night. He had every intention of making her scream his name. But wasn't prepared when Cicely introduced him to his first experience in a claw foot tub.

Walter had taken Madeline's place at Cicely's first doctor's visit. The woman doctor had no issue with Cicely's age, saying Cicely was in excellent physical condition and if she felt up to it she could continue to run.

The weather co-operated, so for Christmas Walter surprised her by taking her to see Shanequa and Tamequa. The Sims's welcomed them with opened arms and Cicely cried the whole time they were there. At least now she knew why she was so weepy. Pauletta and Bernard agreed to let the girls visit a couple of weeks the coming summer after Cicely recuperated from having the baby. Tamequa was a little upset Walter had married Cicely instead of waiting for her.

She and Walter and not taken the idea of foster kids off the table, they just wanted to get their own out of the oven first.

With the help of the lawyer she'd met the 'Perri night' as Cicely called it, she set up her own accounting business out of her and Walter's home. Walter's Crew and his Momma were her first customers. Janice rented out Walter's half of the duplex to a nice single middle aged gentleman. She began to think if her daughter-in-law could go younger why couldn't she? She invited him to dinner.

The first time they felt the baby move Walter was about to make love to Cicely. It freaked him out so much he vowed not to have sex with her again until after it was born. This only lasted for the time it took for Cicely to continuously expose her growing breasts to him.

Oh they had fights. Twice Cicely kicked him out the house, which they attributed to pregnancy hormones. Once when Walter neglected to tell her he was working late and didn't answer his cell, which made her frantic. The second time he did get hurt on the job, breaking two fingers and not telling her until he came home from the emergency room. The pinkie and ring finger of his right hand, wasn't a biggie because he was a lefty.

Their little girl Siobhan (God is Gracious) decided to come early and was born on her daddy's birthday in late May. Cicely did not want to name her after her dead sister. Small, at six pounds, but healthy in spite of being born early, she had her daddy's eyes. Taking advice from her grandmother-in-law Cicely did not allow Walter to see the birth. "As much as a man likes lady parts, they do not need to see a baby coming out of them. Sexual equality be damned." Walter's grandmother's words not Cicely's.

Oh he saw her in pain, but when things started becoming ugly and she had to push, Janice and Diane, Walter's cousin, were by her side and he was banished from the room. The early delivery didn't allow for Madeline and Bernice to be at Cicely's side.

When Walter saw his daughter for the first time, she was clean and nuzzling her mother's breast. The sight was bewildering to him. Cicely had never seen Walter cry, but this was damn close.

The weekend of the fourth of July was the perfect time to celebrate Siobhan's Christening with an outdoor party. It also coincided with Cicely's six-week checkup. Walter and Cicely had never used condoms while making love so it never occurred to them to use them now. She was nursing, so never considered taking the pill. The couple found out the old wives tale of not becoming pregnant while nursing wasn't always true.

Nine months after the Christening of their oldest child Walter and Cicely became the parents of another baby girl.

At which time Cicely told Walter to see a doctor and get it snipped. And if he didn't she would personally take care of it for him.

ACKNOWLEDGEMENTS

I would like to thank everyone that help me get my book finished. Especially my BFF since kindergarten that read and reread every word I wrote. My cousin that promised to keep bugging me until I was done. People that read it and told me how much they enjoyed it and that I had actually surprised them.

Made in the USA
Middletown, DE
18 July 2021

44100194R00229